In a clearing stood a cabin of barked logs, a swaybacked structure with a rock chimney at one end and behind it a rude shed. There was a ruined pole corral and a well-sweep. A small pond near the cabin was frozen over. The roof of the cabin sagged. There was about the crude habitation a loneliness and desolation softened only by snow that mounded every protuberance, and the knowledge that someone had once settled here; settled here and failed.

Martin moved angrily toward Giles. "You can't just leave us here like this! We'll starve! What the devil do we know about living in the wilderness? We'll both be dead in a week, from starvation or wild animals or just the cold!"

"But Andrew!" Belle protested. "Andrew will tell them you . . . you"

"Tell them what?" Giles demanded. I'll tell Andrew you and your dummed lover just decided to go it alone up here. Didn't I fix up this love cottage for the two of you? Didn't I bust my back driving supplies up here for you two lovebirds, cut my leg with an axe splitting shingles, get everything ready for you?" He shook his head. "No, no one ain't going to bother about either of you." His bearded lips twisted in a grimace. "If I wanted to kill you, either one of you, I could of done it a long time ago. But you saved my life onct, Martin, and I ain't forgot it." He turned toward Belle. "And I loved you, woman, till you betrayed me! So I figgered this way out. Now it's up to you and that—that—" He broke off, and finally wept.

ADDITIONAL
READING

1. *The Frontier Years.* Mark H. Brown and W. R. Felton. Henry Holt & Co., New York, N.Y., 1955

2. *Doctors of the Old West.* Robert F. Karolevitz. Bonanza Books, New York, N.Y., 1967

3. *Before Barbed Wire.* Mark H. Brown and W. R. Felton. Henry Holt & Co., New York, N.Y., 1956

4. *Dictionary of the Old West.* Peter Watts. Alfred A. Knopf, New York, N.Y., 1877

5. *On The Border With Crook.* John G. Bourke. Charles Scribner's Sons, New York, N.Y., 1891

6. *Indian Sign Language.* W. P. Clark. Hamersly & Co., Philadelphia, Pa., 1885

7. *The Look of the Old West.* Foster Harris. The Viking Press, New York, N.Y., 1955

8. *Frontier Army Sketches.* James W. Steele. Jansen, McClurg & Co., Chicago, Illinois, 1883

9. *Business-Atlas of the Great Mississippi Valley and Pacific Slope.* Rand McNally & Co., Chicago, Illinois, 1877

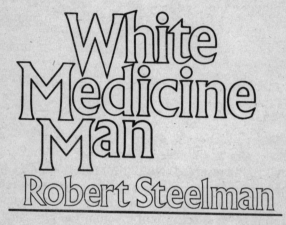

White Medicine Man

Robert Steelman

ace books
A Division of Charter Communications Inc.
A GROSSET & DUNLAP COMPANY
360 Park Avenue South
New York, New York 10010

WHITE MEDICINE MAN

Copyright © 1979 by Robert Steelman

An ACE Original

First ACE Printing: February, 1979

Published Simultaneously in Canada

Printed in U.S.A.

"In 1890, Head Chief and Young Mule, two unruly young Cheyennes, killed a young man named Hugh Boyle. The authorities demanded that the murderers be surrendered, but the Cheyennes wanted to make a property settlement. Although they bid the price in ponies and other property up to a high figure, they were finally made to understand that such an atonement was not a suitable settlement for the spilling of blood. However, they stubbornly refused to allow their young men to be tried and probably hanged. If they had to die, the young men would die as a Cheyenne would die. So the agent, James. A. Cooper, was told that on the appointed day, September 13th, the two young men would ride into the agency at Lame Deer with rifles in their hands, they would attack the troops, and the soldiers could kill them! There was nothing the agent could do but accept this unusual proposition.

"The night before, there were solemn dances in the Indian camp; and on the fatal day the two warriors dressed and painted themselves with great care and selected their best horses for the final ride. A troop of the 1st Cavalry and the Indian police were drawn up in front of the agency, and the stage was set, the Indians in the 'gallery' on the *surrounding hills, for the spectacular tragedy. At the appointed time the two doomed men appeared on the hill to the northeast of the agency, and, singing the traditional death song of their people, rode at full speed down toward the waiting soldiers. Sweeping past, with horses still on a dead run, they fired point-blank into the ranks. On the first pass the Indian police managed to drop one horse and its rider. The other turned, and still shooting and singing, rode deliberately past the ranks again before he and his pony were downed.''*

The Frontier Years
Mark H. Brown and W. R. Felton
Henry Holt & Co., New York,
N. Y., 1955

CHAPTER ONE

No one knew where he had come from or where he was bound for, and there was something in his manner that discouraged inquiry. Not that he was unpleasant or disagreeable; it was only that Martin Holly (such was the name on the passenger manifest of the sternwheeler *Far West*) seemed a private man, intent on private thought.

The passenger was slender and of average height, well-dressed, with straight-combed brown hair, hazel eyes, and a neatly-trimmed beard. He seemed somewhere in his early thirties. Perhaps the only thing that made him appear at all out of the ordinary was impeccable neatness and the delicate long-fingered hands, pale and unmarred by toil.

"A gambler," someone suggested.

"No," another opined. "The man's obviously a gentleman."

A drummer from St. Louis said, "He looks kind of like a doctor." But a miner from the diggings along Big Dry Creek objected. "Hell, he ain't no sawbones! You ever see old Doc Shay at Big Fork? Doctors is always got stains on their hands from calomel and blue mass and such!"

A deckhand lounging nearby while the steamer approached the town had an opinion also.

1

"Fellers," he said, "that man's a safecracker, mark my words!"

When the *Far West* slowed to half-speed and blew for the landing there was still no agreement.

The wharf at Big Fork, the junction with Shotgun creek and the Yellowstone, was cluttered with baled hides, packets of furs, canvas bags of rich ore going downstream for crushing and refining. Soon the Yellowstone would freeze, and travel by boat would be suspended until the spring thaw. Winters in the Territory were frigid, temperatures dropping at times to forty degrees below zero. Anyone who could pay the fare was well-advised to travel down-river at this time of the turning of the leaves, instead of coming up to Big Fork. Otis Spinney, picking up Mr. Holly and his trunk, commented on this fact. Otis was a walking news bulletin for the frontier community, but did not get much satisfaction from Mr. Holly.

"If there had been service farther up," the newcomer said, "I would have gone the distance, believe me." He lighted a stogie and was afterwards silent.

Watching Spinney's buckboard roll toward the Empire Hotel, built largely from the remains of the steamer *Jenny R.*, wrecked on Teapot Rapids just below the town the previous autumn, Giles Dyson, the blacksmith, paused at the forge to wipe his brow. Old man Dancer, reclining in greasy buckskins in a split-bottomed chair, spoke to Giles.

"Looks to me like some kind of a dude."

Jack Flanders, the gambler, thumbs hooked in waistcoat pockets, leaned against a post supporting the porch roof before the Paradise Bar. He watched the buckboard roll past, the bearded man sitting stiffly beside Otis Spinney, a small brown satchel on his lap. Money? Would there be money in that satchel? Flanders decided he would arrange to meet the newcomer, invite him to the nightly draw-poker sessions in the Paradise.

While Spinney struggled with the heavy trunk, the bearded man entered the grandly-named Empire Hotel.

"Where from?" the clerk asked.

Mr. Holly paused for a moment, then wrote "Philadelphia, Pa." in the register.

"Got a nice room second floor front, right at the head of the stairs," the clerk volunteered. "Goes for five dollars a day."

Holly stroked his beard. "I daresay I'll be here quite a while. Do you have a weekly rate?"

"Twenty dollars a week," the clerk said. "Thirty with full board. We got a woman cook, not one of your Chinese."

"Done." The new arrival took a sheaf of bills from his wallet, paid a month in advance, and directed the panting Spinney up the stairs. "Thank you," he said to the clerk, and nodded pleasantly.

Once in his room he bolted the door, took off hat, coat, and flowered cravat, loosened his collar. Opening the satchel, he refreshed himself from a brown bottle, then stared out the window at the scene below.

Though far up the Yellowstone and in hostile Indian country, Big Fork was not as primitive as he at first feared. Some of the buildings were simple log structures but many newer ones were of sawn lumber, made more impressive with elaborately-decorated false fronts. From his vantage-point he could see a sawmill, a harness-shop, the offices of the Diamond-R Freight Company with a corral full of oxen and wagons. There was a wealth of saloons, dance halls, and parlor houses, along with a sagging frame building with a Washington hand press in the fly-specked window and a legend in peeling gold paint that said *The Yellowstone Journal*. Miners and trappers strolled the dusty streets in search of pleasure, teamsters locked wheels in the narrow thoroughfare and swore at each other, a Chinaman in pigtails trotted pony-like, a wicker basket of laundry atop his head. Blanket-clad tame Indians watched the coolie with the wariness of one minority toward another. Dust rose vapor-like in the October sun, veiling the sharper corners of life. It was, Martin reflected, like a scene from Breughel, the Flemish painter who so expertly delineated masses of raw humanity.

That night he ate supper in the hotel dining room; buffalo-hump steak, the first he had ever tasted, along with fried potatoes, applesauce, bread without butter and harsh black coffee. Afterwards, he lit a cheroot and strolled River Street, carrying the satchel.

In the autumn twilight the scene looked different. Shafts of yellow light from gaming-houses lit the dusk, a traveling evangelist harangued a crowd by torchlight from a makeshift pulpit of boxes, a tinkling piano from Big Alice's competed with a Negro musician strumming a banjo in the Ace of Diamonds. Soldiers from Fort Schofield— "swaddies," he heard them called, and not with affection—swaggered with locked arms down the boardwalks. Urchins pitched pennies against a wall, two drunks swung unavailingly at each other while a circle of spectators urged them on and made bets. Somewhere a merrymaker must have shot an anvil. There was a flash of blue-white light and a tremendous explosion, followed by a crash and the sound of breaking glass. After a moment's silence there came a cheer, and River Street returned to noisy confusion. Martin remembered how once, on a dare, he had shot an anvil when he was a small boy. The technique was simple though dangerous. An upturned anvil was loaded with gun powder, filling the small hole in the base, and a train laid to the outer edge. Another anvil was set on top, and the train lighted. The ensuing explosion had tossed the upper anvil through the roof of Mrs. Biedermeyer's chicken house. Young Martin had been tanned for his transgressions.

"Noisy place, isn't it?" a voice behind him asked.

Martin turned. Though the man stood in the shadows under the portico of the Paradise Bar, hat pulled low over his eyes, the voice was friendly.

"Noisy enough, I should say," Martin murmured.

"Name's Flanders—Jack Flanders." The man emerged from the shadows, holding out a hand. A glimmer of yellow light from the Paradise glinted on a diamond stickpin, illuminated a lean face, heavy-lidded eyes, neatly-trimmed goatee.

Martin hesitated, transferred the satchel to his other hand, shook.

"You're new here," Flanders said. It was not a question.

"I guess you could say that. Just came in on the *Far West*."

Flanders smiled, a tightening of lips below the ribbon of mustache. "A drummer, maybe? Selling something?"

Martin shook his head. The buffalo-hump steak lay heavy on his stomach and the coffee had been boiled too long. "No. Just traveling." He turned away, touched the brim of his hat. Flanders called after him. "Didn't say what your name was!" Martin walked on. He was a courteous man but did not like to be importuned.

In the days that followed, he kept much to his second-floor front room in the Empire Hotel. The leaves of the cottonwoods browned, dried, fell in gusts of cold wind from the northwest. The last paddlewheeler left for downriver. He slept much during the day, read by lamplight in the evening, often abandoned the greasy cuisine of the dining room for a can of Blue Hen tomatoes, crackers, and a wedge of rat cheese bought at Terwilliger's Giant Mercantile Emporium—dry goods, liquors, cigars, readymade clothing, saddles, plows and harrows, lanterns, boots, and sundries. Finally, loneliness began to gnaw at him. As the autumn days passed and the countryside turned cold and bleak, his spirits fell, and his usual composure developed a few fissures. In an uncharacteristic way he stopped by Dyson's smithy one day to rub gloved hands together over the coals in Giles' forge. "Cold day, isn't it?"

"There'll be colder," Giles muttered. He was a thick-thewed ox of a man, blue-eyed, thatch of blonde hair wet and dank with sweat as he heated

an iron wagon-tire. His hamlike face was mantled
with smallpox scars.

"Mind if I sit here and warm myself for a
while?"

Giles did not answer directly. Instead, he poured
coffee from a battered pot near the coals and
handed it to the visitor. "This is Dancer," he
grunted, returning to his bellows and nodding toward a whiskered ancient squatting like an Indian
atop an upturned box. The old man stuck out a
gnarled and liver-spotted hand. "That's all I go
by," he explained. "Dancer. I had another name
once, but it's been long forgot."

Martin sat in a sagging reed-bottomed chair, out
of reach of the cold wind whirling through the
open door of the shop.

"Holly," he introduced himself. "Martin Holly."

With Dancer's help Dyson slipped the red-hot
tire around an oaken wheel and plunged the assembly hissing into a tub of water.

"Hawley?"

"Holly. Like Christmas—the holly and the ivy,
or however that old song goes."

"You a mining man?" Dancer inquired.

Martin shook his head. "Just traveling for my
health."

Giles withdrew the wheel from its bath, stood it
steaming on the anvil, ran a critical eye over it.
"Seen you walking around," he said. "Probably
you're used to big cities—places where they got
theaters and fancy restaurants and carriages and
such. Big Fork is a pretty dull place."

"I came from Philadelphia."

"Ain't much doin' at nights here," Dancer said, "except whoorin' and raisin' hell.'"

"I'm not much for either," Martin admitted.

Wind howled around the sagging shack. Giles drew the door shut. "Well," he sighed, "guess that's it for the day! I got to stop at the Mercantile and take home a bag of flour and some onions or Belle'll skin me alive! I already forgot twice."

Outside the door the smith snapped on a huge brass padlock. "If you're lookin' for a little diversion some night," he suggested, "you could do worse than try the draw-poker game at the Paradise. I generally sit in. Then there's Gus Terwilliger and Frank Abbott that runs the Diamond R station and Captain Mapes from the post and Jack Flanders and a few others. It ain't a cheap game but—" Dyson paused, buttoning up his jacket. "Hell, nothing out here ain't cheap, and that's a fact! How's a poor man to support his family?"

Though he had played poker at school, Martin Holly was not a gambling man. Still, the long nights were wearing. More than once he had gone to bed early from sheer boredom only to waken in the dead of night, forehead damp with perspiration, heart pounding with a remembrance of nightmares. With winter soon to come, he needed diversion. One night after a heartburning meal in the Empire "dining room"—fried sidemeat, sour-tasting gravy, beans, and shot-hard biscuits—he paused before the Paradise Bar. In a pool of light from a hanging Argand lamp was a round table covered with green baize. He noticed Giles Dyson's blonde thatch under a fur cap, and the man called Jack Flanders. Red and white and blue chips punctuated the verdant green of the cloth. The players were guffawing at a joke old Mr. Terwilliger was telling. There, in the lamplight, were *bonhomie* and companionship, close at hand. In sudden resolve Martin entered the Paradise, slipped into a vacant chair at the table.

"An open game?" he asked politely.

Terwilliger rolled a cigar around in his mouth. He still wore sateen sleeve guards from his counter at the Mercantile. "Your money's as good as anyone else's," he shrugged.

Giles Dyson shook Martin's hand and introduced him to the rest of the players. Jack Flanders nodded, the others mumbled greetings and went back to staring at their cards.

"Deal me in the next hand," Martin murmured, and handed Flanders fifty dollars for a stack of chips.

During the evening he played conservatively, calculating the odds, watching for telltale signs of bluffing. About nine o'clock a sadfaced man carrying a violin, accompanied by a short-skirted lady with improbable orange hair, came out on the skimpy stage. In response to scattered applause the female sang popular songs—"Lilly Dale," "Finnegan's Wake," and "The Girl I Left Behind Me"—while the accompanist produced whimpering sounds from the fiddle. The Paradise was a high-class place, but down River Street a barkeep ejected a troublesome drunk, and later a brawl broke out in the Ace of Diamonds. Shots sounded, and a female voice cursed in high-pitched dudgeon. In the Paradise, however, all remained genteel. Glasses clinked, tobacco-smoke veiled the hanging

oil lamps. In the corner a roulette-wheel whirred as
the banker chanted his wheedling song: "Make yer
little bets, gents, make yer little bets! All's set, the
game's made, the little ball is a-rollin'!"

Occasionally someone in the barred "office"
tapped a bell and a round of drinks was ordered by
the house. All in all, it was a pleasant evening. At
midnight Martin had lost thirteen dollars, but then
he had once or twice deliberately bluffed so as to be
caught. It was, he remembered from school, a good
way to keep other players off-balance. He was
sorry, however, to see that Giles Dyson had lost
heavily.

"Well," the blacksmith grumbled, staring into
an empty wallet, "tomorrow's another day, I
guess! Maybe my damned luck will change."

Flanders, heavy winner, slapped Dyson on the
back.

"That's all it is, Giles," he comforted. "Luck—
bad luck! You play your cards as well as any man
ever I saw, but you've just had a run of bad luck!
The only thing to do is play out your string, wait
for your luck to change. It soon will, believe me!"

Pleased at the surcease from loneliness, Martin
walked home with Giles Dyson. Overhead swung
Orion with his club raised, and the Big Dipper was
askew in the northern sky. The night was cold;
frost spangled the meadow they crossed, brittle
grasses crunching under their boots. On a slope
above the town, a lamp burning in the window,
stood a small cabin with a sloping lean-to from
whose chimney curled a tendril of smoke. Martin
smelled burning wood; the lamp and the homey
smell of the hearth suddenly moved him. It had

been a long time since he had known a home, a real home.

"Guess Belle's waitin' up for me," Giles muttered. "Oh, won't she give *me* what for when she finds out I lost all my money tonight!" He shoved the fur hat back on his head, dug a toe in the well-swept yard. "I'd invite you in, but—"

"That's all right," Martin said. "Anyway, I just wanted to thank you for introducing me to the game." He stroked his beard and smiled. "Though I admit I felt a little out of place—undressed, as it were."

In the starshine the blacksmith's face was puzzled. "What do you mean by that now?"

"So many of the people in the Paradise wore guns. Even old Mr. Terwilliger had a big old Colt's slung around his middle. Captain Mapes carried sidearms—I'd expect that of an Army officer—but everywhere I looked there were guns, guns, guns! The only person I didn't see one on was you, and I guess Jack Flanders."

"I'm a peaceable man," Giles explained. "If I got a score to settle I guess I'd more 'n likely do it with my bare hands. But Big Fork is a rough place. There's some real hardcases here. I don't fault any man for carrying around a hogleg."

In the weeks that followed Giles Dyson and Martin Holly became friends. Giles, unable to read or write, admired Martin's obvious refinement; Martin came to know the smith as a bluff honest man whose only vice seemed to be gambling. Martin spent more and more time at the Paradise, looking forward to the poker game each evening. He held his own, occasionally won a big pot, and grew to know and like Gus Terwilliger, Captain Mapes, and the other players to whom the nightly game was almost a sacrament. They, in turn, seemed to like Martin's serenity, his coolness in the big pots, his always-unruffled manner. Only Jack Flanders seemed not to cotton to Martin, and Martin was similarly doubtful of the gambler. Flanders was too dexterous with the cards. Martin's eye more than once caught a quick blurred movement in Flanders' deal that made him wonder. Still, the others seemed to accept Flanders without question.

"Where did Flanders come from?" he asked old man Dancer one day.

Dancer, leaning on his ancient Hawken rifle, had just sold a bundle of prime beaver pelts to a trader who had come overland from Omaha in his wagon. The old man was in an expansive mood, and treated Martin to a drink in the Ace of Diamonds, his headquarters when he was in Big Fork.

"Dunno," he said, pouring another drink. "Just showed up one day. Around here it ain't polite to inquire too much about a man's business." He grinned, gargled the gin. "Like you, Mr. Holly."

"Martin."

"All right—Martin! Don't no one know where *you* come from, either, though there's been speculation."

"There's no need for speculation," Martin said. "I'm a physician, from Philadelphia. I was successful there, not only in my medical practice, but in buying and selling property. But I—well, I developed a touch of consumption, and decided to sell out, come West for my health. That's all there is to it, you see. No great mystery."

Dancer slammed the cork in the bottle, threw a coin on the bar. "Well, Martin Holly, I can tell you this! Jack Flanders don't bear you no particular love!"

"I guessed that," Martin admitted. "I suppose in some way I offended him, though I don't remember it."

Standing on the porch, they watched a rain of snow descend on the town.

"People takes offense in all kinds of ways," Dancer mused. "Now you take Jack Flanders. I figger it this way. Till you come, Jack was the only gentleman in Big Fork. Wears paper collars, takes a bath twice a week, bows and scrapes with the ladies, likes to show off, make folks know he's seen better places than Big Fork. Then you come along and put a spoke in his wheel. You're the genuine article, Martin—quality, I mean. Don't never get loud and boisterous, always the gentleman. Maybe Jack Flanders is got his nose out of joint."

"No!" Martin protested. "It can hardly be anything like that! I can't imagine—"

"It's the truth," Dancer insisted. Bobbing his head in farewell, he ambled down River Street toward Big Alice's place, rifle under his arm, the ancient felt hat quickly crowned with snow. Martin remained on the porch, puzzled. Dancer's theory was absurd. Still, Jack Flanders obviously disliked him.

In one of the quick changes common in the Idaho Territory, the weather turned mild. *Sioux Summer*, old man Dancer called it. The half-frozen ground thawed, River Street became a quagmire.

Slogging through the mud one sunny afternoon Martin heard his name called.

"Mr. Holly?"

He looked up. Standing on the boardwalk was a tall angular woman, mahogany-tinged hair tucked under a sunbonnet. She held a sack of groceries in one arm; the other hand clasped that of a tow-headed boy ten or twelve years of age.

"Ma'am?" He climbed up on the boardwalk, scraping mud from his boots on the edge of the planks, and tipped his hat.

"You're Mr. Holly? Mr. Martin Holly?"

"Yes, ma'am."

She was young—in her middle twenties, he judged, and her eyes were blue and troubled. Ill at ease, she stammered. "My—my husband—he's Mr. Dyson, Giles Dyson."

"I'm pleased to meet you, ma'am," he said, and bowed.

"This is our—his boy Andrew."

Martin shook hands with Andrew, a small copy of Giles Dyson. Sensing her nervousness, seeing the covert way she looked about at passersby, he moved to a sheltered alcove off the walk, a passageway to the rear of the brewery, stacked high with barrels.

"Is there something I can do for you, Mrs. Dyson?"

She gave Andrew a small push. "Go play, Andrew. I want to talk to Mr. Holly." From up the hill came the clang of her husband's hammer on hot iron, and she bit her lip. "I hardly know how to start. I—I mean you—you're Giles' good friend, Mr. Holly. He's told me a lot about you. He admires you, with your education and all. You know, Giles never went to school. He's had to work hard all his life."

He nodded.

"But this gambling!" She swallowed hard; her bosom rose and fell under a worn shawl. "I *don't* know what to do about it! Mr. Holly, my husband can't afford to lose money at the Paradise like he's doing! He works hard, God knows he does, and he's a good husband and father! I—I'm his second wife, you know; the first died of the smallpox, and Andrew is his son by her—Mary, her name was. Really, I—I think it's just that there's not much money in smithing and Giles thinks he can win big some night at the Paradise and buy things, better things, for Andrew and me. But I don't want that, Mr. Holly! I just want Giles, that's enough!" She seemed ready to weep, but bit her lip and went on. "These few groceries here—lard and beans and matches. I had to ask Mr. Terwilliger for credit."

"Ma'am," he said, "I know your predicament, I surely do. But your husband is a grown man. If he wants to gamble, I don't know how he can be stopped. With some men it gets to be a kind of fever."

She swallowed again; her face was drawn and worried. "I hoped maybe you could talk to him, make him see—"

"Ma'am, I like and respect your husband. Giles Dyson is a good man, a kind man, a decent man. But I don't see how I could help."

Forcing a smile, she called to Andrew, who was across the street playing mumbletypeg with some companions. "I guess I was a little forward, talking

to you this way, Mr. Holly. But I felt desperate. I
—I had to speak to someone about it, because
when I mention it to Giles he just won't talk about
it. Anyway, thank you. I was pleased to make your
acquaintance."

He bowed; Mrs. Dyson trudged up the hill, sack
of groceries in her arm, holding young Andrew by
the hand. Uncomfortable, he kicked at a loose
board in the walk and succeeded only in scarring
the polished toe of his boot. Otis Spinney, lounging
in his rig in the scanty sunshine, called to him. "Afternoon, Mr. Holly!"

He nodded.

"That Mrs. Dyson is one nice lady! Used to be a
dancer, I hear. Come through here with a theatrical
troupe that run out of funds. That's how she met
Giles."

Perhaps Otis' story explained Mrs. Dyson's lack
of refinement, her blunt and forward manner. Still,
she was in some respects an attractive woman;
aquiline nose only slightly sprinkled with freckles,
a fine bosom under the drab gingham dress, and—
he remembered with a connoisseur's appreciation
—a graceful way of holding her body, certainly a
dancer's legacy.

"That so?" he asked. He selected a cigar from his
leather case and bit off the end.

When Martin did not speak further Otis
scratched a match on the seat of his pants and held
out a light. He tried another tack.

"Nice weather, ain't it? For this time of year, I
mean."

"It seems so."

"I'll be glad," Otis said earnestly, "when snow

comes—I mean the *real* snow—good and deep."

Martin drew on the cigar, let smoke drift from his nostrils. The sun was pleasant; it warmed his back through the heavy woolen stuff of his coat. A dancer—she had been a dancer. He tried to remember where he had seen blue like Belle Dyson's eyes. A cornflower blue, he seemed to recall; that was how one of his lady friends in Germantown had identified the shade. But Belle Dyson was a long way removed from the genteel gossip of Germantown ladies.

"Why is that?" he asked absently.

Otis was glad to give information, as well as to receive it. "Why, it's account of old Wolf Voice and them pesky Oglalas! They been seen lately on top of the Chetish there—" He waved toward the distant mountains, their mauve bulk dusted with snow. "Them brutes bushwhacked three miners last summer! Once it snows good, though, they hole up in winter camp. Then civilized folk can breathe easy—till spring, anyway."

Martin was a well-read man. In the East the newspapers, he felt, had treated the troublesome Sioux situation very fairly. There were even organizations like the National Indian Defense Association which had been formed to take the side of the Sioux, who were being pressed relentlessly from ancestral lands by white men pouring into the Black Hills in search of gold. But out here in the Idaho Territory there was little sympathy for the embattled Sioux; the *Yellowstone Journal* daily inveighed against their depredations. He decided to be circumspect.

"Well," he shrugged, "perhaps some snow will

cool a few hot heads." He thanked Otis for the light and resumed his constitutional. Mrs. Dyson's eyes, he decided, were not really cornflower blue, but more of an aquamarine.

An opportunity to help Giles Dyson came sooner than Martin expected. On a cold November night the snow—the *real* snow—arrived in earnest. At dusk an eerie orange glow suffused the western sky. Masses of black clouds boiled over the Chetish. In three hours the temperature dropped forty degrees. Wind drove down River Street like a hammered nail, freezing the mud into sculptured ridges. Passersby leaned into the gale at an angle, and fire-doors clanged all over town as chunks of resinous pine were crammed into stoves.

At first, only a few flakes fell, spiralling and fluttering in the wind. Then, around nine in the evening, the wind dropped. Snow cascaded in a blanket, falling so heavily that River Street quickly became a fairyland of mounded white, with only a mellow lamplight from frosted windows to indicate human presence within.

That night Giles Dyson, as usual, lost heavily at the Paradise. He began to drink heavily. The blacksmith's broad face became flushed, beads of sweat stood out on his forehead, black stains spread under his arms. At the conclusion of one unsuccessful hand, when Giles' two pair lost to Jack Flanders' three treys, the smith angrily swept the cards from the table and spilled his bottle.

"Take it easy," Martin counseled, putting a placating hand on Giles' massive shoulder. But the smith only shook him off, glaring at Jack Flanders.

"You're too God-damned lucky!" he growled.

The gambler stopped the deal for a moment and looked at Giles with opaque eyes. "It's just the play of the cards," he shrugged, and resumed dealing.

"That's right," Gus Terwilliger grumbled. "Don't be a sore loser, Giles! I already lost forty dollars myself!"

The smith continued to lose. His stake nearly exhausted, he stayed in a big pot, drawing two cards. Flanders was dealing, and Martin blinked as he saw again, or perhaps only sensed, that quick blur. He frowned, shifted in his chair, but no one else seemed to have noticed anything out of the ordinary. Martin himself failed to improve a high pair. Since the ante had been unreasonably high he threw in his cards and settled back to puff at his cigar. "By me!" he sighed.

"Ten dollars," Giles cried eagerly. He shoved his remaining chips forward. "All I got!"

The rest had dropped also, except for Jack Flanders. The gambler called Giles' bet, slowly spreading his own hand on the green baize. "Three kings," he announced.

Giles stared at the cards. His face flooded with color. With an oath he flung down his hand; he had held three nines. As Flanders reached for the pot Giles rose, grabbed the gambler's arm. "No, you *don't!*" he said in a strangled voice.

Flanders stared back, eyes chill under the brim of the black wool hat. "Take your hands off me," he said in a low voice.

Angrily Giles flung the gambler's arm away. "You're a crook!" he charged. "I seen you!" He appealed to the rest. "Didn't you see him? He give himself that last card right off the bottom of the deck! That's how he beat my three nines!"

Captain Mapes tried to make peace. "Giles," he soothed, "you've been hitting the bottle too much! Now why don't you just drink some coffee and sober up? There's no need to call names here!"

"That's right!" Frank Abbott agreed. "This has always been a friendly game. Why don't you two—"

"You called me a crook!" Flanders insisted. He had not moved from his chair; he sat like a graven image, arms folded over his chest. "I have killed two men for less than that, Dyson."

"I don't care!" Giles' big hands worked convulsively at his side. "You're still a damned cheat, Jack Flanders!"

Martin was aware the whirr of the roulette wheel had stopped; the call of the banker was silenced. The faro game broke up. The violin on the stage trailed into a reedy dissonance, the orange-haired lady fled. There was a scuffling of chairs as players left their games and found shelter behind posts, the piano, the long mahogany counter.

"Now we don't want any trouble here!" the barkeep protested, coming quickly forward, wiping hands on a stained apron. "This is a high-class place, gentlemen, and—"

"You have called me a cheat, Dyson," Jack Flanders repeated. "Take it back!"

"I called you a cheat," Giles snapped. "I meant it!"

Again there was that quick blur that had so puzzled Martin. Now Flanders' fist held a derringer. It had, Martin realized, probably been up the gambler's sleeve; that was where such weapons were often concealed.

"Apologize!" the gambler ordered.

Giles' face drained of color but he stood his ground stubbornly. "You know I don't pack no iron!"

Mapes, the Sixth Cavalry officer, had been sitting next to Flanders. Before the captain could object, the gambler flipped Mapes' service revolver from its holster, spun the magazine, noted the brass shells showing at the rear of the cylinder.

"Now just a minute!" Mapes protested. But Flanders shoved the weapon across the table toward Giles Dyson.

"Loaded," he observed. "There's a shell under the hammer. Pick it up, Dyson."

Mapes and Abbott and Gus Terwilliger abandoned attempts at peacemaking and shrank back. Martin Holly was left sitting at the table next to Giles Dyson, near—too near—the line of fire of the derringer. It was a small weapon, physically small, but appeared to be of large caliber. There were two barrels, one below the other.

"Pick it up and defend yourself," Flanders said in a flat voice, "or I'll shoot you where you stand."

Giles swallowed. His face contorted. He wet his lips. One hand crept slowly toward the weapon.

"Wait," Martin said.

The tableau froze. It was as if neither the gambler nor the smithy was aware he still sat at the table, such was the unexpectedness of Martin's voice.

"Give me the derringer," Martin commanded.

Flanders stared at him.

"Give me the gun," Martin repeated. He was serene and confident, with no sensation at all of danger. He felt exalted, a more-than-human being looking down at an earthly drama, controlling the actors as if he were a puppet-master.

"Thank you," he said, withdrawing the derringer from Flanders' fist. The gambler's fingers hung foolishly in midair, bereft of the weapon. "You, Giles," Martin instructed tersely, "get the hell out of here! Go home to your wife and Andrew; they're probably waiting up for you. And don't come back to the Paradise any more. If you've got to gamble, pitch pennies in the street!"

Breaking the derringer, he extracted the shells, handed the weapon back to Jack Flanders. "I'm not sure whether you're a cheat or not," he said coolly, "but I have suspicions."

The roulette wheel was silent. The banker's mouth hung open, his pitch forgotten. The violinist still had the instrument tucked under his chin, but his face was pale and frightened. The orange-haired soprano had fled somewhere offstage, and the rest of the spectators seemed stunned.

"Goodbye, gentlemen," Martin said. He tipped his hat to the company and walked out, aware of a new sound that started as he passed through the swinging doors—a quick buzz of comment. He had wanted to remain inconspicuous, but he had failed.

Outside the Paradise Bar stood Giles Dyson, shoulders hunched against the cold, big hands jammed in his pockets. When he saw Martin, he turned. "By God, you shamed me! If you'd of let me alone—"

"If I'd let you alone," Martin said dryly, "that

red-haired woman would be a widow, and young Andrew an orphan."

Now that his performance at the gaming table was over, he experienced depression, gloom, even fear. Trembling, he stamped away toward the Empire Hotel, snow mantling his shoulders as he walked. He needed something from one of the brown bottles in his valise at the Hotel.

CHAPTER TWO

Big Fork was at last caught in the grip of winter
—full, iron-fisted winter. The river froze a foot
thick from bank to bank. Men were already cutting
ice with long coarse-toothed saws, to be stored in
sawdust against the heat of summer. One departure, the *Thomas McKelvey,* steamed away too
late; the sternwheeler was frozen into the Yellowstone a scant mile downstream.

A thick blanket of snow lay over the town, sof-
tening the harsh outlines of false-fronts and shacks.
With river traffic suspended until spring, the only
links between Big Fork and civilization were the
blue wagons of the Diamond R bull trains, along
with a sporadic delivery of "Star Route" mail by
buckboard, and a tenuous telegraph system con-
necting Fort Schofield with the other Territory
posts, and so back to the War Department in
Washington.

Martin avoided the Paradise Bar, now having
unpleasant memories of his recent experience.
He also avoided Giles Dyson's shop; the blacksmith, embarrassed and angry, avoided him. But
the story of what had happened that night spread
from mouth to mouth in Big Fork. Martin Holly
found himself an unwilling celebrity. He was, pop-

ular report had it, a man of steely courage; a "quiet" man, people said, of the sort who minded his own business but whom it was dangerous to provoke. Everyone seemed to subscribe to this theory except Jack Flanders. The gambler put it out that he had turned over his gun to Martin Holly only to preserve the peace, not because he was afraid of him. Most of the town believed otherwise.

Martin now spent much of his time at the Ace of Diamonds in company with Dancer, the trapper. Dancer was an antidote to Martin's spells of depression. The old man had a sardonic tongue, but he talked entertainingly about the "old days"—before civilization encroached on his way of life with metropolises such as Big Fork and Deadwood and Cheyenne. Dancer's stories helped while away Martin's dreary boredom.

"Now you take the buffalo," Dancer reminisced, sipping a shot of whisky Martin bought him. "Territory's nigh hunted out now, compared to what it was, say, in '60, '62. Why, I seen hunters like old Vic Smith get as many as a thousand prime hides in one season! Used to sand his finger to make it tender, give him a better feel on the trigger! But hell—that's greed! Ain't *no* man got a right to slaughter *that* many critters! That's what's angerin' old Wolf Voice and his Oglalas—they got to ride farther and farther each summer to take their supply of meat."

"I suppose hides bring a lot of money," Martin remarked, lighting a stogie.

"There's hides and then there's robes," Dancer explained. "What you get from a bull is a hide, and from a cow it's a robe. Average quality don't bring no more than three, four dollars, salted, rolled, and piled at the landing. Course, there's special kinds, like white and blue. A good blue robe is kinda mouse-colored. It'll bring up to sixteen, eighteen dollars."

"You say they leave the meat to rot?"

Dancer wiped his mouth, looked thirsty. Martin signaled the bartender to bring the bottle.

"Except for the tongue," Dancer explained. "A hunter cuts that out, usual, and broils slices." His eyes shone with remembrance. "Ain't nothing to beat a good hump steak, though, with onions! Fries, too!"

"Fries?"

"Testicles," Dancer said. "Tender as a bride's kiss, and tasty. A man can make himself a good sandwich with the bread, too."

Martin was still pondering "fries." "Bread?"

"Strip of fat runs from the shoulder right along the backbone." Dancer licked his lips. "The Oglalas call it *ni cha nin*—white folks call it 'Indian bread'. All you got to do is fry it in hot grease, kind of seal it. Then you smoke it. When it's cold, it slices nice. Put a slab of hump meat between two pieces of *ni cha nin* and you got as nice a sandwich as was ever served in any restoorant." He fumbled in the tattered buckskin "war bag" he carried with him. "Got a hunk right here." He handed Martin a billet of mahogany-colored flesh.

"Not right now," Martin declined. "I just had supper."

Not caring for the boisterous card games at the Ace of Diamonds, attended for the most part by drunken soldiers and foul-mouthed teamsters,

Martin no longer played poker, although he missed it. Bored, he thought from time to time of moving on, though where to move in this winter season he did not know. It was possible to get a ride on a bull-train, or perhaps on the buckboard carrying the U.S. mail. But those roads all led back east. That was a direction he did not care to take.

One bleak day, the sky a windswept steel-gray and the thermometer hovering near zero, he paused at the post-office. The building was a sagging shack of cottonwood logs set in the ground, roof of poles covered with dirt. *Letters,* Martin thought. *There are letters in that post-office, letters to people in Big Fork from places back East, places like Philadelphia and Camden and Trenton and Germantown, places that had been home.* He had friends in those places, and relatives, but no one was going to write to him.

On sudden impulse he walked into the shabby structure, looked about at the familiar wicket, crudely-carpentered "boxes," the eye-shaded clerk. Trying to appear casual, he shoved his hands in his pockets and stared at the posters tacked to the log wall. Most were printed broadsides, some adorned with villainous-looking woodcuts. He was deep in this examination, face thoughtful, when Otis Spinney came in, flapping furry arms across his chest to warm himself.

"G'afternoon, Mr. Holly."

Martin jumped, looked quickly away from the posters.

"How's things?"

Otis was an inveterate gossip, but Martin hesitated to turn him away too suddenly lest his close scrutiny of the WANTED posters invite comment.

"Very dull, Otis. Big Fork isn't exactly a Utopia."

Otis' brow furrowed. "I ain't never heard of that place. Down the river, is it?"

"I'm not sure where it is," Martin smiled. In spite of the man's wagging tongue he liked Otis. "But I daresay it's warmer there today than in Big Fork." He pulled on his gloves. "Sometimes, Otis, I think I'll make tracks out of here as soon as I can. Living in a hotel is tiresome, and the food is horrible. I've had dyspepsia ever since I've been here."

"Dy—dy—" Otis gave up. "What is that—what you said?"

"Dyspepsia is a derangement of the digestive function, often aggravated by improper diet. Sometimes it can be caused by spasms in the esophagus, but I think in my case it's caused by the cook at the Empire Hotel."

Otis was stunned, but quickly recovered.

"I hope you *don't* move on, Mr. Holly! Big Fork ain't a bad place. We got plans for a school, and the Reverend Mr. Willis holds Baptist services every Sunday morning in the back room at Big Alice's."

"I'm not very religious," Martin said. "I guess you could call me an agnostic."

Otis was unruffled. "We even take in Lutherans at Sunday morning service! There's room for all faiths." He sighed. "Of course, some of the yahoos gives this town a bad name! Any settlement near an Army post, like Fort Schofield, is bound to have a few rough edges. But Big Fork will be a decent place some day." He scuffed a toe on the dirt floor. "What I mean to say—folks around here likes you, Mr. Holly. You're a gentleman, a real gentleman, that's plain to see. Big Fork *needs* people like you. Some of us citizens got together the other night and a feller—guess it was me—mentioned as how you might be persuaded to run for mayor next spring, when Mr. Ab Drury's term runs out."

Martin was startled. "Me?"

"Yes, sir."

"But no one even *knows* me, where I come from, what I'm—what I'm doing out here in the Territory! I mean—well, I just show *up* here, and people want me to run for mayor?"

Otis was dogged. "We *know* what kind of a man you are, Mr. Holly. What happened in the Paradise told us that! Always quiet, never raise your voice or get drunk like most of the citizens around here! Everyone knows you're a gentleman, a real gentleman! You got a lot of book learnin' too. Look at the way you just told me all about dys—dys—"

"Dyspepsia," Martin said. "But what makes people think—"

Otis waved out the door at a drunken soldier, supported by two of his comrades, who demanded to be transported out to Fort Schofield. "I'd consider it!" he called back. "I'd consider it real serious, Mr. Holly! Don't go rushin' off nowheres till you give us citizens a chanct to discuss it with you!"

By what seemed a coincidence, Martin was sitting in the scanty "lobby" of the Empire the next day when Giles Dyson came in. The blacksmith paused, twisting his hat in his hands, big fingers working hard at the brim. His eyes did not meet Martin Holly's. "Could—could we talk?"

Martin was glad to see him. "Sit down," he invited.

The smith poised his bulk on the edge of a spindly chair. "Been meanin' to speak to you," he said. "I—I wanted to explain about the other night, in the Paradise." He reddened, licked his lips. "Fact is—"

"No explanation necessary," Martin interrupted. "I've had a snootful myself from time to time. Someday, maybe you can do a favor for me, Giles." He held out his hand. "Friends?"

The smith grabbed Martin's hand in his own paw.

"That's decent of you, Mr. Holly!"

"Martin."

"Martin, then." Giles swallowed, stared into the depths of the ragged hat. "There's another thing."

"What's that?"

"I hear—the talk is, anyway—you're planning to move on. It's said the grub at the hotel don't agree with you. They say too, that Big Fork is a pretty raw place for a refined man like you."

"So that's what they say." Martin murmured noncommittally.

"Don't go," Giles said. "Big Fork ain't a bad place! Oh, it gets kinda cold in the winter season! But the rest of the year there's birds singing and good pasture, the trees leaf out and all, and—and—" His rhetoric faltered. "I guess I ain't no poet, but a lot of us has put down our stakes here. We mean to make Big Fork a good place for people to live, maybe people that couldn't cut it back east where everything's crowded and expensive. I come from Cincinnati, thirteen years ago myself. Out here folks can have a cow and some chickens and a little homestead."

Martin nodded. "I see."

"So what I was going to say—" Again the big man consulted the interior of his hat. "Me and Belle was talking. My wife is a good cook, and we got this here kind of finished-off room in the barn —it ain't much, but it's snug and warm and there's a good sheet-iron stove and I cut plenty of wood. I keep the mules in there, too, but they won't bother you none."

"Giles," Martin asked, "are you asking me—I mean, *inviting* me to board with you and Mrs. Dyson?"

The smith nodded. "We wouldn't charge you much. We surely ain't in it for the money. But I guess we—I—owe you something, after you stood up for me that night in the Paradise."

"You don't owe me anything," Martin objected.

"We *want* to do it, Mr. Holly! Martin, that is. Belle and I talked it over, and like old Dancer says, that's the way our chip floats. Will you do it?"

Martin was embarrassed. Giles' offer was so transparently sincere, born only of good-will, that he would have difficulty in refusing. *Otis Spinney,* he thought; *that blatherskite!* Otis talked too much; in the future Martin would have to be careful.

"And I guess I got to be honest," Giles went on. I'm too dummed slow-witted to be anything else. We ain't—we haven't got any school here, and Andrew is eleven going on twelve and can't hardly read big print, even. You seem to have a lot of time on your hands, Martin. Maybe you could teach my boy reading and writing and ciphering. I—I'd hate to have him grow up and be a numbskull like his pa."

Martin rubbed his chin, stroked the beard he had lately neglected; it needed trimming and shaping. Giles' last words put a different light on the situation. Home-cooked food, a place of his own, isolated and private, where he could put his store of books on shelves, read at night without the clamor of River Street below. He would pay them well, of course, could also return their simple kindness by tutoring Andrew, their—Giles', he remembered from his conversation with Mrs. Dyson— Giles' towheaded son. It could not be home, but perhaps an approximation of it.

"You're sure it'll be all right with Mrs. Dyson?"

The smith beamed. "Why, I guess most of it was Belle's idea anyhow! I'm sure glad she thought of it! I was wonderin' how to make friends with you again, and now I've done it!"

Martin took a deep breath. "All right," he agreed. "We'll try it for a while and see how it works out, Giles."

When Giles first brought Martin Holly to the small house above the town, Belle Dyson was digging a hole in the frozen ground for a clothes-pole Giles had promised to put up, but had not found time for. "I'm glad you come, Mr. Holly!" she said, holding out a work-hardened hand. Her face was red and flushed, from effort and from the raw wind stirring the winter sunshine. The wealth of reddish hair was pulled back with a scrap of ribbon, and she wore a man's heavy boots. "I hope we can do for you all right, make you feel at home!"

Otis Spinney had said Mrs. Dyson used to be a showgirl, a dancer with a stranded theatrical troupe. Martin came to know her as imaginative and resourceful, making do with whatever came to hand. She did laundry for the soldiers. She took care of sick children, mixing her own poultices and salves from herbs and medicinal plants. She sewed and mended constantly, making shirts for Giles and pants for Andrew; in the snow behind the house lay the remnants of a huge winter-killed garden.

Giles Dyson was big, with a hearty appetite. Though the household was often strapped for credit at the Mercantile, Belle always managed to feed the three males and herself with appetizing food, in quantity to satisfy Giles' voraciousness and Andrew's boyish, play-sharpened hunger; Martin himself was a scanty eater.

Now he spent most of his days in the small room in the barn. He read, made notes for a medical treatise he would write someday, or often simply smoked a cigar and stared out the single glazed window at the great *massif* of the Wolf Mountains, the range the Sioux called the Chetish. At noon Giles clattered in with his team and wagon; the smith sometimes picked up extra money by hauling supplies to the Ophir Mine at the foot of the Chetish. After Giles said grace, they would have a simple lunch of thick soup and fresh-baked bread with Belle's apple-butter, and perhaps the luxury of a tin of peaches. In the afternoon Martin sometimes napped, sometimes strolled the snowy hills, tramping through the resinous pines mantling the lower slopes, making his way with a stout staff. In the evening, after supper, he usually worked with young Andrew at the kitchen table, teaching the boy his "times" tables, explaining the intricacies of multiplication and long division, how to parse a sentence. Belle knitted and Giles dozed in an armchair after a strenuous day at the smithy. Martin quickly found the boy had artistic talent.

"Look here!" he called, proud as if freckle-faced Andrew were his own offspring. "Look how he's drawn this deer! See the little highlights in the eyes? Look how the face is shaded to show the direction of the light!"

Giles snorted, woke in his chair, looked around. Belle came quickly to the pool of golden light on the oilcloth.

"Why, that's pretty, Andrew!" she said, hand spread over her bosom in surprise. "I didn't know you could draw so good!"

Andrew lowered his head, muttered, uneasy at being the center of attention. "I seen a deer like that last week, up the hill from the barn. I guess I just remembered what the critter looked like."

Giles came too, eyes heavy with sleep.

"Looks real," he agreed. "Wouldn't be surprised to see that white tail pop up and the animal skitter away into the woods!" He yawned, stretched. "I declare—I'm that weary! Belle, you comin' to bed?"

"In a minute," she said. "I'll be up directly."

Giles lumbered up the ladder. Belle sent Andrew to wash his hands and face and don his flannel

nightgown. A moment later they heard Giles'
heavy snore from the loft. Belle came to sit op-
posite Martin Holly, her face in the shadow of the
lamp.

"I—I've been wanting to talk to you, Mr. Holly," she said.

He waited, drawing aimless circles and squares.
"Ma'am?"

She was younger than Giles Dyson, closer to his
own age. At first, when he had met her in River
Street, he had thought her rather gauche, the
auburn hair straggly under the sunbonnet, her
manner awkward. She was hardly a lady in the
Eastern sense of the word, but still, Martin did not
know any "ladies" in Philadelphia who had Belle
Dyson's knack of making-do, surviving, getting
along. Too, her love for Giles and young Andrew
was rich and nourishing; at times Martin felt
almost jealous. And now he was beginning to think
her rather attractive.

"I just wanted to tell you," she said, "how grateful I—how grateful *we*—Giles and me—are for
what you're doing for Andrew." She clasped work-
worn hands before her. "You see, I never had
much of a childhood. I was born Sarah Pickens in
Missouri. My pa was a pig-farmer—he drank a lot
—and mama was sick most of the time. I grew up
fast, I had to. I missed out on a lot of things that
are a child's natural right. When pa beat me, I ran
away with Professor Haley's Great Combination
Troups. I fought my way up to be a dancer, and
finally I had my own act."

"I am sure," Martin said gently, "you were a
fine dancer."

"I was as good as most." Belle stared at the green glass shade of the lamp, the brass filigree work below it. "It was Professor Haley started to call me Belle. "Belle La Tour," he said, "that's your name!' He knew French, and he said that meant 'Beautiful Tower'—I was so tall, you see." She sighed. "It was a hard life! Go here on the cars, there on a stage, across the prairies in a wagon, up the mountains on mule-back! I—I—" The hand stole to her bosom in an abstracted way. "A girl in a traveling show had to do a lot of things. Some of them I'm not proud of. But I don't ever want Andrew to be like me. I want him to be educated, have a good life. Most of all I want him to have the chance I never had—"

For a moment she was silent, staring at the green luminance of the lamp. Belle Dyson was, he realized, a woman of character. Giles was a lucky man the day The Great Combination Troupe was stranded in Miles City.

"Mama!" Andrew shouted from the lean-to kitchen. "There ain't no soap!"

"I'll be there in a minute," Belle called back. To Martin she said, "Yesterday I made a fresh batch from pork-fat and wood ashes. Soap costs ten cents a bar at Terwilliger's!" She rose, smoothing her skirts, and went quickly out to the wash-stand in the kitchen.

Martin's outlook on life quickly improved, helped by homecooking, the peaceful atmosphere of the Dyson household, brisk walks in the hills above the town. Andrew adored his tutor, Giles was proud to have Martin under his roof. Belle kept his tiny cell spotlessly clean, changed sheets and pillowcases weekly, did his laundry, sometimes

brought a pot of tea and oatmeal cookies. Now he
did not feel so much need for the medicine in his
satchel. Life took on a happier aspect.

Big Fork, Martin decided, was not the end of
creation he had at first thought it. Though he enjoyed the winter landscape, even experiencing a
thrilled awe at the blizzards—"whiteouts", old
man Dancer called them because the land was ob-
scured by whirling clouds of wind-driven snow—he
thought with anticipation of the coming of spring.
Long denied by his circumstances, a lust for living
began to rise in his veins.

One late afternoon, a red winter sun descending
into smoky obscurity behind a ragged edge of
mountains, he tramped back to the house, puffing
and blowing with effort. Standing the walking-
stick at the door of the barn, he shucked off the
waterproofed-canvas boots he had bought at Gus
Terwilliger's store and entered the barn in his
socks. The door to his cubicle was half-open. Belle
Dyson was in his room, dusting.

Pausing in the doorway, he watched, intending
to say "Boo!" or some such silly thing before he
was discovered. But as she mounted a milking-
stool to adjust the flour-sack curtains, he saw a
long, well-turned limb and a flash of milk-white
skin above the coarse cotton stocking. Feeling a
long denied flush in his loins, he stood motionless.
It was not until she had finished with the curtain
and descended to pick up his brown satchel to dust
under it that he found his voice.

"Don't touch that!"

Surprised, she looked up. "Mr. Holly—it's
you!"

Confused, awkward, he took the satchel. "I—

I'm sorry," he stammered. "I didn't mean to startle you, ma'am. It was just that—that—"

Belle stood before him, chin slightly lifted, bosom still trembling with surprise. The last rays of the sun lit the mahogany hair. Piled high on her head, she could not have known it was a style eastern ladies called a *chignon*. Her face was flushed from the effort of cleaning. Even on this winter day, a dew of perspiration spangled her brow. The lips, he noted with fascination, were full and moist. "I—I didn't intend any harm," she said breathlessly. She was very close to him; her breath was clear and sweet, like that of a child.

"Belle," he murmured, "I—I—"

Suddenly, moved by an impulse, he drew her to him and pressed his lips hard against hers. For a moment her back arched. She pressed hands flat against his chest, strained to pull away. But he refused to relinquish his grasp. Gradually her body softened, conformed to his own, melted against him, thigh to thigh, breasts soft and yet firm against his waistcoated chest.

"Mama!" Andrew called. "Where are you? Come look at the fish I caught through the ice!"

Gently but firmly Belle pushed him away. Her face was pale, and she breathed hard, mouth half-open. Her hand went to her bosom in a now familiar gesture, protectively.

"I'm sorry," Martin muttered.

Belle said nothing. She picked up the dust-cloth and leaned to retrieve the bucket and mop dropping his dirty laundry into a bag made from the sheets stripped from his cot.

"I'm sorry," he repeated.

The sun had dropped behind the mountains and the room filled quickly with dusk. Hay from the loft overhead smelled sweet. Or was it she—Belle Dyson? It had been a long time since he was with a woman. He knew perfumes, French scents, but this was not a man-made fragrance.

"I—I'll come back later and bring clean sheets," she faltered. Head bent, she walked through the open door. "Yes, Andrew," she called. "I'm coming!"

Of course, he had been an idiot. Now he would have to make other arrangements. Dismal as was the renewed prospect of the Empire Hotel, he had brought it on himself. There was no one to blame but Martin Holly. He cursed himself savagely, knowing he was even a worse scoundrel, for having first thought of the dreary hotel dining room, instead of how he had betrayed the trust that Belle and Giles Dyson—and Andrew, young Andrew— had placed in their boarder. Well, he would get out, at once. Excoriating himself, he flung clothes, books, all his meager possessions into the battered trunk. But he stopped, suspended by indecision, when he heard the call from the house.

"Mr. Holly! Supper is on the table!"

Belle Dyson was calling him to supper!

With shaking hands he slopped water on his face, ran a comb through his hair, put on his coat. *If you go in there,* he told himself, *you are a damned rascal! Please have the goodness, the manliness, to beg off on some pretext or other, and to leave as quickly as you can!*

He went in anyway. Giles, face red and beaming from the rough nap of a towel, sat at the head of the table and began a simple grace: "*Father, we thank Thee for this good food prepared by loving hands. Bless it to Thy uses—let it nourish us to Thy bidding always.*"

Once, during the meal, Belle Dyson's blue eyes met Martin's briefly, then looked away. There was something unfathomable in her gaze. Was she hurt, angry, disappointed, indignant—what?

After supper he excused himself on grounds of a headache. "Aw, gee!" Andrew protested. "You was going to read from your book all about Egypt and the Sphinx!"

"Not tonight," Belle said, putting a hand on the boy's arm. "Mr. Holly isn't feeling well."

Belle herself, Martin thought, looked perfectly well. For a moment he almost doubted the encounter in the barn. Still, it had been real enough. Tomorrow, he knew, he would have to say his farewells and go—it was the gentlemanly thing to do. In Big Fork, at least, he had a reputation as a gentleman. But perhaps he would not leave until the end of December. His board was paid until then.

The next day there were complications. Going in to the Mercantile for a handful of cigars he met old man Dancer riding a pony with a high-piled pack-mule following him.

"Leaving Big Fork?" Martin asked. He hated to see his friend depart.

Dancer spat a gout of brown juice, wiped his stubble of beard.

"Goin' to visit my wife." he announced. "Got me a woman in a Cree village up near Whiskey Butte, along Cox's Branch."

Martin had never thought of the old man as domestic. "Oh?" he murmured.

Dancer grinned, the whiskery hole of a mouth twisting in a grimace. "Got me a few bush babies up that way." He rummaged in his war bag and took out a fistful of peppermint candy canes. "For Christimas they allus loves sweets, no matter what else I bring 'em."

"Bush babies?"

"Younkers," the old man said. When he saw Martin was still puzzled, he chortled. "Children! Sprats! Kids!" Putting the candy back in the bag, he became serious. "Let me give you a little advice, pilgrim, before I light a shuck out of here." Leaning forward, he spoke close to Martin's ear. "Keep an eye out for Jack Flanders."

"Flanders?" Martin asked. "Why?"

Dancer looked cautiously about. "Flanders," he muttered, "has been talking around that you and Belle Dyson are puttin' the horns on Giles."

Martin was astonished. "I? Mrs. Dyson?"

" 'Course," Dancer shrugged, "no one puts any stock in it! But Flanders is of a mind to cause trouble. He ain't never bore Giles Dyson no love, either. So it figgers—he hopes to start trouble between you and Giles."

"Well, it's a damned lie!" Martin protested.

"I believe you," Dancer soothed, "but in a place like Big Fork there ain't nothin for people to do during the winter but gossip." He spat again, a Niagara that flooded the snow with a quick amber stain. "Either way Flanders plans to come out ahead. If folks don't believe his story, then he's hopin' you'll call him a liar in public. Frank's a handy man with a gun, and this time he ain't plannin' to hand it over to you. Sabby?"

Martin nodded. "I understand, Mr. Dancer. Thank you for the warning. I'll be very careful."

Dancer waved, dug moccasined heels into the ribs of his speckled Indian pony. Troubled, Martin watched him as the little train ambled down River Street and turned onto the narrow trail leading toward the Ophir Mine and the Chetish beyond.

CHAPTER THREE

Christmas came; Martin Holly was still living with the Dyson family. He knew himself for a fool and lay in his bed each night reproaching himself. He vowed again and again to leave the Dyson household, to go back to the Empire for the balance of the winter, to go anyplace away from Belle Dyson. But he suspected the attraction would continue to draw him, whatever his refuge. All he could do was groan, toss in his sleep, mutter imprecations.

Back East he had been a successful professional man. He moved easily in society, charming—and being occasionally intimate with—more than one delicate young lady or blooming matron. He had had a reputation as a Lothario, could choose for his dalliance among many females: lissom blonde maidens, unhappily-married ladies with raven tresses and smoldering eyes, red-haired vixens of joy and spirit. On weekends at great estates in Bucks County he had even indulged in backstairs amours with pretty maid-servants. Young, successful, distinguished in appearance—Martin sampled them all, and left them tearful and disconsolate. But now he had been wounded by the genuine article, Cupid's arrow. And from Belle's

covert glances from time to time, as if they shared
a secret, he knew she loved him too.

He insisted on buying the family a fat goose for
Christmas dinner, and also purchased a fine English shotgun for Giles, a China-silk shawl for Belle,
and a folding jack-knife of Swedish steel for young
Andrew. Because the farrier-sergeant at Fort
Schofield died suddenly of an apoplectic fit, Captain Mapes was forced to turn to Giles for the im-
mediate shoeing of several remounts. So this
Christmas morning Giles was still in his shop
shoeing cavalry horses but promised to return in
early afternoon for the festive dinner. Andrew was
on the snowy hills with his playmates, whooping
delightedly as he coasted on the iron-runnered sled
his father had made for him. Belle and Martin were
in the lean-to kitchen where she plucked and
dressed the goose.

He sat in his accustomed chimney corner, smoking. Belle bustled about the kitchen, face pink with
effort, brow spangled with perspiration as the stove
heated. The luxuriant mane of hair fell over her
eyes, and she brushed it away with an impatient
gesture. Again he saw that fleeting glance, a look
that somehow linked them in growing passion.

"Can I help you any?" he asked.

"Damn it, I'll never get this bird in the oven and
done before Giles comes! Martin, put more wood
in the stove, will you?"

She swore only occasionally. What would have
been a vulgarity in a lesser woman became to him
a charming anomaly. He put wood in the fire and
sat down again, watching her. How had it happened? Of course, he had been a long time without

a woman. Perhaps this unexpected proximity had simply brought out his basic male need. Or was it more than that?

Fascinated, he watched Belle stuff the goose, noting her slender waist, fine bosom, the swell of hips below the tightly-clinched waist. *Twenty-two inches, twenty-three?* He was, always had been, a calculating connoisseur. Finally, in a casual voice he said, "I—I—that time, in the barn. I kissed you then. I want you to know I did not mean any disrespect." He paused, examining the smoldering cheroot to cover a growing confusion. Finally the words came in a rush. "I love you, Belle! There, damn it all, I said it! I cannot help myself, and I hope you will understand!"

She had put the goose in the pan and dusted the prickled yellow breast with salt and pepper. The shakers paused in midair. Belle did not look at him. "I—I'll try to understand," she said in a low voice, "but—"

He rose and stood near, willing his hands to stay jammed in his pockets. "I know," he admitted, "that I am a fool! Worse than that, I am a scoundrel, and no gentleman! But here, near to you, seeing you move about, smile, laugh, touch your breast in that little gesture as you are doing now, I am helpless, quite helpless. Belle, what shall I do? What shall *we* do? I think—I *must* think—you have affection for me, too."

She turned to face him, blue eyes grave.

"You can't talk like this, Martin! You mustn't!"

Frustrated, he seized her hand. She did not pull away, only continued to gaze at him with that stricken look. He smelled warm flesh, the perfume of her hair, even the coarse soap with which she washed their clothes.

"You *must* feel something for me!" he insisted. "I've seen how you look at me! A man can't be wrong about something like that! It's in a man's bones!"

Her face was pale, even in the kitchen heat. With downcast eyes she murmured, "Yes, maybe I do. You're a fine man, good-looking and refined and all. Giles—he works so hard. When he comes home at night he's worn out and then he sleeps like a log. I—I—sometimes I wake up, in the night. I lay there looking out the window at the stars wondering what's left in life for me! Am I going to get to be an old hag in gingham and my face wrinkled and dry like the old ones in Big Fork? I was a dancer once, you know that. Men liked to look at me. But not anymore—"

"Belle!" he whispered, and pulled her to him. "Belle—you love me! I know it! I—"

The outer door banged and they drew apart. Andrew burst into the kitchen, pink-cheeked, panting for breath. For a moment he stared uncertainly, first at Martin and then at his mother.

"What's the matter, Andrew?" Belle asked, pushing her hair into place.

Andrew's momentary surprise seemed to pass. "I'm hungry!" he announced. "Ain't it time for dinner yet?"

"Isn't," Martin corrected. He sat down in the sagging chair, picked up his cigar from the broken saucer serving as an ashtray. "*Isn't*, Andrew," he repeated.

"Isn't," the boy agreed. "Anyway, I'm hungry!"

Reaching into the jar he snatched a handful of molasses cookies and ran out, trailing the sled by a rope. Belle Dyson put the goose into the oven while Martin held open the door. They did not speak again until Giles came in at two o'clock and said grace.

On the day after Christmas Martin walked down the hill to Terwilliger's for a handful of cigars. Though the "wheelers" in Gus' stock were hardly of Havana quality, Martin had become used to their rank flavor. Lately he had become accustomed to many raw and crude things in the Idaho Territory. One thing he was not accustomed to, however, weighed heavily on his shoulders. That was the burden of guilt concerning Belle Dyson.

He was relieved to see no one in the Mercantile but Gus Terwilliger, reading the week's *Yellowstone Journal*.

"Mornin'," Gus grunted. "How be you, Martin?"

Martin shrugged. "Well enough."

"Sure miss you at the Paradise," Gus remarked, stuffing Martin's cigars into a paper bag and taking his money. "The games ain't been the same since you and Giles left."

"I miss the games too," Martin said.

"Nice Christmas?"

"Very satisfactory."

Gus grinned, winked. "I hear it's pleasant company up there."

"What do you mean by that?" Martin asked sharply.

The merchant busied himself wiping the counter,

polishing a glass globe containing peppermint candies. "Why, I didn't mean nothin'," he said. "Just —well, I suppose it's nice for you to be with Giles and Belle and young Andrew on Christmas Day. Bound to be lonely for an unattached young man." He peered at Martin over his spectacles. "Ain't it, now?"

Martin gripped the paper bag so hard he was afraid he crushed the bone-dry cheroots. "Yes," he admitted. "It can be lonely. I'm very grateful to the Dysons for taking me in."

In River Street Jack Flanders lounged on the porch before the Paradise. The negro swamper was cleaning the gambler's muddy boots while a few loafers sunned themselves. Flanders watched as Martin Holly approached. The loafers fell silent as Martin passed; the only sound was the crack of the negro's rag as he whipped it over the fashionably sharp toes of Flanders' boots. Martin went by, not looking to right or left. But as he walked from under the roof, out into the thin winter sun, he heard suppressed laughter. Jack Flanders said something which Martin did not quite catch; the snorts and giggles broke into derisive laughter. It was time, Martin told himself, to talk to Giles Dyson.

Captain Mapes had not as yet been sent the farrier sergeant he had requested from Fort Abraham Lincoln. Giles was still busy shoeing remounts, young Andrew giving him a helping hand.

"Hi!" Andrew called as Martin approached the smith.

"Hi, Andrew," Martin said, and gave him a nickel. "Run down to Terwilligers'—there's a good chap—and buy yourself some jawbreakers while your pa and I have a talk."

Cheerfully Andrew obliged. Giles watched the boy go, wiping his sweating brow with the hem of his apron. "Glad for a break myself! Mapes has got three more of these hardmouthed critters waitin'!"

The shop smelled of smoke, hot iron, the acid odor of horseflesh, burned hoofs. Martin cleared his throat.

"I've been meaning to talk to you for a long time, Giles. I don't have to tell you how grateful I am for the chance to live with you and Belle and Andrew. It's been a long time since I've had a proper home. But now—" He hesitated, swallowed. "It can't be any secret to you that there's talk about me and—Belle."

Giles wiped his hands on the apron, watched Andrew disappear into the Mercantile far below.

"It's no secret. It's being mouthed all over town."

"So," Martin said, "I want you to know I'm ready to leave, go back to the hotel, go anyplace. I don't want to hurt Belle—I mean, you and Belle and Andrew. After all, it'll be spring in a few months. I'll probably drift on, somewhere west, maybe California. But I'm ready to go, if that's what you and Belle think best."

Giles kept on wiping his hands in an abstracted manner. He stared down the snowy slope where Andrew had disappeared. Finally he spoke.

"Gossip ain't nothin' new to Big Fork. There's people around here gets their chief enjoyment from hurtin' folks. They got tongues—mean tongues— that's hinged in the middle and swings both ways."

He turned to look at Martin. "I ain't worried," he said. "Matter of fact, I'm proud you're stayin' under my roof. You're a gentleman, any fool can see that, and wouldn't do nothin' out of line. You saved my life that night at the Paradise. I couldn't hardly turn you out, could I?"

Andrew ran up the slope toward them, red woollen cap a spark of color against the snow. From the distance they could hear him calling shrilly in exultation, holding up his bag of candy.

"But I—I—" Martin stammered, was confused. "Really, I think it's best if I—"

"You're my friend," Giles insisted, "no matter what Flanders and Otis Spinney and them bastards say. And that's an end to it."

It was not, of course, that easy. Martin stayed in his cubbyhole in the barn, reading sometimes but more often staring out the window. Belle did not walk into town for grocieries anymore, sending Andrew instead. He wondered if she was unwilling to confront the Big Fork ladies. Giles, too, came finally to change. He was always courteous to Martin, kissed Belle on his invariably late return from the smithy. In addition to his remount shoeing he was now busy with a spate of plows and agricultural implements the settlers in the bottom lands along the river wanted to get ready for spring. But something strange began to creep into his manner; he became preoccupied and thoughtful. After supper he customarily napped for a while in his chair, then arose, stretching and yawning, to go to bed. When Belle and Martin sat in the kitchen, she knitting and he chatting idly, they were often aware Giles' heavy snoring had ceased, that he was lying in the loft above, listening. Martin talked about Philadelphia, the East, about musical concerts and art exhibitions, the time he had met Henry David Thoreau, the great writer and naturalist, when he was a boy in Germantown. Belle, avid for culture, listened raptly, fascinated by his talk of famous folk, romantic places.

The affair came to a head late on a January afternoon with a suddenness and decisiveness that was startling. Giles as usual had to work late at the smithy. Belle put hot soup and a chunk of fresh bread into a lunch-bucket and sent supper to him by Andrew. Together Martin and Belle sat in the cozy kitchen, he sipping coffee and she sewing. A dying winter sun lit the green fronds of Belle's prize Boston fern hanging in the window.

"Boston," Martin reminisced, as the orange orb sank behind a ragged spine of mountains. "I loved Boston! When I was a student, we went boating on the Charles of a Sunday." He remembered drifting under the willows lining the bank—a girl, a warm stockinged knee, the maiden smiling at him in a dim green bower of leaves.

"That was when you went to college?"

A soft thigh, gently yielding, a girl's laugh, the sound warm and delicious in the Sunday afternoon stillness.

"College? Oh, yes! Harvard College."

"That's when you studied to be a doctor?"

"Yes."

The room was almost dark. Only a faint golden glow suffused the frost-spangled window. He moved close to her, put his hand on her knee.

"Martin, don't!"

"I must!" he said irritably. "Damn it all, do you think I can sit here day after day, looking at you, not being able to speak my mind; not being able to show you I love you?" He knelt before her, pulled her fragrant curls down to him. "I love you, Belle," he pleaded. "I can't help myself anymore!"

She trembled at the touch of his hand. Her breasts were warm and full under his groping fingers. "Giles," she murmured. "Oh, Martin—Giles! We can't do this to him! He's such a good man!"

He buried his face in the contours of her breast. "Damn Giles!" he cried, and then was contrite. "I don't mean that, of course! But I've got to have you, Belle! You love me too, I know you do! I can see it in your eyes!"

She dropped the sewing. A rush of passion flushed her cheeks, shook her body. Slowly she bent over him, one arm around his neck, warm wet lips pressed against his, the other hand guiding his.

"Martin!" Her voice was strangled. "Oh, Martin—"

The barn was connected to the kitchen lean-to by a covered roof to permit passage when the snow was deep; in that dark aisle they could not be seen. Inside his little room a fire smoldered in the pot-bellied stove, but they did not need the warmth. As the last light of day faded, they lay together on the patched blue and white quilt, pressed their bodies together. A tide of delight and tenderness swept over Martin. Even with all his dallying it was a feeling he had never before experienced.

When they were satiated Belle laid her head in the hollow of his arm. Gently she touched his cheek. "Your body is so perfect, Martin. So—so straight, and nicely put together. There's no blemish on you at all, except maybe this little scar here. This moon-shaped scar."

He followed her hand to his cheek and held it in his own, saying nothing. No blemish? There was a larger scar on him, a scar that no one could see.

"Where did you get it?"

"Get what?" His mind had strayed far away.

"The little scar."

He thought of a schoolyard in Germantown, long ago. How far from there he had come, in time, in way of life, in prospects!

"A schoolboy fight, when I was small. A boy hit me with a stick. Almost got my eye. You can see how close it was."

For a while she was silent. Then she said in a low voice, "We must never do this again, you know."

He got up, walked to the window. There was a glow from the forge in Giles' shop. A crescent moon hung on the horizon. Everything was still. Together they walked back to the lamplit kitchen. Andrew was there, slicing a ragged chunk of bread from the loaf.

"I wondered where you was, mama," he said, slathering the bread with Belle's raspberry jam.

That night Martin went to bed early. Before he slept he stood outside in the cold clear air, looking up at the infinity of stars prickling the night. Over all loomed the snow-mantled bulk of the Chetish, ghostly in the starlight. He breathed deeply of the crisp air, feeling fit and invigorated. He would probably not need the medicine tonight, now that the male need had been satisfied. Peace enveloped his troubled soul.

As he turned to enter the barn he paused, staring down at the white blanket under the single window of his quarters. There, in deep snow not previously touched, were footprints. Someone had stood only recently under his window, looking in. He felt his heart skip, then resume its beat with a deep insistent thumping.

Andrew? Not likely. Giles? But Giles had been down below, busy at the forge, and Giles wore blunt-toed Wellingtons, scarred and scorched by melted iron. These prints were small, almost dainty. The toes were sharp, like the—the—

Squatting on his heels, staring, he remembered where he had seen boots like that; Jack Flanders, on the porch before the Paradise. Had the gambler been outside the barn, listening, watching, while he and Belle lay together? Martin went inside, disturbed, and did not sleep well.

He had read silly French novels in which men abandoned wives, children, station, honor, in pursuit of a beautiful female. Scoffing at such literature, he thought it not true to life, even for creatures like Frenchmen. But in spite of the danger he and Belle could not resist each other. They continued to cuckold Giles Dyson and the scandal grew. In constant fear they would be discovered, they relished stolen moments of delight. Giles did not seem to suspect. The smith, Martin concluded, was one of those noblemen of nature, so honest and innocent he refuses to believe evil of others, even in the face of hard fact. But this comforting fantasy did not long last.

One blustery day Martin met Otis Spinney in River Street. The drayman reined up his team and looked down at Martin, heavy brows thatched with snow. "Do you know where's Giles, Mr. Holly?"

"Giles?" Martin was puzzled. "Isn't he in the shop?"

Otis shook his head. "I got a cracked tire on my back off wheel, and I can't find him. Shop's closed, padlocked. Now ain't that a hell of a way to run a business?"

That night Giles came home late. He acted sullen, and spoke only in a monotone. Belle fixed his solitary supper, looking concerned but saying nothing. When Martin mentioned his conversation with Otis Spinney, Giles only stared at him, muttered "That so?" and wearily climbed the ladder to the loft. His boots were muddy and his face flushed, either from liquor or windburn. Belle and Martin did not talk, only sat together and stared into the fire.

Giles' absences from his forge grew more frequent, longer. Business, never prosperous, dwindled. At times Giles did not even come home at night. Martin made discreet inquiries but no one in town seemed to know where the smith went. There were only a limited number of possibilities, and Giles did not appear to frequent any of the known places. When he did return, he was uncommunicative. Belle feared to press him. Even young Andrew, worried about his father's strange behavior, met only silence and went about worried and white-faced.

"There, there!" Belle comforted the boy. "Your papa's not feeling well, I guess. But it'll pass—it'll pass." When she looked at Martin, her face was pale and drawn, eyes pained. *What must we do?*

she seemed to ask. *What can we do?*

With the smithy failing, Giles brought home even less money. Martin, over Belle's protests, went to Terwilliger's and bought groceries—lard, flour, beans, sidemeat, a ribbon for Belle's hair, a spinning top for Andrew. In his illicit passion he had neglected Andrew's education, and felt guilty on that account.

As he emerged from the Mercantile, carrying the supplies in a wooden box, Captain Mapes reined up in River Street and called, "Martin, you know where I can find that damned Giles Dyson?"

Giles had been absent for two days. Martin shook his head. "Otis Spinney said he saw him hitch up his wagon and mules and take the old trail up to the Ophir Mine. I remember hearing say Giles sometimes hauls supplies up there."

Mapes shook his head. "Ophir's closed for the winter. No one up there but a caretaker." He swore, tugged at his brushy mustache. "God damn it, I got a field ambulance needs work before spring comes and the Sioux start to raise sand! All Fort Lincoln sends me is a bunch of pimple-faced kids right off the turnip-wagon! Not a mechanic in the lot! Most of 'em don't even know which end of a hammer to take hold of!" He waved a paper. "I got a War Department contract right here. All it takes is for Giles to make his mark and I can keep him busy for a month! But no—the loafer disappears! If I didn't know he was an honest man, damned if I wouldn't suspect him of running guns up to old Wolf Voice!"

The next day Giles reappeared. Driving his mules and canvas-bowed wagon into the yard, he unhitched the animals and grained them, along with a strange saddlehorse. Dusk came early; gray clouds massed over the Chetish and there was a smell of snow in the air. The iron stove alternately roared and murmured as freakish currents of air swirled about the mud-and-stick chimney.

"Giles!" Belle ran to him, tried to embrace him. "Where have you been! We—I—Andrew and I, Martin, too, was worried!"

Giles' chin was unshaven and there were deep circles under his eyes. His broad face sagged. There was a gash in one boot, edged with dried blood.

"Let me look at that!" Martin urged with quick interest. But Giles thrust him aside and slipped off his coat.

"Just a little hide scraped off," he mumbled. "Axe slipped. Nothing to worry about."

"Papa, where you been?" Andrew insisted. "We missed you!"

Giles looked at his son for a long time, affection in the pockmarked face. He reached out a hand, touched Andrew's cheek awkwardly. "Missed you, too, boy," he said. He muttered a solitary grace, then bolted the sidemeat Belle had fried, slopped gravy on thick slices of bread, drank coffee.

"I'm weary," he said finally.

In what seemed a daze he passed a hand over his forehead. The three were silent, watching him. On the slab mantel the clock ticked loudly against the background of a rising storm. "Going to be a real rouser," Giles said absently, staring out the window. The lights of Big Fork had disappeared in a preliminary sifting of snow. He yawned, stretched, shook his head as if to clear it. "Best go to bed," he muttered.

The three sat together in the kitchen while

Martin tried in vain to explain fractions to Andrew. Belle's needles clicked; from time to time she glanced at Martin and then fixed her eyes again on the sock she was knitting. Martin was patient with Andrew, but none of them had their minds on their tasks. In the loft Giles snored. There was not a single creak from the ancient springs. The smith was lying there, they knew, like a log—utterly exhausted.

At eight o'clock Belle sent Andrew up to bed, and a few moments later Martin said goodnight to her.

"Sleep—sleep well," she faltered. "I—I—after while I'll go out and bring in a few chunks of wood for the stove." There was a silent message in her eyes. He nodded briefly and went out, bending in the gale that drove flakes of snow like needles into his face.

Inside he smelled familiar odors of hay, manure, mules, urine. The bigger mule—Nick—whickered. Martin often gave them apples. He patted Nick's soft muzzle, stared at the strange bay, then went into his cubicle and lit the lamp. The stove was out and the room was cold. Soon he would be warm under the buffalo robe, and did not bother to kindle the fire. In the meantime he sat on the edge of the cot and waited for Belle.

In a few minutes she came in, shawl pulled tightly, shivering.

"Martin," she said in a trembling voice, "we can't go on like this! It has got to stop! It's destroying Giles! And think of what it will do to Andrew if he finds out!" In the light of the lamp her eyes shone with unshed tears. "We've both been wrong, and both of us know it! Giles is a good man, a kind man. We've dishonored him, and ourselves, too!"

Martin stared into the lamp, not knowing what to say.

"I haven't been an angel in my life," Belle went on. "I don't suppose you have, either. But I'm honest with myself, and I expect you to be too, Martin. I—I—for a while, I guess I saw a little bit of what life might have been. I loved you, and you brought something I needed into my life. But I loved—I *love* Giles too. In a different way, maybe." Her lips twisted in frustration. "Oh, it's too damned hard to explain! How can I make sense to you?"

It was the end, of course. They had carried on the affair too long.

"Belle," he sighed. "Belle LaTour!" He drew her to him, kissed the hair, her cheeks, felt the wetness of her tears on his tongue. It was late to be a gentleman again, but he had to try. "Kiss me goodbye," he commanded, putting a gentle hand under her chin, tilting the tear-stained face up to his. "In the morning I'll leave. I don't know where to go, but I can't stay here, where you are. The mail is due to go east tomorrow. I'll pack and ride the buckboard, I guess. Anyway—kiss me, Belle, kiss me so I'll remember."

They embraced. She pressed her lips against his. Breasts crushed softly against his pounding heart, she wept. "Martin! *Martin!*"

They were standing so, locked in each other's arms, when the door banged open. A gust of wind drove a feathery cloud into the room. Giles Dyson stood in the doorway, pointing the English shotgun

Martin had given him for Christmas. Behind him Andrew cowered, nightshirt flapping about his ankles.

"Get ready!" Giles blurted. His face was pale, but his grasp on the weapon was steady and unwavering. One broad finger curled around the trigger.

Belle moaned in distress, stepped away from Martin Holly.

"Ready? Ready for what?" Martin paled. "What do you mean?"

Giles spoke to Andrew. "Get your shirt and pants on, boy!" His eyes never left Martin Holly. "Hitch up Nick and old Pansy to the wagon. Quick, now!"

"But, papa—"

"Git!" the smith snarled.

As Andrew fled, Giles stared unwinking at the stunned pair. "You, Belle, go in the house and snatch up that old green valise! Put your belongings in it. Martin, take along whatever you can pack in five minutes!"

"Where are we going?" Martin asked.

Giles Dyson smiled, a strained grimace. "You and her will find out soon enough!"

"But—"

Seeing Martin move forward, hand raised in supplication, Giles twitched the barrel of the shotgun. "Do what I say and no one will get hurt!" he ordered. "But if either one of you makes a move I'll—I'll—" He broke off and his face turned bleak, agonized. "Then I'll shoot t'other one! If you don't value your own hide, Martin, maybe you love her so dummed much you don't want her harmed!"

"Giles!" Belle pleaded. But the smith's gaze turned stony.

"Move!" he growled, "and be quick about it! It's time to put an end to this sorry business!"

CHAPTER FOUR

In the middle of the night they sat—Belle Dyson and Martin Holly—huddled under blankets in Giles' wagon. The smith squatted in a corner, shotgun across his lap, watching them by the light of a coal-oil lantern. Andrew drove the team. From time to time they could hear the boy against the background of wind rippling the wagon-canvas, whipping up the mules, sometimes weeping. The strange saddle horse, tethered to the tailgate, plodded behind them.

"I don't know where you're taking us!" Martin protested, "or what you plan to do, Giles! But can't we at least talk this over?"

"You think I need to be bored for the simples?" Giles jeered. "You think I'm just a dummed stupid mechanic, without no brain in my head? You two been acarryin' on for weeks! It's good thing Jack Flanders caused me to see the light!" A stone jug stood next to him. He unstoppered it, took a long draft. "At first I didn't believe all them tales! I didn't think it, not of either of you. But now I know the truth. The scales has been lifted from my eyes!" He swore horribly, fingering the dual triggers of the shotgun.

"But—but we didn't mean any harm!" Martin pleaded. "I know it looks bad, Giles, but believe me! Both Belle and I decided it was wrong! We were ashamed of ourselves, ashamed we were doing this. You've got to believe me! When you came in on us, we were saying goodbye to each other. I was planning to leave, to go away somewhere, and—"

"Shut up!" Giles waved the shotgun. "You're that smooth, Martin Holly, you could talk the lard off a hog, with all your big words and education! No, I ain't going to listen to you! I made up my mind what to do, and I'm going to do it!"

The mules were toiling up the old grade toward the Ophir Mine. The wagon swayed and rocked, iron tires grating as the animals slipped and scrambled for footing. Behind them the tethered bay picked his way. Near the top of the hill, where the tailings dump was, Giles stuck his head through the canvas to speak to Andrew. "Turn left, boy," he instructed. "Just beyond that dead pine that kindly leans over the road."

"Papa," they heard Andrew say, "I don't see no road there."

"It's there, right enough," Giles insisted. "Don't I know? Pretty poor goin', but Nick and Pansy will make it—if'n the wagon holds together."

The going became more precipitous. The stout oak planks of the wagon groaned, wheels ground and scraped, Belle and Martin were forced to hold on to the wagon-bows as they inched upward in the night, their way lit only by a pale moon glowing through the falling snow. They passed frequently under low growths of juniper and cedar that scratched and tore at the canvas, obscuring even partial vision of the narrow mountain trail. At these times Giles clambered out of the wagon with a muttered threat to them, walking ahead in the darkness, holding the lantern high and calling instructions to Andrew. "Pull over to the right, boy —there's a big boulder here!" Or, "Whip up the mules, Andrew! We got to climb over this ledge crossways in the road!"

Shaking with fear and cold, Martin and Belle crawled together, covering themselves with a common blanket. It was no longer a matter of deceiving Giles Dyson. Martin clutched his satchel. Belle had a carpetbag in her lap, stuffed with whatever she had been able to pack on short notice.

"What do you suppose he's going to do?" she asked. Her voice trembled and she made an effort to keep it steady.

Martin shook his head. "I don't know." He groped for her hand under the blanket. "Whatever he has in mind, it's best not to provoke him; he's been drinking. Men like Giles sometimes go to pieces completely, commit horrible crimes."

She shuddered. "He was always so good to me— and Andrew."

"Men change," he said soberly. "We all change, given enough provocation."

The smith climbed wearily into the wagon. "Gone as far as we can tonight, I guess," he grunted. "We'll wait for daylight. Andrew's building a fire, and I rigged a canvas over some bushes to break the wind a little." He tossed them a paper sack of soda crackers, along with a water bottle. "Git out, eat if you've a mind to, tend to your needs behind a bush somewheres. But remember—" He patted the carved walnut stock of the shotgun. "I aim to keep an eye on the both of you. I'm tellin' the Lord's truth when I say I'll shoot if there's any monkey-business!'

He did not mean to murder them out of hand; he could have done so in Martin Holly's cubbyhole in the barn when he caught the lovers in each other's arms. On the other hand, that might have lead to a murder charge in the Big Fork justice court. Perhaps Giles was hurrying to a secluded spot to shoot them, bury the bodies in an unmarked grave. Still, there would be Andrew as witness—Martin was puzzled. He chewed a mouthful of dry cracker, washed it down with icy water from the canteen.

"The sun is coming up, I think," Belle murmured as they sat, cross-legged, in the meager wind-whipped shelter. Her voice was hoarse, and he wondered if she was catching cold. Why, if Giles intended to kill them, had he brought them so far? Bodies could be dumped in any convenient ravine. By spring there would be nothing left but bones and scraps of clothing, perhaps a button or two. Martin watched Giles standing in the middle of the rough trail, shotgun in the crook of his arm, staring thoughtfully at the orange glow of dawn.

Belle cleared her throat and spoke in a low voice. "Martin, whatever *is* he thinking to do with us?"

"I don't know," he sighed. His eyes were red and weary and on his chin grew a prickly stubble. "But whatever it is, it will be—appropriate. He must have thought this over for a long time."

With the coming of dawn the snow ceased to fall. In slanting orange rays the wagon toiled upward again. Not far above was timber-line, an abrupt cessation of growth that left the peaks bare and sterile. Martin was bruised from the jouncing about and Belle had hurt her wrist when she was thrown against the side of the wagon.

"Can't we get out and walk?" Martin pleaded. "We're getting knocked to pieces in here! The wagon isn't going any faster than a good walk, anyway!"

Giles hooked a finger in the handle of his jug, tipped it on his forearm and gulped. He set the jug down and drove in the cob stopper with a blow of his fist. "There's a time for walking," he growled. "Around noon you'll both be on shanks mare."

At last the wagon came to a cul-de-sac. The trail necked down, narrowed to a foot-path through the chaparral.

"Papa," Andrew called, "we can't go no farther with the wagon!"

Giles climbed out, yawned, stretched his legs.

"Unhitch the mules, boy," he commanded. "Let 'em browse around. And untie me that bay horse and put the saddle onto him."

Stiff and sore, Martin and Belle descended, grateful for the thin winter sunlight. Wrapped in blankets, they watched Andrew saddle the strange bay. From time to time the boy turned a worried face toward his step-mother. Giles, watching him, spoke roughly. "Get a hustle on! We ain't got all day!"

When the bay was ready Giles pulled his bulk onto the animal, sliding the shotgun into the saddle-scabbard. "That way!" He pointed to the path through stunted junipers. "Get goin', you two miserable specimens!" To Andrew he said, "Stay with the wagon, boy! I aim to be back before the sun goes down. If'n I don't, build yourself a little fire and eat some of the grub in the box under the seat."

Andrew's young face twisted in grief. "Mama!" He ran to Belle, threw his arms around her. "Don't go, mama! I don't care what you done—I don't want you to go!"

Belle knelt and kissed the boy, murmuring words of comfort. But Giles, leaning from the saddle, grabbed Andrew's arm and jerked him away.

"None of that, now!" he muttered. "She ain't worth no tears!"

Blanket-wrapped, Belle and Martin trudged along the trail, only dimly lit by winter sun filtering through the snow-laden greenery. Jays and nuthatches flitted ahead. The lovers slipped and scrambled on icy ledges and outcroppings where the warmth of the sun had not reached. Fortunately, the path seemed now to descend. From time to time they passed small parklike meadows rimmed with leafless aspen. A deer stood transfixed in the trail, then bounded into the underbrush, white tail aloft.

"Where are we?" Martin wheezed.

Giles, ambling along on the bay, scowled.

"Git along a little faster," he commanded. "The sun's almost nooning already."

In the meadows the snow was two, perhaps three feet deep. When they crossed a glade at Giles Dyson's direction, they staggered, fell, picked themselves up, fell again. Reaching the far edge they paused, winded. Giles looked at the thin veil of clouds drifting over the sun. "Weather making up," he remarked. "Hurry along! It ain't but another two, three miles."

Belle panted for breath. The glorious hair had fallen over her face and her hands were chapped and scratched. Martin did not look any better. But when Giles growled at them, gesturing with the shotgun, they staggered on.

Neither had any least idea where they were; somewhere on top of the Chetish probably, but the circuitous route, much of it during the night, had completely disoriented them. They were many miles from Big Fork, and many thousands of feet above the Yellowstone. The light rain of snow had resumed, and they did not even know where north lay.

In late afternoon, to judge from the dying light, Giles rode ahead, scanning the trees. "Here she is," he announced. There was pleasure in his voice, and something poignant. When they caught up with him, gasping for breath, he pointed. "There!"

In a clearing stood a cabin of barked logs, a swaybacked structure with a rock chimney at one end and behind it a rude shed. There was a ruined pole corral and a well-sweep. A small pond near the cabin was frozen over. The roof of the cabin sagged. There was about the crude habitation a loneliness and desolation softened only by snow that mounded every protuberance, and the knowledge that someone had once settled here; settled here, and failed.

"What—" Belle's voice faltered. "Giles, who lives here?"

"You do," he growled. "You and your dummed paramoor, or whatever a man's called when he sneaks into your house and steals away your wife right under your nose!"

Martin was astounded. "We? Belle and I? Live here?"

"You two love each other so much, now you're going to stay here and make a go of it, you hear?"

"But—but—"

"There'll be six, eight, ten feet of snow before long. You can't git out—you can't git away from each other! And you'll be alone at last! No need to jump and run when you hear Giles, good old dummed Giles, acomin' in!"

Belle pressed a hand to her breast. "You can't mean it! Please, Giles—"

"This is the place Mary and me built when we first come out to the Territory," Giles went on, ignoring Belle's entreaty. "Mary had Andrew here, and then died of the smallpox. I was going to raise sheep, have a cow for fresh milk for the child, maybe cut a little timber, hoped I'd find gold in the hill back there." His eyes glinted with a sparkle of moisture. "Anyway, when Mary died, me and Andrew went down to Big Fork. That was the end of it." He dismounted. "I been coming up here, bringing a little stuff like flour and lard and tea and sugar, patching up the place. There's an old musket in there that once belonged to Mary's pa, and powder and ball. You two can make your way, if you've got the guts to do it. Anyway, it's a hell of a lot more than Mary and me started out with!"

Martin moved angrily toward him. "You can't just leave us here like this! We'll starve! What the devil do we know about living in the wilderness? We'll both be dead in a week, from starvation or wild animals or just the cold!"

Giles turned the shotgun on him; Martin shrank back. But aware of their perilous situation, he continued to argue.

"You can't get away with this! Why, it's—it's against the law! People will see we've disappeared, Belle and I, and they'll ask questions! They'll say you took us on the Chetish and murdered us, that's what they'll say! They'll say you killed us and buried us in some unmarked grave, and there'll be charges filed!"

Wearily Giles shook his head. "Not in Big Fork, Martin! Everyone there knows what you done to me. No matter what happens, they'll figger you and her got your just deserts."

"But Andrew!" Belle protested. "Andrew will tell them you—you—"

"Tell them what?" Giles demanded. "Why, I'll just explain it to the boy when I get back down on the road. I'll tell Andrew you and your dummed lover just decided to go it alone up here. Didn't I fix up this love cottage for the two of you? Didn't I bust my back driving supplies up here for you two lovebirds, cut my leg with an axe splitting shingles, get everything ready for you?" He shook his head. "No, no one ain't going to bother about either of you." His bearded lips twisted in a grimace. "If I wanted to kill you, either one of you, I could of done it a long time ago. But you saved my life onct, Martin, and I ain't forgot it." He turned toward Belle. "And I loved you, woman, till you betrayed me! So I figgered this way out. Now it's up to you and that—that—" He broke off, and finally wept. "You ain't no whore, Belle LaTour that was Belle Dyson, but you cheated me, you deceived me, you shamed me and Andrew!"

Shoulders sagging, Giles trudged to the patient bay, swung his bulk again into the saddle. The snow was falling harder; in the downpour his figure was indistinct. Barehead, he leaned over the saddle-horn and muttered a prayer:

"Lord, these here two don't know what they done to me. I can't kill no one, I ain't never been that kind of a man. But this here is the best way I can think of to set things straight. I hope you'll forgive me if I done wrong but it was all I could come up with. Amen."

Belle watched him wheel the bay, trot back toward the rude trail, now indistinguishable among the serried ranks of trees. Martin ran after him.

"Don't leave us here!" he shouted. "Giles, come back! We'll do anything!" Big Fork was frontier enough, strange in its scenes and practices, but this abandoned dwelling in the depths of the wilderness struck terror into his heart. "Giles—"

From the silent gloom of the forest the shotgun roared. Twigs, pine-cones, torn bark fell in a shower on Martin's bare head as the heavy balls cut a swath through the branches. He threw himself to the ground, buried his face in snow and pine-needles, panic-stricken. After a while he got slowly to his feet, brushed dirt from his face and hands, walked back to the abandoned cabin. Belle hurried toward him.

"Martin, did he—did Giles hurt you?"

He shook his head. "I don't think he meant to. He only wanted to scare me off, keep me from following."

Standing together before the rude cabin they watched the snow swirl thickly down. Already they could not make out the opening in the trees where Giles Dyson disappeared. They were marooned; marooned as completely as any shipwrecked sailor —and with as little hope of rescue.

Belle pressed his hand, drew close to him.

"At least," she murmured, "we're together."

"Yes," he said, almost absently.

Inside, the cabin was decrepit. The two small windows were of thin-scraped deerhide, cracked and yellowed so that only an amber glow filtered through. In one corner stood a bed of rough lumber strung with leather thongs. On it lay a soiled mattress stuffed with long-dead cornhusks. There was a rickety chair, a home-made table of planks, and a cupboard. Belle pulled at the cupboard knob and the door fell off, raising dust from the earthen floor.

"Giles had every right to be angry," Martin complained, "but there was no call for this! I would have preferred he shot us both where he found us, instead of leaving us to starve to death in this hovel, or freeze, which is more likely!" He sprawled in the chair, blanket pulled around his shoulders, staring at the yellowing calendar tacked on the wall. The last page, tattered from the attacks of a chewing insect, was May of 1861; the calendar advertised a firm of wagon builders in Cincinnati.

Belle examined the contents of the cupboard, peering up onto shelves, looking into sacks. "I never wanted to hurt him," she confessed. "That was sin enough, what we did. But more than that, we committed adult—adult—"

"Adultery."

"Yes, that's it, what the Bible says! That's a greater sin than just *hurting* someone!"

He shrugged. "Perhaps."

"There's flour, in this sack," Belle called. "And a flitch of bacon, but it's frozen." She opened a can. "Hmmmmm—tea. And sugar."

The wind blew snow through the broken door. Belle picked up a hatchet and a box of rusted nails, hammering the leather hinge in place again, closing the door.

"What's the use of that?" Martin complained. He slumped in the chair, satchel on his lap. "We'll be dead before morning, anyway!" He was utterly defeated.

She knelt beside him. "Martin, don't be gloomy! We're not dead *yet!*" She stroked his cheek. "There's a pile of wood outside," she said. "Giles must have cut it for us. There isn't much, but you can start a fire and I'll put snow in the iron pot to melt. A little tea will warm us up." In spite of his protests she put her arms around him and kissed him. "We'll show him—we'll show Giles Dyson! I've been in worse fixes than this when I was with Professor Haley's troupe! I come out a little banged up, maybe, but I made it. And we'll get out of this, too, you'll see!"

With a small fire in the fireplace, they lay that night on the rude bed, covered by the burr-pricked horseblankets Giles had given them during the wagon trip. The wind howled unceasingly. More than once during the night they were sure animals were prowling outside. "There's that old musket in the corner," Belle whispered. "Why don't you get up and load it, just in case?"

He burrowed deeper into the stinking blankets. "What do I know about loading a relic like that— powder and ball and flint and things?"

"I'll bet I could do it," Belle insisted.

"Then do it!" he blurted, "and let me sleep!"

For a moment she was silent. Then she murmured, "Martin!" in a hurt voice.

Wearily he turned toward her, one of the rawhide thongs snapped as he did so. "Belle," he protested, "I'm sorry! But if a grizzly broke in, the whole thing would come to an end faster, surely more mercifully! Starving to death, freezing to death, can be a long-drawn-out and horrible experience!"

Unable to cheer him, she snuggled close. Grateful for the warmth of her body, he finally slept.

In the morning Belle hacked chunks from the bacon and fried tough little cakes of flour and water and salt in sizzling bacon grease. The meal turned Martin's stomach sour. When they tried to open the door, they found it piled almost to the lintel with snow. By their combined efforts, aided with a rusty shovel, they forced it open. Outside, snow still fell. The stuff walled all four sides of the cabin, almost obscuring the windows. The end of the wellsweep stuck up from the snow like a signal for help. The frozen pond had completely disappeared, and the tall pines surrounding the meadow were heavily freighted with snow. From the forest came an occasional *shhh—thunk* as snow slid from overburdened branches.

"Look there!" Belle cried, pointing.

Martin looked. Emerging from the dark depths of the forest was a kind of ragged trough in the snow, punctuated by deeper holes. A large animal of some kind had circled the cabin, even approached the door.

She clung to his arm. "Oh, Martin!"

"This time of the year I suppose the wolves are hungry. I recollect old man Dancer saying the deer come down to the lower altitudes for the winter, so the wolves left up here get pretty thin—and vicious."

She stared at him. "Why are you talking that way?"

"Talking what way?"

"Dwelling so on gloomy things like that! Anyway, I don't think a wolf would eat a person!"

"You never know," he said.

Angrily she pressed the hatchet into his hand. "There's some fallen trees at the edge of the meadow! Go out and cut some limbs for firewood! Last night we used most of what Giles left us!"

He hacked off a few of the smaller limbs and dragged them into the cabin. Belle was dusting the shelves with a rag. Somehow the sight seemed to infuriate him.

"Damn it!" he shouted, "don't you realize we're in a serious situation? How can you potter about like that, dusting—my God, *dusting*—like you were in your own house?" The scar on his cheek tightened, glowed red.

She looked at him, lips compressed in a tight line. Finally she snapped, "Go blow your nose, Martin, do! It's running!"

During the next few days it continued to snow. They huddled before the fireplace wrapped in blankets, hungry and shivering. The bacon was half gone, only a few cups of flour were left, the tea exhausted. Some cornmeal remained, dotted with frozen weevils. Martin sank deeper into passivity. Alarmed at a cough he had developed, Belle floundered through thigh-high drifts herself to cut wood for the scanty fire, pulled her own blanket around his shoulders to warm him, told jokes.

"We'll pull through!" she insisted. "We're bound to!"

He shook his head. "We're dying, that's all—and you don't even know it!"

"I sure as hell don't know it!" she cried. "And so long as I don't know it, I'm not going to admit it! And so long as I don't admit it, it's not going to happen! Anyway—" She tossed her head. "I wouldn't give Giles Dyson that much satisfaction!"

Her face was gaunt and smudged. The mahogany hair was tied up in a bun, bound in place with a dirty rag. One buttoned shoe was split; her toes showed through the wreck of the stocking. Martin stared at her, shook his head, hunched down in the chair again.

"Suit yourself," he said gloomily.

Soon, to Belle's further alarm, he seemed to drop into a delirium. Nothing touched him. He smiled to himself, muttered aimlessly, sat all day in the chair, even all night, rebuffing her pleas to come to bed. He might be dying, she thought. She remembered how, days before the end, her grandfather had sunk into the same kind of peaceful inaction, eventually dozing his life away.

"Martin!" she insisted, "get out of that damned chair! You've got to move about, keep the blood flowing in your veins!"

He stared at her, smiling vacuously. "Flowing," he murmured. "Flowing! Why, I'm flowing along right now, Belle! On a river! It's the most beautiful river you ever saw! Water, warm water! Palm trees are bending over the water, and a soft wind is blowing." His eyes rolled upward in ecstasy. "No ice, no snow! Just warm water!"

Frustrated, she pulled him to his feet. Though the rigors of their privation had weakened her also, she wrestled him upright and held him by the soiled lapels of his coat, glaring into his lackluster eyes.

"Stop that silly grinning! Stop it!"

She slapped him hard on the mouth, but he only licked his lips and stared at her. "Water," he murmured. "Warm tropical water!" He made vague paddling notions. "I'm swimming in it—swimming in the warm water. Belle, come on in!"

Hopeless, she let him sag into the chair. There was nothing more she could do. Resignedly she picked up the hatchet—the handle had split but she repaired it with some rusty wire she found in the shed—and floundered out into a lead-gray morning. The small fireplace consumed an astonishing amount of wood even to keep the temperature of their habitation above freezing. At night the snow-water in the iron kettle froze rockhard while they slept.

By now they had almost exhausted the dead wood at the edge of the clearing, and were forced to go deeper and deeper into the forest. Hacking one day at a fallen limb, she straightened in panic at a low growl. In the underbrush a great dog-like creature stared at her with glowing eyes. Panic-stricken, she dropped the limb and ran to the cabin. Once inside, she bolted the door and leaned against it, hand over her pounding heart.

"There's a wolf out there!"

Martin sat at the table, his satchel before him. Several vials littered the table and he was holding one to his lips. He peered dazedly at her. The brown bottle dropped from nerveless fingers, contents spreading a dark stain across the unpainted wood.

"A wolf?" He blinked.

Puzzled, she approached him, picked up the satchel and looked within. Bottles, many small brown bottles, and more money than she had ever seen; packet after packet of greenbacks. She stared at him, then back at the money—and the small brown vials.

"What's in those little bottles?"

When he only grinned she grabbed his shoulders and shook him.

"Martin Holly—*what is in those bottles?*"

His voice was slurred. "Peace. Contentment. Palm trees, Belle—happy—warm—"

Suddenly she knew. With a wrench of her heart she knew. There had been a man in Professor Haley's Great Combination Troupe—the banjo player, she remembered—who took opium. The symptoms were the same. She stared at Martin, trying not to believe.

"Is it opium?"

He swayed in the chair, mumbling. Again she grasped his shoulder. "Opium?"

The words were muffled. "Laudanum. Tincture of opium. Boats sailing on the water, Belle! Come along!" He giggled, tried to put one of the small bottles in her hand. "Warm—boats—happy, happy!"

Aghast, she stared. "Martin! You're a —you're a *doper*!" Now she understood the significance of the satchel he was always so particular about. "You've been taking that stuff!" How often he had seemed serene, unruffled, even in times of stress!

Then, she had thought it an admirable trait of character. But now—Was it only the effect of opium?

"Medicine," he mumbled. "It's only medicine!"

Suddenly she was furious. These last days, when their existence hung on the thinnest of threads, Martin Holly had been swigging opium to escape their dilemma. He had dosed himself into insensibility while she cooked, chopped wood, dared wolves, covered him with her own scanty blanket, fought winter and starvation and wild animals and despair. With a frustrated cry she upended the satchel, swept the bottles from the table.

"Medicine? I'll show you what you can do with your damned medicine, Martin Holly!"

The bottles were of thick glass. She gathered them up and hurled them against the log walls. Only a few broke; she snatched up the rest and flung them again and again at the walls until they shattered, contents dribbling down the walls.

"Stop that!" Martin wailed.

Aghast, he staggered to his feet and tried to retrieve some of his vials. But she stamped on them with her feet, grinding the contents into a stew of liquid, dirt, and shards of glass.

"Stop that!" he insisted again.

With more energy than he had shown for days he grabbed her arm, wrestling with her. But he was weakened by the drug; Belle Dyson, in addition to being a strong woman, was made stronger by indignation.

"You—you damned worm!" she screamed, and knocked him sprawling. "Swigging that cursed stuff, leaving me to go it alone!" The auburn hair fell over her eyes. One breast emerged from her shift where his grasping fingers had torn it. She had cut her foot on the broken glass. "You worm, you, Martin Holly!"

Whimpering, he crawled about the earthen floor, searching for an unbroken vial. At a loss for words adequate to express her indignation, she stamped hard on his hand. Perhaps the violence of their encounter had mitigated the soporific effect of the drug, because Martin roared with pain and anger. Catching her about the legs, he tripped her. They rolled on the dirt floor like catamounts, scratching, biting, and kicking.

"You devil!" he panted. "That was a hell of a thing to do! You broke all my bottles!"

"Here I thought you were a *man*!" she cried, "and I find out you're just a damned good-for-nothing—" When his fingers, apparently attempting to strangle her, got too near her mouth, she bit him. He cursed, swinging his hands in pain.

"You don't know what you've done!" he howled. "Damn it all, you've *ruined* me!"

In the melee the satchel had fallen to the floor; the room was awash in a litter of greenbacks.

"The money, too!" he wept. "Look what you've done to the money!"

She ground greenbacks into the earthen floor with her heel so they were only shredded paper.

"*That* for your money!" she shouted, "wherever you got it!"

Face livid, he struck her across the mouth. She hardly noticed. Snatching up a billet of firewood, she struck him over the head. Martin collapsed like a suddenly-folded umbrella, telescoping into a welter of mud, laudanum, glass, and greenbacks. Breasts heaving, Belle swayed on her feet, watching

him with loathing and contempt. This was Martin
Holly, the man she loved! This was the man for
whom she had abandoned a perfectly good husband, Giles Dyson the blacksmith!

"Doper!" she spat.

For a while she attempted to think of other
epithets but this was the vilest she could imagine.
In the seamy world of a traveling theatrical troupe,
Belle had seen the under side of life. Nothing had
disgusted her more than the banjo-player who
abandoned his responsibilities to retreat into
drugged dreams. The world was real, life was hard;
a man—or a woman—had to be able to face up to
it.

Suddenly she became aware that she was cold.
Her shift had been torn half away, one of her shoes
had come off, her feet were like ice. As anger faded,
the flushing of hot blood through her body ceased.
She began to tremble, not only from cold but from
the inevitable reaction to violence. Taking Martin's
soiled collar, she pulled him across the room,
heaved him on the sagging bed. Covering him with
the mangy blanket, she looked down at him. He
was soiled and disheveled. There was a bump on
his skull the size of a walnut. He lay like a rag doll,
limp and lifeless. Finally he snored, in drugged
placidity.

"My suffering Jesus!" she muttered, and made
herself a cup of tea from the spoonful of leaves
remaining in the canister. Now that she was alone,
she let go with a good cry.

CHAPTER FIVE

Belle sat at the edge of the sagging bed. Chin cupped in her hand, she stared at Martin. Her anger with him, her contempt, had faded. Now she was only hungry and frightened. For the first time she was discouraged, and did not know what to do.

It was late afternoon, the sun sinking fast. Waning light suffused the squalid room, laid a deathlike patina on Martin's face. His breathing was slow, and at times completely stopped for a few moments. Then, with a smothered gasp, he resumed breathing and Belle sank back in the chair, pulling the shawl tightly about her.

There was left only the stub of a candle. To conserve it she fashioned a rude lamp from a crockery cup filled with bacon grease, the wick a strand of hemp pulled from a rotten coil of rope found in the shed at the rear of the cabin. It sputtered, and smoked vilely, but with the coming of darkness it was a comfort.

Anxious to do something, anything, to relieve her mind, she sat at the rough table, lamp beside her, and counted out the money she had retrieved from the floor. That, and the further packets in the satchel came to—She frowned in concentration. Arithmetic had always been a mystery to her. But there must be—there were—thousands of dollars! She gasped.

Intrigued, she dumped out the entire contents of the valise. There were several other bottles; not the small brown ones that contained opium or whatever it was, but larger, and of clear glass. She twisted open the glass stopper of one and smelled. Alcohol, it was; the odor was familiar from the time Andrew stepped on a rake and old Dr. Shay cleansed the wound with the mediciny-smelling stuff. There were other bottles, too, filled with pink and brown and blue pills. Some resembled the Blaud's tablets that Doc prescribed for her when he suspected her of having anemia one spring. Others looked like calomel, to be taken when the bowels were bound up. And last there was a contrivance of rubber tubes with a kind of bell at one end. She held it in her hand, gingerly, as if it were a serpent. Then she recognized it. It was a steth—a steth—. She could not remember the name, but Doc Shay had once put one to her chest and listened when he thought she looked peaked. Remembering, she hooked the tubes into her ears and placed the bell-like device on her chest. *Thump,* thump; *thump,* thump, *thump,* thump. Fascinated by the steady pounding, she smiled. What a wonderful thing, to be able to go right inside a person's breast and listen to the heart! She was so engrossed that she heard the yowling of the wolf for some time before she realized what it was. The steady beat of her heart quickened, missed, raced wildly. Tearing the tubes from her ears, she sat paralyzed. The yowling was near; the animal must be just outside!

Martin groaned. She jumped in panic, hand to

her throat. He sat bolt upright in bed.

"Who is it?" he called out in delirium. "Who's there?"

She ran to him, put her arms around him. "It's me, Martin," she said. "Here—lie down, let me cover you!"

He resisted, and it was then she noticed the trickle of blood on his cheek. The ear was filled with dried blood, and a fresh trickle stitched down. The dirty blanket on which he lay was also stained with dark red spots.

"Lay down," she coaxed, trying to force him down on the bed. "You've got to be quiet or you'll hurt yourself! Please, Martin—lay down!"

Finally he relaxed and obeyed. She covered him with the blanket, put her own shawl over him, but now he began to shiver uncontrollably. Paroxysms shook the bed.

"I'm cold," he protested. "I'm freezing! Where am I? It's like an ice-house in here!" He opened his eyes, stared at her. "Who are you? Why in hell don't you turn some heat on the ward? These people are sick—they'll die!"

To comfort him she slipped into bed, still in the remnants of her clothes, and pressed tightly against him, her body seeking the contours of his. "It's getting warm," she said. "See how warm it's getting, Martin! Everything will be all right, you'll see. Everything will be fine!" She stroked his stubbled cheek, and finally he slept.

Blood, she thought. *Blood!* Taking away his tincher of opium or whatever it was called should not make him bleed from the ears. Suddenly she froze, in new apprehension. Had she hit him on the head too hard with that billet of firewood? Was that what caused the bleeding?

Moving carefully so as not to disturb him, she crawled from the bed and slumped in the chair, listening to the wind howl. The sound reminded her of the wolf. Though her eyes were red and smarting from lack of sleep, she had to do something about that beast. The wolf was hungry, she knew. It would be dangerous to go outside any more for firewood, even for snow to melt for water.

She knew little of guns. Back in Missouri her pa and her brothers always carried guns. Pa boasted he could bark a squirrel at forty rods, shooting only close enough so the eruption of bark would stun it, kill it without a mark on the hide. Vaguely she tried to recall how the men handled their long-barreled guns. Picking up the old musket, she examined it by the sputtering light of the oil lamp. With the gun there was a horn of coarse black grains she supposed must be gunpowder, and a sack of leaden balls. Drawing back the curved metal arm, she felt something click inside. When she pulled the trigger, the metal arm snapped forward and there was a spark. Yes, that was it! The spark lit the powder, and the explosion fired out the ball!

Trying to remember how her father had handled guns, she poured powder into the muzzle of the weapon. Enough? She did not know. To make sure, she poured in some more. Now she remembered about the patches. Tearing a piece from the dusting rag Martin had so resented, she wrapped it around one of the heavy balls, forcing it down into the barrel with the ram thing—ramrod?—that rested in a kind of clip under the long barrel.

Martin whimpered, struggled for a moment, then lay still again. Belle sat with the musket across her knees, thinking. There was something else. The gun had to be primed—was that the word? Primed, like a pump? But how did a person do that? *Flash in the pan;* that was a saying. Pan—yes, there was a pan in the gun. Nodding with satisfaction, she poured a few grains of powder into the pan, closed the cover. Now she was ready for whatever might come. She dozed, hearing the wolf howling now some distance away, but she was not as frightened as before.

In the thin gray light of dawn she woke. The fire had gone out, starved for its meager ration of fuel. Martin was awake. Puzzled, he looked at her, "Belle?"

"I'm here," she said.

He licked lips. "God, I'm thirsty!"

Happy to see him better, she broke the ice in the bucket and brought a gourd of water. He drank greedily. "My head!" he complained. "How it hurts!"

Now, instead of suffering from the cold, Martin was sweating. She rubbed his arms, back, legs. "Cramps!" he muttered. "Oh, such cramps!" His face twisted in pain, and she knelt before him, working with strong hands at the knotted muscles, so hard they seemed almost like boards.

"You've been sick," she told him. "Very sick! You didn't know me. You kept calling out, wanting to know who I was. You said the sick people in the wards would freeze unless they got some heat."

He stared about the room and a thought seemed to strike him. Half naked, clothes stained with his own filth, he ran to the satchel, spread it open. Shocked, he clapped a hand to his brow, remembering. "My medicine! You broke all the bottles!"

"Yes, I did," she admitted, "but believe me, it's better for you. That stuff is poison, Martin! I knew a man once—he was in Professor Haley's troupe—"

Angry, he pushed her away. "You broke all the bottles, God damn it! You broke all my bottles!" Furious, he clenched his fists, raised them high above his head. She was afraid he was going to hit her.

"Belle, you don't know what you've done!" Shaking with passion, he stalked the room. "Here I am stranded without any—any—"

"Laudanum," she said coldly. "Opium! Tincher of opium! You admitted it yourself."

"Tincture," he groaned. "That's right. Tincture of opium! I've been taking it for a long time. Strong solutions; stronger and stronger, I guess. I know it's bad, but I have to have it. I'm *accustomed* to it! And when you're accustomed to it you've got to have it. I've seen patients who were deprived, and they went through hell—vomiting, loose bowels, sweating, cramps!"

"Like you," she said, without sympathy.

He licked his lips, nodded. "Like me! That's right, like me! But how can you stand there and look at me in that cold-blooded way, let me suffer? God damn it, Belle—"

She became angry. "Cold blooded, is it? Suffering Jesus, you don't know what *I've* gone through these last days, trying to feed you, keep you alive

and clean, comfort you, see you were warm! Cold
blooded, is it? Why, I—"

She broke off, seeing him rub his cheek and his
fingers come away stained with red. He stared
down at the crimson smear. "Blood!" he muttered
incredulously. He stuck a finger into his ear, pulled
it out, looked again at the blood. "Bleeding from
the ears. Now I remember! You hit me over the
head with that stick of wood!" He groaned. "Was
ever a man so put upon? First, you took away all
my laudanum. Then you hit me over the head for
some reason, so hard you gave me a concussion,
maybe a comminuted fracture of the skull! Damn
it, Belle—"

He ran a hand through his hair, clutched his
arms about him to quiet their trembling. "I haven't
got my laudanum!" Distraught, he began to weep,
paced the rooms, arms wrapped about his chest.
She was stricken to see how thin he had become
these last few days, and tried to coax him back to
bed. But he was restless, excited. "Something's
coming over me, Belle—a kind of a fit! I warn you,
I'll not be rational! Jesus, what's a man to do? I
need my medicine!"

Gently she pulled him by the arm, got him to sit
on the edge of the bed. "What you need is food,"
she decided. "You haven't eaten a bite of anything
for days, Martin! Let me boil you up some cornmeal and make a little mush. With some of that
bacon-grease poured over it—"

He bent over, vomited. The sour stuff stained the
hem of her skirt but it was already soiled beyond
the powers of soap, even if she'd had any. Martin
collapsed on the bed like a dirty rag doll, arm flung

over his eyes while she wiped his face with a rag. "Belle," he moaned, "help me! It's coming on—I feel it!"

"Stop whining!" she cried. "Let it come! We'll beat it, like we've beat everything else so far! Just you sit tight and grit your teeth! I'll make do for both of us!"

Giles, she thought savagely. *Giles Dyson did this to us; to both of us!* She hated Giles. But then there was Andrew. She swallowed, felt a lump grow in her throat. How was poor Andrew to get along, with no mother?

The effects of his deprivation from laudanum were bad enough. Now, perhaps from the blow on his head, Martin had frightening spells of delirium. Once, in a paroxysm of terror, he prowled about the cabin carrying the rusty butcherknife, seeing Belle as a hunting lioness that threatened him in a tropic jungle. Fearful, she ran out into the snow, heedless of the terrible wolf. When she came back he was lying in bed again, spent and sweating.

Pale and thin, he developed a racking cough, finally a fever. Lying exhausted on the bed, apparently too weak to move, he would suddenly spring into frantic action, spouting gibberish, flailing at imaginary demons.

Though she could get him to eat little food, and certainly little remained, he had a prodigious thirst. She seemed constantly to be melting snow-water. That took wood. Carrying the musket, she cut up what deadfall she could find, musket propped against a tree-trunk. She did not see the wolf again, and was grateful for that.

Losing track of the days, she knew only that for
both their sakes she must prevail. The meager supply of food Giles had left them was nearly gone.
Belle dug for acorns under the snow-laden oaks.
Parching them in the ashes, she ground the meats
into meal which she boiled to make gruel. Rooting
beneath winter-killed bushes, she found roots re-
sembling withered potatoes. She cooked them in
the bacon-grease that remained, though it was be-
coming sour. With the hatchet she cut a hole in the
ice on the frozen pond. Using the bent pin for a
hook and strands from the coil of rotten rope for a
line she caught several tiny fish. They ate them
broiled, heads, tails, insides and all. But even with
her frantic foraging she and Martin were beginning
to die. She knew it, though Martin was too de-
lirious to appreciate their peril. What they needed
was meat, fresh meat—red meat! Her mouth watered when she remembered the venison old Mr.
Dancer had once brought Giles. She had been to
the Mercantile and stopped at the smithy on her
way back when the old man came in, carrying a
bloody haunch. Then and there, hungry for flesh,
Belle hacked off chops and Giles cooked them on a
shovel-blade over the coals of the forge. Meat! She
licked her lips.

Rabbits were in the vicinity, giant white rabbits,
plump and juicy. She improvised snares from
strands picked and braided from the rotten coil of
rope. Indians used snares, she knew, but though
she had a dozen of the things laid in their shallow
trails she could not catch a rabbit. The deer were
gone, drifted down to the lower reaches of the
Chetish. Hungrily she eyed a jay perched on a

snowladen branch, jawing at her. She even raised the musket and drew a bead on the sassy creature, but even if she managed to hit it there would be nothing left but a handful of feathers.

Was it her imagination, or was Martin making more sense? He seemed not to sleep so much now; the cramps had left him. He did not gag or vomit. Or was it simply that she, exhausted and starving, had become irrational herself, losing perspective, slipping into his own confusion and delirium? She could not trust her own senses anymore. But when he reached for her hand, his eyes did seem clear and unclouded.

"Belle," he murmured. "Ah, Belle! You take such good care of me!"

She was ashamed of her appearance, thinking it the first time he had seen her clearly. Her hair was dirty, fingers worn and scratched, nails grimy and broken. She had slept in her clothes for weeks, and there was no soap to wash anything.

"You are beautiful." His fingers touched her straggling curls. "Diana, Circe, Heloise—and Belle, my beautiful Belle."

She didn't know who those women were, but supposed they were ladies he had known back east, when he was a doctor.

"I'm hungry," he murmured, "Is there anything to eat?"

There wasn't, but she made a sudden resolve.

"For supper," she promised, "I'll make something special."

Smiling wanly, he sank back. Her heart ached as she looked down at the sunken cheeks, the skin stretched over his bones, the moon-shaped scar on his cheek grown large and white against the scanty skin. The Reverend Mr. Willis in Big Fork had been a chaplain with the Union forces, and was taken prisoner and put in a jail called Andersonville down south. She remembered him describing the starving prisoners, hungering for Jesus as they hungered for food, Mr. Willis said. He had a picture in a book to show. Martin looked like one of those starving Union prisoners. Of course, she supposed women had a little more flesh on their bones, and were thus better able to withstand hardship. But she had to do something for Martin and do it quickly.

The sun was low in the western sky. In this season of short days it seemed always to be dark, or getting dark. Holding the musket at the ready, Belle stumbled round the perimeter of the clearing, looking for tracks; perhaps a fox, a late-migrating goose, a porcupine—did they sleep in dens in the winter, like bears?—or even a fat squirrel.

There were many small tracks on the hard-crusted snow but no sign of a live animal. Fearfully she looked into the depths of the forest. It was dark and gloomy, only the very tops of the bull-pines lit by the declining rays of the sun. Making up her mind, she plunged in, holding the musket ready. Even a catamount was edible, she supposed, though they roamed mostly at night.

In a dank glade, so thick with growth that snow had hardly reached there and the ground was slippery with brown needles, she saw the wolf. He had just made his kill, forelegs spread wide as he gnawed the fat white rabbit. Seeing her he paused, one foot on his still wriggling prey; his eyes glowed yellow-green. The wolf growled, the dog-like nose wrinkled, black lips stretched tight to reveal rows of fangs. She stood stockstill, hoping the beast would not resent her presence. The wolf stared back, foamy spittle dropping from the open mouth like a spider sliding down a strand of web.

Suffering Jesus, she thought. *Dear Jesus, save me!*

Slowly, very slowly, the wolf advanced stepping delicately and quietly for such a huge beast. The amber eyes remained fixed on her, the big head dropped. The wolf had forgotten the rabbit, and was intent on a larger kill. She raised the musket.

"Back!" she quavered. "Back, sir! Get back!"

Startled by the sound, the wolf paused, snarled, again wrinkled the black nose. Once more it prowled toward her, growl deep within its throat. The ruff of hair rose around the powerful shoulders that thrust up and down through the fur as the animal slunk nearer.

"Back!" she screamed. She raised the musket, sighted at the massive head. "I'll shoot!"

Her own voice sounded shrill and desperate. As she saw the haunches tighten, the animal prepare to leap, she pulled the trigger.

There was a flash of light, an explosion that deafened her. She was thrown violently backward. Her head crashed against a stump and she lay dazed and helpless, waiting for the end. Try as she would, she could not move. Lassitude enveloped her. Eaten by a wolf—what a strange end! Giles, she thought fiercely, would be sorry; he would really be sorry!

After a while she began to feel cold. Hesitantly

she moved, stretched out an arm, a leg. Rolling over, she sat up on the slippery needles, surprised to find herself alive and whole. In an almost involuntary gesture she patted her hair back into place, readjusted her shawl. Not three feet from her lay the wolf.

She shrank away. Her hand touched the musket and she snatched it up, holding it like a club. But the wolf was dead. The yellow-green eyes were open and staring, but the deadly light had gone. The jaws gaped, the tongue lolled, the furry body lay still. Gasping, she tottered to her feet.

After a while, still trembling, she stumbled back toward the remnant of daylight in the clearing. But remembering the rabbit, she ran back to retrieve it. The poor thing was still alive, looking at her with piteous eyes. Quickly and expertly she wrung its neck, as she had often done with chickens when she and Giles had enough money to enjoy that luxury. Floundering, breaking through the crust, her legs were scratched and bleeding when she reached the cabin, rabbit in one hand and musket in the other. Recklessly she threw their remaining wood on the fire. Then she gutted, skinned, and cut up the rabbit. She had often done this also, rabbits being cheaper and more plentiful than chickens in Big Fork. By the time Martin awoke she had a savory-smelling stew bubbling in the pot.

"What's that I smell?" he asked, struggling up in bed.

"What I promised you," she smiled. "Something special!"

He tottered from the bed, holding himself upright with a hand against the wall. "I feel better tonight," he murmured.

She helped him to the table, wrapped the ragged blanket about him. The fire was bright and cheery; their shadows moved darkly against the peeled logs. Martin ate two bowls of the stew, wolfing it down and asking for more. "Meat!" he rejoiced. "Real meat!" He held out something on his spoon. "Whatever is this?"

"I don't know," she said. "A root. I found them under the snow behind the shed. I guess they're kind of a potato, or a turnip. I've heard of Indian turnips. The Sioux dig them up in the woods."

"And the meat—"

"Rabbit."

He looked at the musket standing in the corner. "You—you shot it?"

She did not deny it, not wanting to upset him with the story of her encounter with the wolf.

"And now," she said, "you had better sleep. You're weak, and must rest!"

For a moment they stood beside the sagging bed with its broken rawhide thongs. She had planned to use some of those thongs against the day when she feared she would have to tie him down to restrain him.

"Belle," he murmured. He clung to her, buried his face in her hair, one hand against the small of her back so she was pressed against him. "Belle, thank you!"

"None of that now!" she protested, pulling his hand away. "We're alive! That's enough for now, I should think!"

He put his hands on her cheeks, holding her face gently. "I've come through," he said. "It's all very muddled in my mind and I only seem to remember bits and pieces. But I believe I'm cured of the habit! I feel almost healthy, and God knows I'm happy, just to be here with you. Has it been a long time? Do you know what the date is?"

She laughed, picked up a shingle with black marks on it. "For a while I used charcoal from the fire to mark off the days. Then, when you got sick I lost track. I think it's still February. No, that can't be! It must be March!" She put a hand over her mouth. "My goodness! March?"

Lying propped-up with a pillow, he motioned her to bring the brown satchel from the shelf where it rested.

"But you must sleep!" she protested.

"In a little while," Martin insisted. "But first I must explain something to you."

She sat beside him, the sputtering lamp on the shelf. He opened the satchel, took out the packets of money, the bottles, the thing of rubber tubing. "After all we've been to each other," he said, "there should be no secrets between us. Isn't that right?"

"I suppose it is. But—"

"This," he explained, "is a stethoscope. It's used to—"

"I know what it's used for," she interrupted. "It was just the *name* I didn't know."

"These are pills, medicines, powders, things like that. Ipecac, jalap, choloroform, nux vomica, asafetida, Dover's Powder, alcohol, and so on. I threw away all my surgical instruments; just kept the medicines."

"I knew you were a doctor."

A shadow crossed his face. "I—I was. A damned good one, in fact. A surgeon—chief of staff at St. Anthony's, in Philadelphia. But a doctor sees a lot of pain and suffering. He works long hours, and much of the time he's under great strain. When you're around drugs, it's easy to take a little something now and then to quiet you down. Some doctors did it with bourbon; I took laudanum. It relaxed me, stopped my worrying. When I was on laudanum, I felt ten feet tall. Nothing stopped me. I could do miracles, I thought."

"I didn't want to believe it," she murmured. "You seemed so—so refined, so quiet, such a gentleman. You never got angry or upset." Suddenly she put a hand to her mouth. "That night, when you saved Giles' life at the Paradise—"

"Laudanum," he admitted. "I always took an extra dollop when I played poker. It seemed to help me keep cool, play better." He shook his head. "When I took away Jack Flanders' gun, I didn't even know I was in danger." He shook his head sadly. "You've heard of Dutch courage—liquor out of a bottle to make you brave? Well, this was Dutch courage, only it wasn't liquor; it was tincture of opium." He buried his face in his hands. "I wasn't brave at all! I was only a dammed fool!"

Again she remembered the banjo-player in Professor Haley's Great Combination Troupe. The banjo player eventually died from his addiction. But Martin lived; now he was cured. She stroked his cheek.

"That's all past now," she soothed.

Martin wanted to talk.

"I couldn't do without it, after a while," he went

on. "That was when my work began to suffer. I got
so I didn't trust myself in surgery any more. People
were beginning to talk. Finally I made up my mind
never to touch a scalpel again. I resigned my position, came out to the Territory, hoping if I got
away, found new sights, new people, new friends, I
might manage to cure the habit." He grimaced,
wryly. "But I damned sure had the foresight to
bring along a supply of laudanum in that satchel,
just in case!"

She pulled the blanket up around his chest, feeling with a wrenching of her heart how thin and
fragile his bones were. But he pushed her hand
away, saying, "Now, about the money."

"The money?"

He pulled out a packet of greenbacks and threw
it on the blanket. "You must have wondered."

"I supposed you were rich, that's all."

"Let me explain. I was a good surgeon. People
brought hopeless cases to me, other surgeons sent
their failures. I got high fees from rich men with
ailing daughters or crippled sons. I did operations
no one else would touch, and brought most of
them off. So I had a great deal of money. I bought
stocks on the Exchange, had rents coming in,
things like that. When the laudanum started to ruin
me, I had my accountants cash in all my interests
and took the money with me when I left."

She only smiled and pushed him back against the
pillows, rearranged the shabby blanket. The room
was for the first time warm and comfortable. Lately the weather seemed to have moderated. Perhaps
an early spring was on the way. "Well, anyway,"
she said, "there's nothing out here to buy with

money! Money doesn't mean a thing to us, does it?"

He kissed her. "What you have given me, done for me, couldn't be bought with money, any amount of it! I'll never forget it, Belle LaTour!" He grinned, the first smile in a long time. "Beautiful Tower, eh? Well, you have been a tower of strength to me. Somehow, someday, I will find a way to repay you!"

For a long time she sat in the chair next to the fireplace, rubbing her shoulder where the gun had kicked. The flames waned, smoldered into red-eyed coals. When she finally went out into the night to relieve herself, she was grateful the wolf was dead; no longer need she be frightened. Martin was over his ordeal, and they were both alive. With luck they might make it through the rest of the winter.

Returning to the cabin, she passed the window and noticed a disturbance in the snow, outlined by a moon riding high in the sea of clouds. They were prints, footprints, the prints of a human being. The snow was so deep she could not further identify the prints; they were only ragged holes. They were not her prints, she knew, nor Martin's. The prints circled the cabin, passed under the window, then disappeared into the forest in a direction she did not remember ever walking.

Giles? It could not be Giles. Giles had abandoned them. Indians? The Sioux stayed deep in their winter camps, not stirring until spring. What, then?

Frightened, she hurried into the cabin and bolted the door. His breathing slow, regular, and peaceful, Martin slept. Forcing herself not to panic, she loaded the musket—she should have done it immediately she shot the wolf—and sat all night in the chair, watching, listening, fearful. At last she slept a troubled sleep.

CHAPTER SIX

The world was white, covered with snow as far as they could see. Even the thick stands of juniper and spruce and bull-pine were nearly buried in the stuff. They had lost all accounting of time, and—it seemed—space, also. Nothing remained but a trackless wilderness of crusted snow blanketing the Chetish. Winter sun shone with a dazzling brilliance as they stared down at the footprints beneath their window.

"Indians, I suppose," Martin muttered the next morning, looking down at the dark holes in the snow. He inspected the tracks, noting where they disappeared in the encircling forest. "*An* Indian, I think—no more than one."

Belle shuddered. "One is plenty." She pulled the ragged blanket around her shoulders. "Mr. Dancer said the Sioux holed up in their camps all winter, didn't come out till spring."

"Maybe a hunter. Anyway, he didn't harm us."

"But he might come back!"

In sunlight, after his long confinement, Martin Holly looked like a gaunt bird. Hair and beard were long and straggly, cheeks sunken and hollow, his eyes deepset in their sockets. But he tried to summon up optimism.

"Probably not. Anyway—" He laughed, a croaking sound.

101

"What's so funny?" Belle asked, pushing strands of hair back into place.

"If you could see yourself!"

She was annoyed. "Well, Mr. Martin Holly, you're no prize either!"

He touched her arm placatingly. "What I meant was—I wonder any self-respecting Indian would come near us, badly-used as we both look!"

Then she laughed too. They returned to the cabin. Belle heated the rest of the rabbit stew and appeared to have forgotten the footprints. Martin did not, however. They were in danger. Wolf Voice and his bloodthirsty Oglalas would hardly tolerate them on this mountain—Wolf Voice's own mountain, so he claimed. But what could they do, a sick man and half-starved white woman? It was a struggle merely to exist.

They did not perish. Perhaps it was Providence; Belle thought it was. Martin ascribed their continued existence to luck. In the next days a natural physical resiliency asserted itself. Flesh began to clothe Martin's bones, eyes lost their lackluster glaze and took on brightness. He found strength to make a crude chair from loose boards he pulled from the sagging shed. To dine, they could now sit across the table from each other. With Belle's help and the rusty kitchen-knife sharpened on a stone, she trimmed his beard and hair, though raggedly. Belle, horrified at seeing her face in a pan of melted snow-water, washed her hair and bathed, laundered ragged clothing in left-over water, mended them as best she could with threads pulled from a blanket. To celebrate Martin's recovery they ate an extra portion of stew, the table lit by the stub of the nearly-vanished candle. They toasted each other with snow-water.

Holding the rusted cup high, Martin said simply. "To the woman I owe my life to—Belle LaTour."

She touched her crockery mug to his.

"It's been a long stretch," she agreed. "But now it's over, and I'm glad. Not just for you, Martin, but for me too! I was beginning to think I'd never look, never feel like a natural woman again, a *real* woman! It's nice now, to have a man do for me."

He laughed. "*Do* for you?"

She bridled. "It's a good old Missouri expression!"

"I know what it means, all right! It's just that I can't *do* much of anything yet, for you or for myself! But I mean to try." He scraped the bowl clean of the last smears of stew. "I must say, that was one big rabbit you brought in! We've been eating rabbit for over a week!"

When she seemed ill at ease he was puzzled.

"What's wrong?"

"Nothing's wrong!" she said.

"I know when something's bothering a woman!"

She averted her eyes. "It's not rabbit, then."

"Not rabbit?" He looked at his spoon, the empty bowl. "What is it?"

"Wolf," she said faintly.

He rose, staring at her. "Wolf?"

"At first I didn't want to tell you. You weren't well, and I was scared telling you about the wolf would upset you."

"Don't talk in riddles! What's all this about a wolf?"

She told him, finally, how she had come on the

wolf with the squeaking rabbit under its paws, how she had shot the beast, snatched up the rabbit, run back to the cabin. "When all the rabbit was gone," she went on, "I thought we were going to starve. But old Mr. Dancer told me once sometimes the Sioux eat dogs. They strangle them with a string—"

Martin turned pale, sat down.

"Are you going to be sick? Because a wolf is just kind of a big dog, really! If Indians can eat dog and prosper on it, why I figured we could too! So I've been going back and cutting chops off that ugly old wolf—"

In spite of his malaise he started to grin. After a while he broke into laughter, mirth that left him weak and winded. Taking her in his arms he pressed her against him. "I declare!" he gasped, "you are a *champion*, Belle LaTour—a real champion! Wolf! Wolf stew! Little Red Riding Hood met the wolf in the forest and made stew out of him! Oh, my stars!"

Afterwards, they lay together in the sagging bedstead. It was snowing again, a light feathery downpour that seemed to melt as soon as it hit the crusted older snow. They were warm and comfortable in each other's arms, the only sound the murmur of their breathing, the rustle of the dying fire.

"What are you thinking?" Martin murmured.

She stirred in the hollow of his arm. "Andrew."

"He'll get along all right. Andrew is a smart boy."

"And—Giles."

He stiffened. "Don't think about him!"

"Still, we did a shameful thing to him, Martin."

"And he a worse one to us!" he muttered. "Giles

reads his Bible regularly. Doesn't it say in there someplace 'Thou Shalt Not Kill'? Well, he tried to kill us, and would have too, if it hadn't been for you!"

"I guess so," she sighed, and spoke no more about it.

There were no further footprints. But Martin, recovering, and grateful for freedom from the long craving for drugs, did not forget the peril. Soon the Sioux would stir from their winter camps. It was probably only a matter of time till he and Belle were discovered. But where *were* they? And where would they go, even if it were possible to cross the snow-deep wilderness? They could never return to Big Fork, and Big Fork was near the western extent of civilization—except, of course, for the Californias.

"Do you remember hearing anyone speak of a place called Fitch's Landing?" he asked Belle one afternoon.

She had found the secret of extracting bull-pine seeds from the cones, having watched the squirrels do so. Grinding the rich oily meats between two flat stones, she molded the meal into cakes to be baked on the hearth. That, and a few of the potato-like roots and a little wolf-meat were all the food that remained.

"No. Leastways, not that I recall. Why?"

He cleaned neglected nails with a pine splinter. "I had a map with me when I came out to the Territory. It was put out by the Rand McNally Company in Chicago. I'm trying to remember the details. It seems to me that upriver, maybe a hundred miles or so from Big Fork, there was a town called Fitch's Landing."

She placed the cakes on a stone slab near the fire
and wiped her hands on the remnants of the dress.
"It might be. But what good is that? Omaha is over
that way, too." She waved toward the east. "We're
not likely to reach there, either."

"I don't know about that," he said thoughtfully.
"I don't want to get your hopes up, but I've been
thinking."

"Well," she said, "you've got a pile of thinking
to do if you plan to get us out of this fix! I've been
thinking too, don't imagine I haven't but it appears
there's nought to do but stay here and starve, or be
scalped."

He put his arm about her shoulders. "Now,
Belle! That's not like you, to give up!"

Forcing back tears, she clung to him. "Oh,
Martin! Whatever are we to do?"

"Why, we shall prevail," he said gently. "You
taught me that, and I'll not forget it! After escaping
that fiendish drug, there is nothing I can't do!
You'll see!" Placing her in the crude chair he had
made, he sat across from her while the mealy cakes
simmered on the hearth. It was late in the afternoon; a dim amber light filtered through the
scraped-hide windows. "Listen to me now—hear
what I have to say!"

Wiping her eyes with the hem of the dress, she
squared her shoulders and took a deep breath.

"That's my Belle!" He patted her hand. "Now
from what I remember of that map, and I studied
it a lot, we are in a little valley on top of the
Chetish. Giles took us in his wagon up toward the
Ophir Mine. Then he turned off left, short of the
diggings, and took us higher into the Chetish. We
crossed one ridge, then another, I remember a

good-sized stream we forded—do you recall when the wagon broke through the ice, and Giles made us get out and push? Well, that was an upper branch of the Tongue, I think, or maybe even the Rosebud. Anyway, I've formed a half-way respectable idea of our present location. I think, if we plan carefully, we have a good chance of reaching Fitch's Landing."

"But how do we know what direction to go?"

He pointed upward. "The stars! I've calculated a west-northwest course will bring us sooner or later to the Yellowstone. Then we'll just go upriver till we find Fitch's Landing."

She was doubtful. "If we could do all that, however would we travel? The ground is covered with snow, deep snow, with a crust on it. You know yourself! All a body has to do is walk a few steps and you fall through and bark your shins something dreadful!"

"I've thought of that too." He showed her a frame made of a peeled juniper branch, tied into a roughly oval shape. "You remember our good friend the wolf?"

Puzzled, she nodded.

"He's kept us alive for a long time. Now he's going to get us out of here! We'll skin what's left of the beast! I took a solemn oath never to touch a scalpel again, but I guess I can bend it enough to dissect Mr. Wolf and stretch his skin over frames like this to make snowshoes."

A glow of hope shone in her eyes, but there were still doubts. "What do we eat, while we travel?"

"You can make some more of those bull-pine cakes. With the musket maybe I can kill a deer or a moose. Anyway, what's the odds? Better to starve *doing* something than squat here and starve to death!"

She looked at him a long time. Finally she said, "Martin, I took care of you when you were sick. Now I guess you'll have to take care of me, and I'll be in your hands. I'm a good cook and housekeeper, I'm strong and healthy, I know herbs and can make poultices and salves and things, but I never traveled down a mountain on snowshoes in the middle of winter amongst savage Indians. But like old Mr. Dancer used to say—if that's the way our stick floats, I'll do the best I can." She picked up the rusted bucket and opened the door.

"Where are you going?" Martin asked.

"Going out to dig up some more of those bull-pine cones, as long as the light holds. We'll need a lot of them little cakes."

The sun was swinging northward on its annual pilgrimage but the winter landscape showed no appreciable change. The nights were still bitter and snow continued to fall, though in diminishing amounts. Were they in February, or early March? They did not know, but worked swiftly to prepare for the journey. The wolf had frozen hard but they dragged the carcass into the cabin and thawed it enough to permit Martin to strip the hide. With only a rusty knife and a dull hatchet it was a difficult job, taking a long time. Soon the carcass began to smell; the stench almost drove them from the cabin. But finally the last shreds of meat had been scraped off. They rubbed the inner surface with oily bull-pine meal instead of the deer-brains old Mr. Dancer recommended for dressing hides. Belle baked scores of meal-cakes. They dried what was left of the wolf-meat before the hearth to make pemmican. Belle's shoes were only scraps of leather secured around her ankles with broken string so Martin made her moccasins from scraps of hide remaining after he had finished two pairs of snowshoes.

"Mr. Terwilliger gave Andrew a book one time," Belle recalled. "It was called 'The Swiss Family Robinson'. Andrew read part of it to me, though he had trouble with the big words. It kindly seems to me we're like those Swiss folks, making do with whatever comes to hand."

"A man can do a lot if he puts his mind to it," Martin said. He quoted a line from *Invictus: "I thank whatever gods may be for my unconquerable soul."* Then he added hastily, "I thank them most of all for *your* unconquerable soul! It was you that brought us this far. Now I can play the man's part and take us the rest of the way."

Belle had a lively curiosity and a good brain. He taught her the rest of Henley's *Invictus*. Whenever things went wrong she muttered the words as a kind of rebuke to the fates. She loved learning, and it pleased Martin to instruct her as they worked together sewing, packing, wrapping the precious store of black powder in a pouch improvised from the wolf's bladder, fitting Martin's brown satchel with a strap to carry over his shoulder.

"Say something in French," Belle coaxed. "You said you studied it at school."

He obliged.

"It sounds like you're talking through your nose."

"I am."

"Is that how they talk? Really, I mean? Them Frenchmen?"

"Those Frenchmen," he corrected.

"Which Frenchmen?"

He sighed. "I mean, you mustn't say *them* Frenchmen! Not *them* anything! You say 'those Frenchmen'."

She bit off a thread. "How about 'them Indians'?"

He sighed again, doggedly, but went on to explain. She at last understood, but objected, "They're only Indians! I don't see why you have to call them 'those Indians'!"

He taught her also a smattering of grammar, and some arithmetic.

"Ciphering," she admitted, "always bothered me. I never was sure Mr. Terwilliger was toting up my bill right."

By rote she learned most of Spartacus' address to the gladiators, and could even recite verse-perfect Shakespeare's sonnet beginning *Shall I compare thee to a summer's day?* It had long been one of Martin's favorites. She spoke the words carefully, entranced by the images they brought up.

"There!" she said at last. "How's that?"

He kissed her. "We will have our own summer day before long," he promised. "I owe you no less."

Teaching her, he thought also of Andrew and how he had tutored the boy. He hoped Andrew would somehow continue his learning, but thought it hardly likely. The boy was slight, not fitted for apprenticing to his father's smithy. Who knew what would happen to Andrew?

First trial of the snowshoes was at least partially successful. Elated at the easy going atop the snow,

Martin tripped and fell over his own invention, breaking loose the bindings. Belle laughed at him as he struggled in the drifts.

"Nothing's the matter!" he protested. "They just need a little wider strap to give more strength!"

His modifications greatly improved the unwieldy snowshoes. Soon he was expert with them, and Belle quite passable. "Tomorrow," he said finally, "we'll leave. We can't risk staying here any longer."

She looked about the cabin. "In a way I kindly hate to leave."

"*Kind of* is better," he said, "though that's a colloquialism too."

"A what?"

"*Rather* hate to leave," he said. "That's even better."

"Well," she sighed, "I druther hate to leave in a way. After all, this has been a home, even though 'twas hardscrabble and icicles most of the way."

Frequently he was delighted by a picturesque turn of phrase. It seemed a shame to spoil her by book learning.

"I suppose so," he agreed, watching her stir acorns leaching in the pot. "Yes, I guess you're right." He ran his hand along the smooth peeled logs, pushed mud chinking back into place. "I'll remember this place. It's where I came back from a long nightmare. It's the place where you fought the demon laudanum, and won me back." He smiled. "Some day I'll come here again and bring a bronze tablet to fasten on the door!"

She put down the wooden spoon and regarded him speculatively. "You don't crave the stuff anymore?"

He pondered for a while. "I've got to be honest.

Right now, if I had some, I don't know whether I could resist taking it or not, Belle. I suspect it's a habit a man never really gets over. On the other hand, I haven't *got* any laudanum, and am not likely to get any! So that's that! I get along without it, and I guess that's all I can ask for."

Going out that day for another run on the snowshoes he trudged far to the west, where a snow-choked ravine met the meadow on which their cabin stood. Panting, he tramped to the head of the canyon. Below stood their wilderness home, the crude structure black and square, indomitable against the winter. Smoke curled from the mud-and-stick chimney, and behind the cabin was the plundered shed and the pond—in a way, his own Walden pond. Their footprints circled the cabin, radiating outward like the spokes of a wheel.

He was leaning against a slab of rock, getting his wind back, when he saw the Indian. Above him, outlined against the gray winter sky, stood a solitary figure, hand raised over the eyes to protect them against the harsh light. A rifle was slung over the man's back, and he wore a fur hat with the tail of some animal dropping behind. The rest of his body was hidden by a rocky ledge.

Martin dropped quickly behind the boulder. Had the intruder seen him? Maybe not; Martin's route to the top of the draw had been largely screened by trees growing from the rocky cleft. Too, the man's attention had been so turned on the cabin that he was probably not aware of a white man's presence.

For a long time he waited, pulse pounding in his temples, mouth dry and cottony. What if the Indian summoned others, started down the canyon toward the house? He was unarmed, and Belle unsuspecting. He chanced a quick glance. The man was still there, staring downward. As Martin watched he unslung the rifle, held it easily in the crook of an arm.

Even if he could reach the cabin, warn Belle, see to the loading of the musket, the priming, they would have no chance against a band of Oglalas intent on eradicating white interlopers from the Chetish. Slowly he straightened, peered again over the ledge, but this time the Indian was gone.

He waited fearing the man and perhaps his friends had slunk into the forest to approach the cabin by a stealthy and roundabout path. Finally, feet almost frozen and joints cramped, he summoned up enough courage to plod down the slope, hair on the back of his neck prickling as he shuffled along. A light mist of snow was falling and he was grateful for the reduced visibility. But if the Indians could not see him, perhaps he could not see them either. Were they watching with grim and savage satisfaction, waiting to dash toward him, tomahawk him, rip away his scalp?

The cabin seemed leagues away. Shrinking small, peering about, he reached the door and slipped within, barring it behind him.

"Martin!" Belle straightened from the hearth, the wooden spoon he had carved dripping mush. "What's wrong?"

He swallowed hard, trying to still his labored breathing. "Up there!" He nodded. "On the ridge! There was an Indian! He—he didn't see me, I guess, but I saw him. He watched the cabin for a long time. I didn't know what to do. You were down here all alone, but if I called out they might —they might—"

She ran to him, threw her arms about him. "What must we do?"

"Get out of here! Get out immediately! The man went away, I guess, because after a while I didn't see him anymore. But he'll be back, probably with a band of cutthroats. We can't be caught here, in this cabin!"

"But it's almost night!"

Fire arrows, he thought. He had read about them in Fenimore Cooper. *The Indians wrapped arrowheads in pitch-soaked rags, shot them onto the roof, through the windows.*

"Shouldn't we wait till morning?" Belle asked.

"No! Certainly not! We've got to start right now! Take all our things and get out of here before they decide to come back and burn us out!"

Dutifully she got their belongings together. Martin helped, throwing away odds and ends he judged were not worth the burden.

"But your old shirt will make good rags!" she protested. "And what's left of my shoes—we can cut strips from the leather and use them to some purpose!"

He threw them in the corner along with other unnecessary items.

"We've each got a heavy load. We must travel light if we're going to save ourselves!"

When they stepped from the cabin the sun was an orange ball in the smoky haze dimming the western sky. The snow still fell. A crow flapped away in alarm, croaking, to roost in a nearby tree.

"Goodbye, cabin," Belle said. Carefully she

closed the door after her. "I'm ready."

Martin adjusted the makeshift pack, perhaps twice as heavy as the one Belle carried, and picked up his satchel. Together they trudged up the rise to the tree Martin had blazed to mark west northwest, so far as he was able to calculate from the stars. At the edge of the forest they paused, looking back. A tendril of smoke wavered upward but the cabin looked lonely now, deserted. Together they turned and plunged into the depths of the forest.

Somewhere near midnight, exhausted, they bedded down on a pile of pine-needles, covering themselves with their threadbare blankets, winding bodies tightly together for warmth. A night wind moaned in the tree-tops. Martin thought dismally of a Grimm Brothers tale about two children lost in the woods who later were discovered, lying in each other's arms, frozen into eternal companionship.

"Martin?" Belle whispered.

On velvet wings an owl flitted over their heads. Perched above them, it hooted plaintively.

"What?"

"I wanted you to know I'm not scared."

He pressed his lips against her cheek. "Brave girl!"

After a while she slept, or he thought she did. Utterly weary, he slept also. When he awoke it was full morning. Slanting shafts of sunlight cut through the greenery, laid geometric patterns on the pine needles and the snow, sent slashes of light zigzagging across the boulders encircling them. Belle still slept, nestled in the crook of his arm.

They were, he observed with a pounding heart, encircled in other ways. Peering over the giant boulders were painted faces. Swiftly, silently, the Oglalas crawled over the rocks, slipped down like cats, ringed them with deadly speed. A brown hand darted out like a snake and snatched away Martin's musket. A man with wavy yellow bands painted across the bridge of his nose pointed a lance. Another, a tall man in the fur hat he remembered, face speckled with white dots, knelt beside Belle and took a lock of her hair between his brown fingers, examining its texture. It was then she awoke, and screamed.

Martin scrambled up, seizing the hatchet, the only weapon left him. Strong arms pinioned him from behind. Something struck him heavily on the crown of his head. The morning world reeled, blackness enveloped him. He toppled and fell, trying to break the fall but unable to raise his arms. The last thing he remembered was Belle's shrill voice screaming—screaming—screaming.

CHAPTER SEVEN

He awoke with a headache. Lying in the gloom, looking at sticklike figures painted on what seemed canvas, he felt his skull throbbing with each pulsebeat, and grimaced in pain. With a reflexive movement he reached for the satchel. It was then that he found his hands—and his feet—were tightly bound.

"Belle!" he called in sudden panic.

She was gone. Screwing his eyes shut against the pain, he remembered; the Oglalas, Belle screaming, finally the crushing blow on his head.

He was not dead. He lived; the pain in his head was evidence enough of that. Now he realized that the strange sticklike figures were drawings on the sun-washed skins of an Indian lodge. He lay bound and helpless, a prisoner of Wolf Voice and the bloodthirsty Oglala savages.

He did not know how long he lay in the mellow gloom. Sounds filtered through the thin-scraped hides; children laughing, the whinny of a horse, a woman's voice singing a chantlike song with a strange descending melody. Twisting and wriggling, he tried to free himself. The rawhide cords cut his wrists and ankles and finally he lay quiet, dripping with sweat.

What would they do to him? What would they do to Belle? In panic he strained at his bonds. But a sudden shaft of sunlight bathed his face. He turned away, blinded.

"Who's that?" he quavered.

No one answered. After a moment he turned his head toward the doorflap of the lodge. Framed in the brilliantly-lit opening was the figure of a man, a tall silhouette with no visible detail.

"You!" the man grunted.

Martin rolled over, managed to struggle to his knees.

"You come."

The tall man untied his limbs. Martin tried to rise but his limbs, long confined, would not support him. Muttering, the tall man jerked him to his feet and shoved him through the door. "Hopo!" he snarled.

Prodded by a ribboned lance, Martin stumbled out to a winter morning. Blinded by sunlight on snow, his eyes watered copiously. Fearing his battered head would fall off, he held it between his palms, staggering along a path beaten into the snow by moccasined feet.

"Where are you taking me?" he asked.

There was no reply; only another jab of the lance.

"All right, all right!" he cried. "I'm going!"

As his vision cleared he got his first sight of a hostile Sioux camp. It was large, much larger than he had imagined, and neatly laid out and organized. The tall conical *tipis*, they were called, dotted a snow-deep mountain meadow in a series of concentric rings. Before each lodge stood a kind of meat-rack, from which hung frozen sides and quarters—of venison, he supposed. At the foot of a canyon that debouched into the meadow was a brush corral filled with splotched and painted horses, small enough to be called ponies back east, but lively and full of spirit as they neighed, kicked up their heels, bit at each other's hindquarters. On the slopes beyond the camp children coasted on makeshift sleds. Beyond the outer ring of lodges with their smoke-blackened apexes was a a spidery line of scaffolds supported by poles. He wondered if these were the elevated burials he had once read of in a book.

Looking fearfully about, he saw that their progress had attracted a crowd along the path. Women, braids dressed in fur bindings, stared curiously at him. Small children, eyes sparkling with curiosity, peered from behind their mothers' skirts. Now Martin saw the face of his captor, and knew it for the man in the fur hat, the one who the day before stood high on the ridge behind their cabin, rifle in the crook of his arm, watching—the man whose white-spotted face had loomed over him just before that crushing blow to his skull. *Belle screaming, screaming, screaming—*

"Where is she?" he demanded. "What have you done with her?"

In spite of the cold the women of the camp appeared only lightly-clad, most in loose garments of what he supposed was deerskin, but some wore calico. The children were nearly naked, but healthy enough in appearance. One reached out to touch him, eyes wide with curiosity, but he pulled sharply away.

"Where is she?" he demanded again, stopping in the path to face his oppressor.

At first he thought the white spots on the man's face to be the relict of some disease. Now he observed they were dots of white paint, worked on the skin in a complex pattern of swirls and spirals. Following the intricate tracery, his eyes came at last to the contemptuous glare of his captor. Suddenly, so quickly he had no chance to defend himself, the man slapped him across the mouth with such force that Martin fell sprawling.

"You—go!"

Prodded with the lance, Martin staggered again to his feet. The woman giggled, the children burst into laughter. One small urchin threw himself howling into the snow in wide-limbed mockery of Martin's fall. Muttering between clenched teeth, he trudged on toward the large tipi, as large as three of the others, to which the path seemed to lead.

Several warriors clustered near the entrance to the great lodge. They lounged indolently about, chatting and smoking, watching Martin and his captor. They were tall men, broad-shouldered, dressed in barbaric finery. They wore shirts of some kind of skin with trailing fringes, beadwork and bands of what appeared to be dyed porcupine-quills across the chest. Many had leggings of buckskin with a broad stripe of colored glass beads down the leg, a heavy twisted fringe from knee to ankle. Others' brown thighs were bare, but they sported calf-length moccasins heavy with beadwork and painted designs. One man wore a scarlet trailing breechcloth, a foot wide, reaching from his belt to the ground. Most had feathers stuck in their black braids at a rakish angle. A man Martin remembered from the attack of the night before, the man with the wavy yellow bands painted across his face, now wore a full bonnet—a magnificent headpiece of feathers set into a decorated headband, trailing almost to the ground.

"*Hopo!*" his captor called, and shoved Martin again. The man with the feathered bonnet grinned, holding aside the painted doorflap for the pair to enter the lodge. As Martin stepped across the threshold the man with the bonnet stuck out a malicious foot. Martin tripped, sprawling again, while the loungers snickered at the schoolboy trick.

Inside, the great lodge was only dimly lit, the interior smoky from a small fire smoldering in the center. On a dais of what Martin recognized as Army ammunition boxes sat a stern bronze figure, probably Wolf Voice himself. Around him squatted the elders of the tribe, somber gray-haired men with wrinkled paunches and faces so lined and furrowed they resembled the crazing of old lacquer. Others lay on scattered buffalo-robes, smoking. Some, probably minor officials, lurked at the circumference of the lodge among the scattered chests, boxes, and leathern trunks, painted with the mystical designs Martin had first observed on the walls of the lodge where he was imprisoned. This, then, was Wolf Voice's seat of government, the capital whence he conducted his campaign against the white men.

"Belle!" Martin cried in surprise.

In the flickering flames he saw her standing near the fire, hair in disarray, hands clasped before her. Jerking free of his tormentors he ran to her, pressed her in his arms. "What have they done to you? Have they hurt you? By God, if they have, I'll —I'll—"

"No," she whispered, "I'm not hurt. They—so far they used me well enough, I guess. But I don't know what's going to happen now."

Surprisingly, no one moved to stop him. He glanced around. The Oglalas stood silently, some squatting, some reclining, watching him with a detached interest, almost as when he had once studied through the microscope a slice of diseased liver.

"Don't worry," he muttered, with a bravery he hoped did not ring completely false. "We got this far! I'm not going to let a bunch of mangy Indians stop us now!"

"But what are we to do?"

He patted her arm reassuringly. "I—I don't know, but don't worry. I'll think of something. After all, if they were going to kill us they'd have done so, wouldn't they? Back there in the forest?"

Wolf Voice uttered a bark of command. The man with the spotted face dragged Martin away, forcing him to stand before the chief. For a moment Wolf Voice stared sternly at Martin. Then he rose, going into a long harangue. The language was harsh, choking, and sibilant, accompanied with swift gestures, fingers flying like startled birds. Not understanding, Martin could only watch, wonder what Wolf Voice was saying.

The chief also was tall, well over six feet in height. Martin had seen many of the peaceful Rees hanging around Big Fork in tattered blankets. They cowered, small and dejected. But these Oglalas seemed uniformly big, wideshouldered, and spirited. Wolf Voice let his scarlet blanket fall so that it dropped around his waist, kilted there by a wide leather belt with a white man's brass buckle. *Probably, Martin thought, despoiled from some murdered settler along the Yellowstone.* But he had to admit the chief cut a handsome figure.

Wolf Voice's features were prominent, sharp, and regular, the cheekbones high and prominent and the lips thin, very severe. The body, glowing with a faint rime of perspiration in the light of the fire, was slender, sinewy and muscular. Scars were prominent on his upper arms and chest. Martin remembered old Dancer telling him about the barbarous Sun Dance of the Sioux. They skewered arms and chest with wooden pegs tied to rawhide thongs, then were hoisted to tiptoe where they hung, lips set against pain, until the flesh tore or someone mercifully cut them loose after the prescribed period. Savages, utter savages! What hope did he and Belle have against such cruelties?

Wolf Voice broke off his harangue, stared at Martin with bright black eyes. Martin's captor nudged him, muttered in his ear. "He say—what you and woman do here, in his mountain?"

Martin folded his arms across his chest. He would do well to try to maintain a composure as dignified, as fearless, as these untutored savages.

"Tell him—" he said. He paused, wrapping arms more tightly about him as he realized he was trembling. "Tell him this woman and I are only peaceful travelers. We were lost on this mountain, and were only trying to reach a place down below—" He waved toward the northwest. "A place called Fitch's Landing."

His captor translated in a swift flow of the jumbled and chaotic language that sounded like the grunts of a wild animal. The dialogue went swiftly back and forth, Wolf Voice fanning himself with something that looked like a dismembered eagle's wing and interrogating Martin, the man with the white-dotted face translating and then repeating Martin's words to the chief, accompanied always by the swift hand signs that appeared to be a supplementary language among the Sioux. The audience stared, listened; one old man leaned forward, cupping a wrinkled ear to hear better.

"Do you know this is a place where no white man can come? Do you know the Chetish is my mountain—our mountain? Those white men are trying take away everything else, but the Chetish is our holy mountain!"

"I know. We meant no harm. But we were lost. And not all white men want your land. *I* do not want your land." *Philadelphia,* Martin thought, *was worth the whole Idaho Territory.*

Wolf Voice motioned. An ancient with a hooked nose, once broken, apparently, and wearing a distinctive vestlike garment with the fur turned out and a headpiece ornamented with buffalo-horns, tossed an object at Martin's feet.

"What is that?" the chief demanded.

It was his satchel.

"There are colored powders in there," Wolf Voice observed. "Bottles. All kinds of little round things like rabbit-droppings."

Pills. Drafts. Alcohol. Dover's Powders. The old man with the buffalo horns was probably the shaman, the medicine man, trying to see what white man's sorcery might be contained in the satchel.

"I was a doctor," Martin explained. "Back there." He waved. "These are medicines, to make people well."

Wolf Voice was not satisfied. "Is there some magic stuff in there, white man's devil-medicine to hurt us?" He turned crafty. "Did they send you here, you with your powders and rabbit-droppings, to do harm to us?"

Martin tried to interrupt, to explain. But Wolf Voice would not be stayed. Hurling down the eagle-wing fan, he stormed into an impassioned diatribe, pointing his finger sternly at Martin and Belle. Pressed for some effective defense, Martin finally shouted back at him.

"Tell him he will be sorry if he harms us! Tell him there are a lot of soldiers at Fort Schofield, with guns and cannon! Tell him if this woman and I do not reach Fitch's Landing in safety, then soldiers will come and punish the Oglalas! Tell him that!"

When Wolf Voice heard Martin's translated words, spoken in a trembling voice by the spotted man, who appeared almost frightened as he relayed the meaning, the chief went into a towering rage. The circle of wizened faces about him shrank back at his vehemence. Wolf Voice stalked the dais, scarlet blanket trailing, raising clenched fists over his head and gesticulating.

"He say—" The translator faltered, trying to keep up with the impassioned oratory. "He say—"

With a swift gesture Wolf Voice tore away the bright blanket girding his loins, snatched off the beaded buckskin breech clout, exposing his genitals in a contemptuous gesture.

"Look!" he howled. "I am a man! I am not afraid of all the whites in the world! Let them come against me! They will die—they will all die! The Oglalas have gods, great gods, to kill the white men with thunder and lightning if they come into this holy place!" His manner was regal, a great sovereign threatened by a minor nation.

The circle of elders nodded, grunted something that sounded like "How—how!" in apparent applause. A man at the edge of the circle of firelight capered about, beating a drum made from skin stretched tightly over a frame of wood, whooping a war-chant. Another took a knife from a beaded scabbard at this waist, a scabbard decorated with long strands of hair that might have once belonged to a white man, and ran a brown finger along the cutting edge.

Belle pressed fearfully against him. "What's going to happen now?"

Lean features once again in majestic repose, Wolf Voice squatted on the dais. He made a gesture, and Martin's captor seized his arm in a powerful grip. Martin knew somehow that this was the end. The audience was finished; they were now —he and Belle—to be taken out, tortured, slain.

"Wait!" he cried.

Wolf Voice frowned.

"Wait!" Martin insisted. He snatched up his satchel. In the quickness of his gesture it spilled. Vials and bottles, twists of powders, packets of greenbacks rolled on the hardbeaten earth.

"Tell him the white men have gods too!"

Searching in the confusion he found his bottle of alcohol and held it high. "Tell him the gods of the white men give great power to their children!" With a thespian flourish he drew out the ground-glass stopper of the bottle. Turning to conceal his movements behind Belle's ragged skirts, he poured the volatile fluid over his hands and arms, rubbed it into his face and hair, let it saturate his sleeves, the ragged trousers.

"Martin!" Belle's voice rose in panic. "What are you doing?"

Turning, he lurched toward the smoldering fire. He thrust out a hand and the alcohol flashed swiftly into flame. In an instant he was bathed from head to foot in a bluish glow, outlining his defiant figure as if illuminated by a kind of St. Elmo's fire. He felt an almost electric shock as the uncanny glow licked his hair, his arms, bathed his chest.

"Magic!" he shouted. "White man's magic!"

For a moment the Oglalas stared, transfixed.

"Magic!" Martin shouted. "By God, you never saw anything like that before, did you?"

Frightened, the Oglalas drew back. Even Wolf Voice, brave in battle, was unnerved.

"Fire!" Martin screeched, waving his glowing arms. "Fire magic! Great magic! I know the Fire God personally, and he gives me this power—me, his friend!"

Rooted in fear, the old men blanched and trembled. The younger braves rolled their eyes, and one sidled hastily from the lodge, overcome. Wolf Voice stood his ground, as a great chief must, but was shaken.

"Martin!" Understanding, Belle ran to him.

"What a damned fool trick! You've hurt yourself!"

Seizing a blanket, she was about to throw it around him to smother the darting flames but he drew away and spoke through clenched teeth. "Not now, damn it! Don't spoil the effect!"

"But you—"

"Follow me," he said tightly, "and bring the blanket."

Drawing himself proudly up, the blue flames still glowing about him but weakening, he stared at Wolf Voice. Then, with iron dignity, he stalked toward the doorflap. Belle followed as a retainer might trail in the steps of a royal presence. The Oglalas shrank back from the small retinue. Those not struck powerless or dumb made small wondering noises and gestured in awe.

Outside the tipi Martin snatched at the blanket and pulled it tightly about him. Belle rubbed out the remaining small flames with the hem of her skirt and gentle hands. "Martin!" she wailed. "Why did you do it? You've killed yourself!"

Gasping for breath, scorched lungs laboring, he stumbled down the foot-beaten path to the tipi where he had been held prisoner. Oddly, he felt no pain. But he had treated burned men before and knew it would not be long before the scorched flesh would rebel.

"Worked, didn't it?" he demanded. "So far, anyway!"

She got an arm under his and helped him walk. "All the same, it was a crazy thing to do!"

Clutching at her for support, he peered from under scorched brows. "We've still got our hair, haven't we? Sometimes the crazy thing is the only thing to do!"

Already the frightening scene in the lodge seemed to have been transmitted to the village. No one was in sight except a few children who peered from doorflaps and then were drawn quickly back. The barbarically-dressed warriors no longer lounged in the sun; a pall of silence lay on Wolf Voice's village. Even the blotched ponies in the corral seemed uneasy, no longer prancing and nickering but standing like statues, regarding all with solemn eyes.

"By God, we scared the hell out those people!" Martin croaked. "No one's going to monkey around with a personal friend of the Fire God!" He sat down on a robe, shoulders slumping. "It's beginning to hurt." He twisted, shrugged his shoulders, stretched his neck. "My God, how it stings!"

She had picked up his satchel in the lodge, hastily thrown in the scattered contents. Now she searched through it again. "Maybe there's something in here." Frowning, she held a bottle to the light. "I can't read this, but—"

Wincing, he shook his head. "I only brought a few things with me from the east. Emetics, diuretics, seidlitz powers—things like that. God, how I wish I had the laudanum you splashed all over the walls of our cabin! It would kill the sting!"

Kneeling beside him, she touched him gently on that one part of his reddened brow that did not seem to have been scorched. "Anyway, I've got to admit it was a brave thing you did."

He grasped her hand and held it tightly. "I got

you into this mess, Belle LaTour, and I guarantee to get you out of it somehow in spite of the whole damned Sioux nation!"

"Try to sleep," she urged. "Maybe that will help."

After a while, still holding her hand, he did sleep, only occasionally making small painful sounds in his troubled slumber.

That night food and a sweetened drink were brought to them by an old woman with sagging bosoms. Rolling-eyed and frightened, she sidled into the lodge, laid down the bowls and cups. Belle tried to talk to her, speaking gently and amicably, but the old woman fled like a deer. When Martin woke she fed him, told him about the visitor. "I think they're good and scared of you," she said.

In spite of his pain he grinned.

"Maybe I haven't got a buffalo-horn hat and a long stick with ribbons and scalps tied to it, but I taught them there's more than one kind of medicine man!"

"At any rate," Belle said cheerfully, "our belly needn't stick to our backbone any longer. We've got food!"

Next morning the camp was still silent, seemingly deserted, the dismal mood accentuated by a dull and overcast dawn. Soon a spring rain started to fall. Belle stared at the grayish triangle of light where she had pulled wide the doorflap.

"I wonder," she mused, "what's going to happen to us now."

"God knows," Martin sighed. "I didn't expect to be alive to see it rain this morning!" Sitting up, he grimaced in pain as the maltreated flesh rebelled.

"How do you feel?" Belle asked anxiously.

"I'll live." He shrugged. "But I'll think twice before I ever do *that* again!"

She stared at the doorway, not knowing at first what she had seen. Then it came again, a quick disturbance of the gloomy triangle. Intrigued, she crawled close, watching. It was then she saw it for sure; the small head poked round the corner, the wide dark eyes, the fat cheeks of an Indian child. The boy—she thought it was a boy—stared at her. When neither of them moved, the child continued to regard her with stolid curiosity.

"Come in!" she invited, beckoning. But the sudden movement startled the boy, and he waddled quickly away.

"Did you see that?" Belle marveled. She loved children, all children, even Indian children. "A boy, a little boy! He stuck his head into the tent! Curious, like all children!"

Martin's pain honed an edge of annoyance into his voice. "Nits make lice!" he grumbled. "Haven't you ever heard that saying? Some day he'll grow up to scalp peaceful settlers."

"I suppose so," she said. "Still—"

Each day food was brought to them. Though they knew little of Indian fare, it was apparent they were being offered the best the village had to offer. There were stews, chops, roasts—boiled potato-like bulbs of some sort, greens simmered with smoked meat, broiled fish, a thin sweet syrupy liquid in wooden cups. Martin kept to the tipi, fearing to emerge until his red and peeling face and hands healed lest his image as a powerful magician suffer. But the dark and limited confines of the tipi were beginning to oppress Belle. When Martin turned moody and silent with his pain, she could hardly stand it. There were by now even small clashes of temper.

"Cabin fever, that's what it's called," she told Martin.

"I guess so," he said, picking at a scabrous patch of skin on his cheek. "Belle, I'm sorry."

One day, while he slept, she emerged blinking in the sunlight, screwing up her courage to the utmost. The frozen brook running through the circle of lodges was now tumbling joyously, released from the grip of winter. Rivulets of melted snow-water ran round the tipis in small ditches dug for the purpose. But the greatest change was in the citizens of the Oglala village. The frightening vision of the fiery man behind them, they had recovered some measure of their composure. Children played again at blind-man's-bluff on the hillside. Men sat at doorways, shaving in a crude way by tweaking hairs from chin with clamshell tweezers. Women cooked in outdoor shelters of green boughs. The scene was sunwashed and tranquil.

Strolling down the path in the meadow, Belle tried to whistle a tune but her lips seemed frozen and unresponsive. At last she managed to get out a few bars of "A Frog He Would A'Courting Go." She must look a fright in her tattered blanket, with long and unkempt hair straggling every which way. Resolutely she pushed it back, trying to smile at the Oglalas as she passed their dwellings.

At first they only stared back, some hostile, some impassive, some curious. Many of the men scuttled into the lodges to peer from the doorway, uncertain. But the children were more receptive.

Before long the game of blind-man's bluff broke up and a string of urchins tagged after her. When she stopped, turned, smiled, they fled. Resuming her whistling, she trudged along the muddy path, aware her makeshift wolf-skin moccasins were sodden and muddy and her feet like ice.

Sitting on a rocky ledge, she turned her face gratefully to the sun. The children clustered at a respectful distance. When she waved to them they only stared back. But the little boy whom she had first seen edged near.

"Come!" she invited, patting the ledge beside her. "Come sit with me!"

Thumb in mouth, he sidled closer, staring with his dark luminous eyes. Struck by a sudden idea, she pulled threads from her ragged blanket and knotted them together. Andrew had loved her to play cat's-cradle when he was small, clapping baby hands in glee as she wove fantastic patterns with a string stretched between her fingers. Really, she had been quite good at it.

The children watched her fingers fly, making complicated networks. The little boy, thumb in mouth, came closer yet. Finally, after one intricate web disappeared into empty air with a flick of her hand, he laughed.

"Sit down," she invited again. "I don't bite!"

Finally he came to sit in her lap, round-eyed and giggling, just as Andrew had once done. He was too small to know fear, real fear. Encouraged, the rest came too, and sat around her. When she judged it time to return to the tipi to see to Martin's wants, they walked back with her, shrilly begging for more tricks, though she did not understand a word of their jargon.

Martin was deep in thought, inspecting a stubborn ulcer on his arm where the flames had bit deep.

"A penny for your thoughts," she joked.

Startled from a reverie, he looked up.

"I was thinking," he murmured, "how to get away from here as soon as we can. When I can travel—"

"You're skin and bones!" she protested. "You're not able! Why, you're still weak as a kitten!"

"Nevertheless!" he insisted. "Nevertheless! We put a good scare into them, and it's beginning to wear off already! It's best to get out of here quick as we can." Gloomily he contemplated the sore on his arm. "And you'd better be thinking about it too, instead of playing with those children. I saw you!"

"I'm not ashamed of it!" she said stiffly. "They're just little ones! At that age they don't differ from what Andrew was, from what you probably were!"

He grumbled, shrugged, said no more. Belle bit her lip, and finally came to embrace him silently. He was hurting from his burns, she knew.

Soon she became friends with more children, and through them with some mothers. Neither spoke the other's language, but the Oglalas had a kind of hand-talk she dimly comprehended. One day, when she rushed back to the lodge, Martin watched as she rummaged in his scuffed satchel. "In Heaven's name, Belle—what *are* you doing?"

"Do you have any calomel in here?"

"Calomel? What for?"

"That little boy's mother, the boy that sat in my lap that first day. She seems to have trouble with her bowels. I thought—"

"Good God!" Sighing, he shook out a single pill. "If you've got your mind made up to help savage Indians who will soon be spreading out all over the Territory, even Big Fork—"

"I don't think that poor woman is going to hurt anyone!" she protested. "She's in too much discomfort with her bowels!"

"Have her take that, then," he shrugged, "with a glass of water at bedtime."

She laughed. "And come and see you at your office in the morning if she's not better! I'll tell her to bring along fifty cents for your fee!"

In the morning the little boy's mother was better, signing graphically that she felt better, holding out wondering hands to indicate the immensity of the relief.

Martin also improved. Soon she persuaded him to walk about the village with her. The sight of the magic fire man created a small consternation among the Oglalas. But with Belle as intermediary they seemed to accept him, though keeping a respectable distance apart from such strong medicine. As they walked, arm in arm, Belle pointed out sights of interest.

"That's where a fat lady with a wen lives. She made me tea the other day, the first tea I've had in a long time, and gave me these new moccasins. Down there, in the meadow, the young men race their horses. I watched them one day. They seem to bet a lot: blankets and knives and tobacco, things like that. In that next lodge there's a sick woman, something wrong with her stomach. Anyway, it's all swelled up and sore. I stayed with her one afternoon, and we sat that way till almost dark, her hand in mine."

He appeared not to have heard. "Up there," he muttered. "That big rock! That's just about west northwest, I'd say! Maybe we could talk them into giving us horses, now that the snow is melting, and we could reach Fitch's Landing."

"I bet you never even heard me!" she protested.

"I did too! You were talking about—about a woman with some kind of abdominal problem."

They stopped in a sunwarmed glade at the perimeter of the camp and sat on boulders emerging from the waning snow. Water ran about their feet, sucked and gurgled down the mountain toward the distant Yellowstone. In the mud a trace of green showed—blades of new grass.

"Could you do something for her?"

He was still contemplating the distant rock. "For who?" he asked absently, peeling a veil of dead skin from his arm.

"For that poor woman I told you about!"

He shrugged. "Probably a tumor of some sort. Anyway, they've got their own medicine men. Don't you remember the old man in Wolf Voice's lodge, the one with the fur jacket and the buffalo horns on his head? He's the local sawbones."

"I'm serious!" she insisted. "Can't you help her —do *something*? She's young, no older than I am, and she's sick and afraid!"

"It's a tumor, or maybe an abscess of some sort. It would take a surgeon."

"You're a surgeon!"

Bleakly he turned to stare at her. "I *was* a surgeon. But I took a mortal oath never to touch a scalpel again. I mean to keep that oath!"

"Then she'll die!"

He stared down at the muck at their feet, the rivulets of glass-clear snow water, the patch of green. "Belle, for the love of Heaven, how would you expect a surgeon to operate in a primitive place like this? No lights, no table, no sponges, no retractors, no chloroform—"

"There's chloroform in your satchel!" she cried triumphantly. "I saw the bottle! I sounded out the letters one day while you were asleep! C—H—L—O—R—"

"Look," he said patiently. "Look here." Gentler than he had been for a long time, he took her hand in his. "Right now we've got a little credit with the Oglalas. They're scared of me and my big medicine. But if I were—don't get your hopes up, now —even if I *were* to try to help her, what if it went wrong? Opening up the belly is a serious matter, not to be done outside a proper hospital. If anything went wrong, they'd blame me, wouldn't they? They'd think I killed her, just like—" He broke off, bit his lip. "Anyway, I say we ought to trade on whatever credit we've got with them, ask for horses. Maybe a guide to show us the way to Fitch's Landing, get the hell out of here while we're ahead. Doesn't that make sense?"

She shook her head. "They're not stupid, Martin! They're people, I've found, just like Giles and Mr. Terwilliger and Mrs. Captain Mapes and even Andrew—my own Andrew! They'd know you were trying to help Star Woman and would give you credit no matter what happened." She pressed his hand. "Won't you at least try?"

Defeated, he sighed. "I'll look at her, if you insist. But don't expect any more than that! I refuse, absolutely refuse, to go any farther than that. Do you hear me?"

She heard him, but was too delighted to argue. Pulling him from his perch, she said, "It's that little lodge by the brook, the one with the orange sun painted over the doorway! *Hopo*!"

Puzzled, he stared at her.

"Hopo?"

She laughed. "That means 'let's go'!"

CHAPTER EIGHT

The tipi where the sick woman lay was oppressive, filled with a smell of sickness and despair. The woman—she was young—lay on a slatted mat of willow rods stretched with sinew, the whole suspended from a low wood frame. A small fire of buffalo chips smoldered nearby. Next to the bed sat the shaman, the medicine man; the ancient wearing the buffalo-horn headpiece whom Martin remembered from his late fiery exhibition in Wolf Voice's great lodge.

"That's High Bear," Belle whispered. "He's an old fraud, and is doing her more harm than good with his goings-on."

The shaman glanced at the intruders with annoyance, but went on with his chants and incantations. Waving a feathered rattle over the swollen abdomen, he sang in a high-pitched nasal singsong. Finishing his caterwauling, he took a leather sack from a pouch at his waist and shook yellowish powder into a wooden cup of water. Mixing it with a paddle, he took a mouthful, gargling. Then, to Martin's disgust, he spat a stream onto Star Woman's swollen stomach, rubbing it into her skin while she groaned in pain.

"You see what I mean?" Belle murmured.

Another man sat at the head of the cot, huddled

in a blanket. At the foot of the bed a gray-haired crone, several fingers missing from each hand, rocked back and forth in grief. The man raised a fold of the blanket, gesturing for Martin to approach the sick woman. Martin started, with a sudden intake of breath; the man's face was covered with a whorl of painted white spots. It was the brave who had captured him and Belle, almost broken Martin's skull with a club, and brought them to Wolf Voice's winter camp as prisoners.

"It's all right," Belle explained, drawing Martin near the bed. "That's Bull Head. He's Star Woman's brother. He looks horrible, but they all paint their faces kind of queer. Those white spots only mean he did some brave deed in a snowstorm." She knelt beside Martin. "The old woman is Magpie. Her husband passed away not long ago and she cut off some of her fingers. That's how they show grief, I understand."

He sniffed. "You seem to be a walking compendium of information about the Sioux!"

She was not rebuffed. "Bull Head speaks a little English," she said cheerfully. "He's been to Fort Schofield for treaty talks. He told me a lot about Sioux names and customs and things. His actual name is *Ni Ka Win A,* you see, or something like that, but it means Bull Head. When I said you were a doctor, he wanted me to bring you."

Cautiously Martin palpated the swollen abdomen. It brought a quick reaction from High Bear, the shaman. He pushed Martin angrily aside, glared with small dark eyes boring like augers from beneath heavy folds of skin. "*Na, na, na!*" he protested.

Bull Head threw aside the blanket, pushed the

old man away. He gestured to Martin. "You do—do medicine. White man's medicine!"

High Bear was furious. Spouting imprecations, he gathered up his potions, charms, and amulets and rushed from the tipi. They could hear his complaints long after he had left.

Bull Head gestured again. "Medicine!" he commanded. "Do!"

Gently Martin probed the stomach again. "Now look what you've got me into!" he complained to Belle.

His patient looked up at him with eyes veiled by the proximity of death. Martin guessed she was in her mid-twenties. Once, as he probed, she bit her lip but this time did not cry out. He felt her brow, looked at her tongue, winced at the foul breath. The pulse was weak and threadlike, the temperature greatly elevated. With a sigh he sank back on his heels.

"Can you tell what's wrong?" Belle asked.

He puffed his cheeks, blew out a long breath. "Not without exploratory surgery. It looks like an ovarian cyst, but that's only a guess. Anyway—something infected, filled with pus, ready to rupture."

Bull Head peered at Martin, trying to understand. The aunt, Magpie, clasped maimed hands before her in a gesture of supplication.

"But surely there's something you can do for her!"

He shook his head. "I've been away from surgical practice a long time, Belle. And I swore never again to touch a scalpel, after I'd misused it so back home. I swore that, and I don't take an oath lightly. But if all those objections were overcome, it would end up the same. An operation like this woman needs has to be performed in a surgical theater, with capable assistants and everything nicely laid out—instruments, sponges, sutures—"

"But she'll die!"

Bull Head understood that. He spoke in low tones to the old woman. Magpie burst into tears, rocking faster and faster on her round bottom, hands clasped around her knees.

Unhappy, Martin got to his feet, dusted his hands. "I can't play God, Belle! This is just one of those things that happens!"

Clutching his arm, she followed him to the doorway. "But there's a chance, isn't there? I mean —if she's going to die anyway?"

The smell was of new grass, rich moist earth, growing things. He was glad to be outside again even if it was raining, a feathery downpour.

"Maybe a small chance," he admitted. "But it's very small—not enough to warrant the effort. No, hard luck as it is, I'm afraid she can't be saved."

Belle followed him into their lodge, still protesting, and finally turning angry. He, too, became annoyed at her harassment. Many of his burns had healed but there was still that troublesome ulcer on his arm. When she accidentally touched it with an imploring gesture, he almost snarled. "Will you leave me alone?"

She drew back, stared at him. "I know what's wrong with you, Martin Holly—don't think I don't!"

He lay down on a robe, one arm flung across his brow. "Then tell me what's wrong with me, damn it!"

"You're scared!" she cried.

Propping himself upright, he stared at her. "Afraid? Afraid of what, pray tell?"

"You told me back there, in the cabin on the mountain! Don't you remember—you said you didn't trust yourself in surgery anymore because of the laudanum you had to take! You told me that! So you ran away, from Philadelphia or wherever it was! You had a duty there, as a doctor, and you ran away from it! You took dope, too, and that was a kind of running away! You ran away from Giles, and I did too. We—"

"He dragged us away!" Martin objected.

"Nevertheless, we were glad to get away because we were ashamed of what we did to him! So that was a running away too, don't claim it wasn't! And now you're running away again, not helping that poor woman, because you're a coward! You're off that dreadful laudanum now, and you can doctor the way you used to—like you told me! You said you were a damned good surgeon, didn't you?"

To shut out her railing, he put hands over his ears. Fiercely she pulled them away.

"You love me—you say you do! But I sure as hell doubt the love of a man that won't lift his hand, a doctor's hand, to save a poor sick woman!"

"It's impossible!" he protested.

"I guess you thought it was impossible for the two of us to keep from starving in that old cabin on top of the mountain, but we did it, didn't we?"

He groaned. "I didn't give much for our chances, I'll admit!"

Sensing victory, she pounced. "Then you'll do it?"

"I haven't even got a scalpel! I threw away all

the cutting instruments! I was afraid of them, any-more."

Triumphantly she took an Oglala knife from the folds of her ragged skirt, a knife with a bone haft and shiny blade, a long tuft of hair hanging from the butt.

"Where did you get that?" he demanded.

"A present. Anyway where I got it isn't impor-tant!" With a quick gesture she took a lock of her unkempt hair and sliced it with the well-honed blade. "See how sharp it is! It will cut anything!"

He snatched the knife away. "You silly goose! Don't do that to your hair!"

"Then you'll help Star Woman?"

With an oath he threw down the Oglala knife. "Good God, Belle, have you no pity?"

Picking up the knife, she pressed it into his hand, looking eagerly into his eyes.

"You surely use a man hard!" Martin muttered. "You don't know what you're doing to me!" Frus-trated, he drew her down on the robe beside him. "I—I've got to explain something, Belle. Listen to me!"

She pressed against him, head in the hollow of his shoulder. "I'm listening, Martin."

He took a deep breath. "I didn't tell you every-thing, that time in the cabin. I *was* a good surgeon, maybe the best on the staff of St. Anthony's, and St. Anthony's was the finest hospital on the East Coast. But—" His voice broke. She looked up questioningly. "I botched some operations, there at the last, when I was on that damnable laudanum. I—I overestimated my ability, I guess. There was a little girl—" Again he broke off.

"Go on," Belle said gently. "It's only me you're

talking to, you know. And I love you, Martin."

"Well," he said, "I botched the surgery. I was sure I knew what I was doing, but I didn't. Laudanum does that to you, you know. You think you're ten feet tall, can do anything. So—she died, you see. She died. And it was my fault!"

His body moved convulsively, and she threw her arms about him. "Martin, it's all right! Everything's going to be all right! You don't have to worry about it any more!"

He swallowed hard, not looking at her. "It's not that—not that simple, Belle."

"But you're over the laudanum, Martin!"

"I'm not over something else," he said. "Belle, the little girl's father was a rich man, head of a big iron works. When his daughter died, he almost went crazy. He found out, somehow, that I'd been using the drug, and swore out a warrant for my arrest, on criminal charges. I guess I'd known something like that was coming, so I was prepared. I'd sold off my properties, converted everything into cash, and I—you're right—I ran away. So—"

He looked at her, face agonized. "Do you—do you still love me, Belle?"

"Martin," she whispered. "Oh, Martin! How could I do anything else?"

The scene reminded Martin of his student days at college. But instead of the peering eyes of first year students, intent on old Mr. Hartmann's swift sure strokes and accompanying comments, there were savage Oglala faces, no less interested and intent. Ringing the makeshift surgical theater, set up in the sunny meadow for best light, stood Wolf Voice's people, restrained to a proper distance by old Spotted Elk, the camp crier, and a contingent of guards from one of the warrior societies, dressed for the occasion in their best. Wolf Voice himself sat on a rocky ledge overlooking the scene, fanning himself with his eagle-feather fan and calmly smoking a long beribboned pipe.

Nerves tight as fiddlestrings, Martin stood by his patient, arranging his equipment on a rickety deal table; the decorated Oglala knife, honed to a razor's edge, bottle of chloroform, clean rags, makeshift retractors fashioned from old spoons, thread and a sewing needle loaned by Magpie.

Belle, acting as surgical nurse, murmured in his ear. "You can do it, I know you can. Remember what you told me! You said we'd gotten this far, and you weren't going to let a bunch of Indians stop us now. Remember that?"

Star Woman's litter had been raised to table height by ammunition boxes. Pale and wan, she lay almost comatose, Belle shading her face against the sun. Martin bent over her, took her hand, spoke gently, though he knew she could not understand his words. "Ma'am, don't worry about anything! We're going to put you to sleep now. You won't feel anything. Just breathe deep, very deep."

At his signal Belle crumpled one of the rags, placed it over Star Woman's nose and mouth. Lifting the chloroform bottle, Martin let the clear liquid drop onto the rag, saturating it. Star Woman struggled briefly; a whimper escaped her tight-set lips at the unfamiliar smell. But Belle stroked her brow reassuringly, and she relaxed.

"Eh?" Holding the bottle high, Martin turned at the sound of an inquiry.

Belle gestured toward Wolf Voice.

"He say—" Bull Head translated for the chief. "He say—" For a moment he struggled with the English words, brow furrowed. "He say—you burn out devil in her?"

In spite of his anxiety Martin's lips twitched in an involuntary grin. Burn out the devil? His fiery exhibition in the great lodge had certainly impressed the Oglalas.

"No," he said. "No fire—this time, anyway. Tell him I will go inside this woman, find the devil, and pull him out for the people to see, to throw stones at, to beat with sticks."

Star Woman lay quiet. Martin put his head near her breast, listening to the dull throbbing. Pushing aside the bangles and bracelets on the slender brown wrist, he laid his fingers there and counted. *One, two, three, four—*

"I think you'd better hurry," Belle murmured. "They're getting restless!"

At his nod Belle pulled back the cotton shift, exposing the operating field. *I've never really believed in a God, any God,* Martin thought, *but God, if you're really there, help me!* With a great effort to steady his hand he picked up the Oglala knife, stared down at the distended brown abdomen. This was his field, his arena, the place where he had always felt at home. But now—

"Are you all right?" Belle whispered.

His brow was wet with sweat; it felt cold and dank in the slight morning breeze.

"Yes," he muttered. "I'm all right."

In sudden resolve he tightened his grasp on the knife, sliced quickly into the skin. Blood bubbled from the incision. At his command Belle blotted it up with a rag. "Retractor," he ordered. Hooking the bent handle of the spoon over the edge of the wound to widen it, he instructed her to hold it while he placed another, further enlarging the cut. "Hold that one too." He cut again, deeper this time, into a layer of yellowish fat, avoiding muscle tissue as best he could.

Sweat from his forehead dripped into the incision and he shook his head impatiently. Suddenly, unaccountably, he was no longer tense, no longer fearful. He was eager to get at it, to open the disordered belly and find the source of Star Woman's trouble. Swiftly, surely, he worked, a long-forgotten rhythm guiding his hand. The Oglala knife was fine steel, almost as keen as one of his imported Solingen scalpels.

"There!" he muttered to Belle. "Look! Ah, the ugly thing!"

Fascinated, yet horrified, she peered at the obscenity of the tumor, a veined and flaccid bulb nested within the surrounding organs.

"I was right!" Martin enthused. "A damned ovarian cyst! Look at the ugly thing! It's rotten, absolutely rotten—ready to burst. Another few hours and it would have popped like a balloon and snuffed her out!"

For a moment Belle swayed; he heard the quick intake of breath, and steadied her. "You're not going to faint, are you?"

She laughed, shakily. "Of course not! You—you go right ahead—doctor!"

With bloody hands he lifted the mass slightly, explored round it with his fingers. If he handled it carefully, managed to cut it free without rupturing it, then he could peer beneath it, know how in-

timately the obscene mass was connected to the
rest of the organs. Juggling the cyst like an armed
mine, he cut carefully, freeing it from the web of
tissue and blood-vessels. He knew Lister's precau-
tions for asepsis, but there was nothing he could do
about asepsis in this crude operating theater.

Some of the people, awe-struck, crowded closer.
Martin, intent on his work, snarled at them. Old
Spotted Elk rumbled a command and they shrank
back. "Blood," Belle whispered. "It's the blood.
They're worried, Martin! They think you killed
her!"

Feeling Star Woman's body flinch under the
probing blade, he barked an order. "Sprinkle more
chloroform on that mask. Ten drops, no more!"

Finally he had the growth excised. "Here!" he
commanded. "Take this thing and wrap it in some
of those rags."

Face pale, Belle gingerly took the cyst, weighing
at least eight or ten pounds, and dropped it into
what appeared to be, incongruously, an old lace
tablecloth, probably looted from some settler's
cabin.

"More retractors!" Martin ordered. "There are
things down here that have to be mended!"

Mopping his forehead, he peered again into the
cavity. He no longer knew, or felt, the presence of
the savages. For the first time in a long time he was
confident, fulfilled, at home. Fingers moving swiftly, surely, he tied off blood-vessels, pushed dis-
placed organs back into place, soaked up blood
with the rags Belle handed him.

"Not too bad!" he muttered. "Not too damned
bad! It's close to a proper job, by God!" Straight-

ening with a sigh of satisfaction, he said "I can close now. Hand me the needle and thread, please."

While Belle held the edges of the great wound together with her fingers, he started to stitch. Suddenly he clapped a hand to his brow. "Damn!"

"What is it?"

"Drainage!"

"What's—drainage?"

"The wound has got to drain for a while, get rid of the pus and blood and liquids that are bound to accumulate. At the hospital we had wooden tubes for that, but here—" He gazed round, blinking in the strong light. The Oglalas stared somberly back.

"There!" he cried. "Right there! That'll do the trick!"

Belle looked at him uncomprehendingly. Martin ran to the rocky ledge where Wolf Voice sat. With a muttered apology he snatched the pipe from the chief's lips and hurried back to the litter, wrenching the cherrywood stem from the bowl. Wolf Voice, offended, rose indignantly. Some of the warrior retinue rushed forward, brandishing lances and rifles. Belle's face blanched.

"What—what have you done?"

Hurriedly Martin inserted the tubular wooden stem into the wound. "No time for explanations! There! Now she'll have to lie on her side for a few days, but when the wound is well-drained I'll pull the tube out and close the hold with more stitches."

Belle looked nervously around. The warriors stood near, lances raised, looking to Wolf Voice for a signal to destroy the arrogant white man. But the chief only looked bemused; he sat down again, pulling thoughtfully at his lip.

Quickly Martin stitched up the incision, pulling the thread tightly. Star Woman stirred, moaned. He laced the rag over her face with a few more drops of chloroform.

"There!" he said in satisfaction, wiping his hands. "That's all any surgeon could do. From now on it's up to her."

Under the direction of Bull Head four men carried the litter back to Star Woman's lodge. Martin, through Bull Head, gave instructions for the patient's care to old Magpie. Murmuring among themselves, the crowd dispersed, with sidelong glances at Martin Holly. Wolf Voice, followed by his courtiers, retired.

"I—I think you did a great thing," Belle faltered, "however it turns out."

Martin looked down at his blood-stained hands, the litter of rags, Magpie's sewing needle and thread that had had to make do for proper sutures. Someone carried away the ugly cyst, wrapped in the tablecloth.

"We'll just have to see," he said, suddenly weary. "She's a young woman, in good health otherwise. The surgery was a shock to her system, of course, but—" He broke off, scrubbing at the stubborn stains while Belle gathered up the litter. Together they walked in silence to their own lodge. Martin lay down and slept heavily. In the middle of the night he awoke, listening. Belle was murmuring something that sounded like a prayer, and rain drummed on the taut skins. He clasped her in his arms, and together they fell asleep again.

When he visited Star Woman in the morning, her color seemed better. The incision, of course, was giving her pain. But she was fully conscious, and greeted him with a wan smile.

"Lie quietly!" he warned. "Don't move! You will be well. I know it."

Bull Head sat near his sister. Martin nodded reassuringly to him. Magpie was grinding what appeared to be dried weeds in a stone mortar. She spoke inquiringly to Martin, and held up the mortar. "She—she—" Bull Head rubbed his forehead in concentration. "She say my sister hurt. She—" Bull Head pointed to Magpie. "She make medicine there. Give my sister, she no hurt."

Martin shrugged. Perhaps Star Woman had a confidence in magical herbs. He knew the placebo effect, had himself often used sugar-pills on rich Chestnut Hill ladies with vague complaints.

"All right," he agreed.

The next day Star Woman was still better. The post-operative pain, which should have been agonizing, appeared to have vanished. Though lying in an uncomfortable position, she joked and laughed with her brother and Magpie. When Martin knelt beside her to take her pulse she grasped his hand and held it to her cheek in an endearing gesture.

"She feel good!" Bull Head grinned.

Martin was amazed. Magpie went on grinding desiccated stems and grasses and flowers in the stone mortar. "What in Heaven's name *is* that stuff?" Martin asked.

Bull Head spoke to the old woman and Magpie went into a long discourse. One word, one phrase, seemed repeated; *wo po it, wo po it, wo po it*. Martin watched as she poured the grayish powder into a tin cup of hot water and handed the brew to Star Woman. "*Wo po it!*" Magpie announced.

Whatever it was, the brew had remarkable pain-assuaging properties. Martin determined to look into it. The Oglalas, it seemed, had a pharmacopoeia of their own.

On the next day he was able to remove the makeshift drainage tube and close the incision completely. In a few more days Star Woman was able to sit up, take solid food. Soon she was walking unsteadily about the lodge, Magpie helping her. In another week she insisted on resuming her household duties in the lodge she shared with her brother.

Bull Head knelt and placed Martin's hand on his head swearing eternal friendship. Wolf Voice, at first affronted by Martin's *lèse majesté* in appropriating his ceremonial pipe, declared that there were some white men who were good; not all, he said, were evil.

Now the Oglalas brought Martin and Belle new clothing to replace their rags; intricately beaded moccasins, fringed leggings and a buckskin jacket for Martin, a dress for Belle cut from a precious bolt of trade gingham. Meat was always ready on the rack outside their tipi. Fresh mushrooms, turnip-like roots, wild onions and other vegetables filled their pantry. One spring day there was declared a holiday, a great celebration at which Martin and Belle were to be the guests of honor. Together they sat on a daïs while the men of the Fox Society beat their drums and young men raced their best horses back and forth before them.

Puzzled, Martin said, "I don't know what this is all about. It's kind of like the Fourth of July, only there aren't any firecrackers, just those men firing their guns into the air."

"You see," Bull Head promised, grinning.

With great ceremony old Spotted Elk held up a stained cloth heavy with some kind of burden. Martin suspected it was the cyst taken from Star Woman. After a long speech, delivered in a bull-like bellow, Spotted Elk threw the thing high into the air. Instantly the Oglalas rushed at it, men, women and children, beating it with sticks and clubs, kicking it with their feet, driving it before them like a ball in some mad game. Finally, having beat it to shreds, the Oglalas cast the remainder into a bonfire and danced around it far into the night. Star Woman's devil had been cast out by Martin Holly's powerful medicine. Before, his calling up fires from nowhere had greatly impressed them; many feared him. Now, with the curing of Star Woman, he and Belle became well-regarded figures, a kind of totem that gave the Oglalas great importance.

"I guess we pulled it off!" Martin exulted after the celebration. "Now we're surely entitled to animals and provisions to get out of this damned place—get on to Fitch's Landing!"

She looked at him oddly.

"What's the matter?" he asked.

"Nothing."

"But I *know*!" he insisted. "You're not a mystery to me any more, Belle—nor I to you, I suppose. But I certainly know when something's bothering you!"

She shrugged. "It was just that—well, I don't know how to say it."

"Don't you want to get out of here, same as me —be able to speak English to white people again, drink decent coffee, eat white bread—even at a backwoods settlement like Fitch's Landing?"

"Of course!"

"Then what—"

"I was just thinking how wonderful it was for you to save Star Woman's life. Yet all you think about is you 'pulled it off', like some kind of cheap trick. Now you can use that to get us food and horses, to—to run away again!"

He stared in astonishment. "You don't mean—you can't mean you want to *stay* here!"

Angry and frustrated in trying to express her tangled thoughts, Belle could only stammer. "No, I don't—I don't mean that at all, and you know I don't! It's just that—that—" She threw up her hands. "If you don't know what I mean, Martin Holly, there isn't any sense in trying to explain!"

She ran back to the tipi, weeping. When he got there, walking slowly and in perplexity, he did not attempt to comfort her. Instead, he thought himself badly used.

CHAPTER NINE

It was the month the Oglalas called *The Moon When the Buffalo Bulls Are Fat*. In the high country the mountainsides oozed water from melting snows; thousands of small springs gushed glass-clear icy liquid. Water ran everywhere down the Chetish, finding its way among the tumbled blocks of granite, refreshing the stunted pines clinging to the earth at their base. Ducks quacked and honked on ponds and lakes. Though the heights above were still mantled with white, in the meadows there flourished vernal grasses, harebells, forget-me-nots, and sunflowers. Along the creeks greened thickets of wild roses. Titlarks and butterflies flew about. Grasshoppers chewed their tobacco and sunned wings on flat rocks, breathing slowly. Full spring had at last come to Wolf Voice's mountain.

With spring also came preparations for war against the white men, the Men With Hats, the Oglalas called them. The various warrior societies —the Bad Faces, the Strong Hearts, the Scalp-Shirt Men—went about their ancient rites. They painted their faces, prayed to Rock, the god of war, renewed the paint on their war-ponies. A straight horizontal line, dripping red, meant an arrow wound had been dealt the mount. A red dripping disk signified a wound from a bullet. A red hand indicated the horse had been struck by the enemy, and a scalp hanging on the bridle-bit meant the horse had been used to run down a fleeing enemy.

Martin, now strolling freely about the village, was interested in the various facets of the complex Oglala society. Bull Head, one of a group of the younger and more rash warriors, explained much to him. Martin even began to pick up a smattering of the Oglala tongue, and Bull Head's English improved.

"That old man!" Bull Head grumbled one day, gesturing toward the chief's great tipi. He spat into the fire. "Talk, talk! Too much talk!"

There was much talk going on in Wolf Voice's lodge. Emissaries had come from the Miniconjou Sioux, from the Brulés and the Hunkpapa and the Sans Arcs, from the Cheyennes to the north, to confer on a course of action against the white interlopers. Two Moons attended, Young Man Afraid of His Horses, and other leaders. But in spite of weighty and continued deliberations it became clear to Martin the authority of the chiefs was a nebulous thing, depending more on persuasion than authority. In fact, many of the younger men, impatient with the talking of the elders, had already left the camp on tentative forays down to the river. By twos and threes they rode away, tails of their ponies tied up for war, a sack of pemmican and a wooden cup hanging from the saddle, a blanket strapped to the cantle. They rode fitted out with knife, bow, and a quiver of best arrows, good rifles of a modern pattern, ammunition in leather pouches, painted buffalo-hide shields. Little Bear, Bull Head's best friend, cantered past Martin, grinning with anticipation. Unlimbering his bow, he

pulled the string, hissing "Tccchk!" as he passed, a
noise like ripping silk in imitation of the sound of
a loosed arrow. Involuntarily Martin shrank back.
Little Bear thought this a good joke.

"That old man!" Bull Head renewed his complaint against the chief. "He treats us like chill—
chill—"

"Children?" Martin suggested.

Sullenly Bull Head nodded. "Like chillern! We
ought to fight, not talk, talk, talk!"

Martin didn't know what to say. He liked and
respected his Sioux friends, and thought they had a
good case against the white interlopers. On the other hand, he was himself a white man; he could
hardly look with equanimity on the killing of white
settlers. Was there not some way the two sides
could get together, talk things out?

Nevertheless, he was grateful to Bull Head and
Star Woman and Magpie for all they taught him.
His Sioux was getting to be more fluent, and he
had even developed some facility with the *wibluta*,
the hand language. In their spoken language
ahuyape meant bread, which they enjoyed when
they traded for it. Corn was *waka masa*. Potatoes
were *bello,* sugar a jaw-breaking *chahumpiaska*.
Fish, for which the women and children went on
long and festive excursions down to the Yellowstone, were called *tam was no,* and caught with nets
of woven willow-shoots. The sweet drink which
Martin had first tasted when he lay badly burned in
his lodge was water laced with sap from the box
elder—*mish ke mai mapi,* the Oglalas called it.
They loved candy, raisins, anything sweet. Magpie
asked him one day if Martin could possibly put her
in the way of a raisin tree. She understood the Men

With Hats had great groves of raisin trees. Any Sioux would willingly trade a bundle of prime beaver pelts for a sack of raisins.

Not all the Oglalas were friendly. High Bear, the shaman, felt Martin had infringed on his territory as the authority on magic and sorcery. Each time the old man passed Martin he shook his rattle, muttered incantations, glowered. Once Martin found a small feathered bundle at his doorway. Opening it, he saw it filled with rabbit-droppings, a remnant of snakeskin, a bit of broken mirror, jay-feathers. A charm, obviously; a malediction, a curse. Showing it to Belle, he laughed. But she was uneasy.

"You'd better keep an eye on that old man! He hates you!"

Martin grinned. "My magic is more powerful than his!"

"Nevertheless, it's no laughing matter!" She was helping Star Woman cook in the outdoor kitchen of new willow boughs the Oglalas put up each spring. She and Star Woman had become fast friends, sharing secrets and at times giggling together like two schoolgirls. But now Belle's face was serious, concerned. "You're a white man too," she said. "A Man With A Hat. You're a special white man maybe—right now—but that old fraud could turn them against you."

"Don't worry," he said, kissing her. "I'm one too many for him."

Gradually he had come to develop a grudging respect for the Oglalas, for their beliefs, their ceremonies and customs, the way they lived close to nature and saw the hand of God—*Wakan Tanka,* they called him—in everything. While Rock, Thunder, Buffalo, and others were a pantheon of deities to be called on and prayed to in specific cases, Wakan Tanka was the Great Spirit, the Chief Of All Gods. One reason for Indian restlessness this spring was the fact that Wakan Tanka loved the smell of tobacco. They had long ago run out of trade tobacco; Wakan Tanka needed to be propitiated, and soon.

Old Magpie became a firm friend of Martin. His brain, long turned away from the practice of medicine, tingled now with the potentialities of her herbs.

"They work!" he told Belle. "There was this old man, you see, down by the brook, with a very irregular heart rhythm. A bad heart, accumulation of fluid around the ankles, dropsy. But do you know what?"

She was braiding her hair, binding freshly-washed locks in otter-fur wrappings given her by Star Woman. "What?"

Triumphantly he held up a dried weed. "This is what Magpie recommended—an infusion in water."

"What is it?"

"Foxglove! The Sioux have known about it for centuries, Magpie says. Even before the Englishman—William Withering—discovered what it could do for the heart a hundred years ago!" He pulled up his sleeve. "And look at this!" Where the painful ulcer had been was now only healing flesh. "She made up a salve from roots and things and it cured the damned ulcer!" Excited, he paced the lodge. "She even has a scurvy remedy made from boiling fish bones! Belle, do you know there is a whole Indian armamentarium of drugs, a pharmacopoeia our doctors don't know anything about? Emetics, blood-purifiers, salves, painkillers—the range is endless! And old women like Magpie keep it all in their heads!"

When she did not respond, he looked curiously at her. "Don't you understand? This could be a great thing!"

She nodded. "I guess I understand. It's just—well, when you get too excited and talk so fast and use so many big words I—I have trouble following you. I never had much schooling, you know that, Martin. But I'm glad for you, if you think it's important."

In a pile of rubbish he found an old calendar. It was from a Moline plow manufacturer, probably pilfered from a ravaged settler's cabin. Though the paper was old and yellowed, it was good stock. He made a notebook to record descriptions and sketches of the grasses and herbs and medicinal plants. Martin threw himself into his research, sitting at the old woman's feet while she mixed her remedies, wandering the meadows and glens with her in search of plants, roots, shrubs, flowers, mushrooms. There was *me emi a tun,* leaves from the sweet pine, for coughs. *Wi tan ots,* the cat-tail flag, served for stomach complaints. *Pat se wots,* a kind of wild onion, was ground into a paste to draw poisons from boils and carbuncles. *Ot ka wit ko,* an herb infusion, was used by the women to prevent conception. *His se yo,* yellow flowers steeped into a tea, were effective when a woman's menses ran too long. Enthusiastically Martin followed Magpie about, hardly seeing Belle except to return to sleep. Absorbed, he watched Magpie grind and shred and boil and mix while he made notes and sketches and

pressed specimens into his notebook to dry. Someday, he promised himself, he would compile a great
treatise based on his observations of Indian medicine.

One day, the air washed clean and fragrant by
the rains and smelling of sweet grasses and
burgeoning buds and rich loamy earth, he was returning from a collecting trip near the river when he
saw old Spotted Elk cantering about the camp.
Martin did not understand the crier's brazen
bellowing, but from the general movement of the
people toward the northwest notch that led from
the camp it was apparent someone was coming.

Carrying his bag of plant specimens, he joined
the spectators. Soon he saw the reason for the commotion. Little Bear and a small band of warriors
had returned from a raid. Proudly they rode down
the slope, sitting their ponies like conquerors, bearing the fruits of their victories. Stopping before the
chief's lodge they unloaded the plunder from pack-
horses; cooking pots, axes, an ornate mirror with a
gilt frame, several books including a Bible with
gold stamping on the cover and spine. Martin
picked it up and read the flyleaf; "To Homer from
Emma with Lov Your Berthday May 16 This Year
of 1859."

Little Bear himself had a small hairy object on
the tip of his lance. A scalp? Someone thrust a cold
hand into Martin's own. Belle had joined him.

"They've killed someone," she said in a toneless
voice. "Some settler."

"Yes," he admitted, his voice dismal.

When Wolf Voice, aroused by the voices,
emerged from his tipi there was sudden silence. The
chief looked imperiously about, then bent a stern

gaze on Little Bear. His face was somber, impassive, not at all illumined by the joy Little Bear and his friends had exhibited.

"*Onhey*!" Little Bear exulted, brandishing his lance. It was the Sioux cry of victory—*I have overcome!* Proudly Little Bear pointed to the pile of homely furnishings. "*Onhey*!" he insisted, looking proudly about, beaming with accomplishment.

"*Hau*!" the people responded. "*Hau! Hau!*"

Wolf Voice's stern visage did not change. Little Bear had gone on a foray obviously displeasing to the chief. Little Bear had struck The Men With Hats hard—plundered, killed, brought home trophies of victory, including the thing on the end of his lance, while Wolf Voice and the war council and the emissaries were still planning the course they would take. The people approved of the raid, but Wolf Voice was angry at the transgression.

"*Onhey*!" Little Bear insisted. He looked puzzled. Turning, he sought encouragement from his friend Bull Head. But Bull Head was uneasy. He tugged at his braids, coughed, looked away.

There was tension in the air. The only sound was the babbling of water in the stream, a hoarse cry as a crow flapped overhead, a pony's shrill neigh from a distant corral. Wolf Voice turned curtly on his heel, dropped the doorflap after him, disappeared.

Embarrassed, Little Bear kicked at the pile of loot. The crowd dispersed. Some muttered among themselves, spoke behind their hands to the discomfited Little Bear. Others sighed, looked troubled. Walking back to their lodge, Belle said in a low voice, "Martin, we've got to get out of here! There's bound to be trouble soon, big trouble!"

"But we can't leave yet, Belle," he argued.

"There's so much to be done! Why, I've only begun to appreciate the full scope of the Indian medicine!" In the tipi he held up his sheaf of calendar pages. "Look here—and this is only a small part of it!"

She was silent, arranging a bouquet of harebells and forget-me-nots in a dented tin pot.

"I've been away from medicine so long, Belle! You can't imagine how this excites me! What a remarkable chance to make a contribution, a real contribution, to medicine!"

She was still silent. He knelt beside her, looking into her troubled eyes. "Are you afraid to stay a while longer, or is it something else?"

"What do you mean?" Her tone was careful. Arranging the flowers, she would not look at him.

"I think you're remembering Giles." A shadow crossed his face. "And Andrew."

She shrugged. "Maybe."

"What do you mean? Either you are or you aren't!"

"I mean—" She swallowed. "I mean—well, damn it, you don't pay me much attention any more! You're always busy. You go out with Magpie all the time. Then you come back and sleep like a log. In between times all you do is write in your notes and make sketches and things. I might as well not exist!"

"But it's important! After all, you're the one that got me started into medicine again, aren't you?"

Her anger kindled. "That doesn't mean I want to be treated like a stick of wood! I don't know how many times lately I've laid there beside you at night and heard you snore and felt lonesome. I've got feelings too, you know! If I'd thought you were going to go into this thing head over heels and—"

"I'm sorry, Belle," he said placatingly. He put a hand over hers but she pulled away. "It's just that I've been caught up so in the whole thing. It's so fascinating, important—"

"I thought I was important too!" she flung at him. "But lately we're more like brother and sister than—than—" She broke off. "Anyway, that's all I meant when I said I might be thinking of Giles. You're getting to be just like him! You're too busy, too tired! You—you—" Her chin quivered.

"I'm sorry." Contrite, he took her in his arms. "I guess I've been a little blind."

That night they lay together a long time in each other's arms, but there was little savor in it for either of them.

There were among the Oglalas, Martin had discovered, some few women-men, what were called *ber da cha;* men, biologically speaking, who in early youth were denied by their visions the traditional male role and became essentially female. These youths grew up in the company of Oglala women, moving gracefully about and speaking in soft well-modulated tones. They had male lovers, they cooked and mended; many showed extraordinary talent in singing and dancing. They were never reproached. The Oglalas reasoned that the gods simply wished it so. The gods had mischievously withheld from the *ber da cha* the lance and gun ordinarily held out in a vision to the young boys, handing them instead the wooden spoon, the cooking pot, and the sewing needle.

One of Belle's good friends was Gentle Horse, a *ber da cha*. Belle accepted the youth casually, just as she did her friendship with Magpie and Star Woman and the rest of the females. Martin tended to be standoffish with Gentle Horse. It went against nature, he insisted. But in spite of his misgivings about the *ber da cha,* and a suspicion that some of them could function as real men if they wanted to, he acknowledged that Indian children were certainly the happiest children on earth. There was little punishment, much love, almost a total lack of discipline as he had known it in his youth. Yet somehow the children were being prepared inexorably and unobtrusively for adult roles. The boys played warrior games, girls made dolls from twigs, fur, and feathers, preparing doll feasts as Philadelphia little girls had tea parties for their bisque and cotton-stuffed dolls. Eagerly the children followed Magpie and Martin about on collecting expeditions, helping hunt for herbs and plants and grasses according to the old woman's instructions. Sometimes they made a purposeful game out of it. Like hunters the boys stalked the plants, pouncing on their prey with a war-whoop. The girls carefully arranged the finds to dry in the sun, like the strips of meat they would in adulthood sun-dry for their husbands and children, meanwhile singing in the soft bemused way of the Sioux female at her work.

At times the little band left camp far behind in search of the elusive *sto wa tsis* and *o haa ino*. Accompanied by the children, he and Magpie wandered far down the mountain. From a ridge they could see the waters of the Yellowstone below, muddied by the spring rise. Magpie, astonishingly agile for such an old woman, had with Martin far outstripped the playful children. Picking berries for a snack, they came suddenly on a smoldering campfire, a tethered horse, a pack-mule. Over the fire sizzled a brace of trout. Someone had just departed.

Fearful, Magpie retreated, waddling quickly away. Neither was armed, though Martin did carry a borrowed knife at his belt. Looking, listening, even sniffing as the Oglalas did when uncertain, he stood stockstill. Satisfied there was no one watching, he started to move stealthily backward in his own tracks. That was when the muzzle of a gun poked through the greenery.

"Stand, you! Don't move ary muscle!"

Martin stood, tight with fear.

The unseen marksman spoke in what sounded like Oglala to Magpie. Cautiously the old woman returned, apron still filled with berries.

"Now what in hell you two doin' in my camp?"

A whiskered face emerged behind the gun. Two button-bright eyes stared down the barrel of the muzzle-loader.

"Dancer!" Martin cried in astonishment. "It's you!"

The whiskered hole of a mouth worked in perplexity; the gun muzzle dropped. Pushing the battered felt hat far back on his head, Dancer scratched his tangle of iron-gray hair.

"Who in tophet—"

"It's me!" Martin cried. 'Martin—Martin—" For a moment he stammered. "It's Martin Holly!" For a moment he had not known his own name. "Don't you know me, Dancer?"

The trapper's eyes widened in surprise; bushy

brows wigwagged. "Holly? Martin Holly? But you're dead! You and Miz Dyson, the two of you—"

"It's all right!" Martin grabbed Dancer's buckskin arm, gestured to Magpie. "He's a friend—*wa kin so*!" Delightedly he pumped the old man's arm. "Well, I never!"

Dancer laid down his gun, squatted beside the fire, poking the trout with a peeled stick. "I never either," he grinned. "You was supposed to be dead, you and Giles Dyson's woman! Giles went up to his cabin and come down all broke up. Said you and Miz Dyson starved or froze to death during the winter, and your remains was carried off by critters."

"Giles? Giles did that? I mean—went up there to see what happened to us?"

Dancer offered him a slab of trout on a piece of bark. Magpie sat respectfully a little distance away, sorting berries.

"He repented what he done, he said. Went up to rescue the pair of you, then found nothin' but a chewed lady's shoe and some torn scraps of clothes. When he come down the Reverend Mr. Willis spent all his spare time for a month prayin' with him, and Giles asked forgiveness, even if he did have a good case against you. Oh, when he saw you was gone, Giles took on something awful! Prayed like a horse, and kept sayin' 'I'm a murderer, a dummed murderer!' He kept sayin' he ought to be condemned to perdition for what he done!"

While the wide-eyed children surrounded them, Martin chewed on the fish, reflecting.

"So how in hell," Dancer demanded, "did you

get out of there? And just how came you to be sashayin' round the Chetish, dressed up like a Oglala, with this old lady and a passel of young 'uns?" His brows drew together, suspiciously. "They ain't your'n, are they?"

Martin laughed. "No!" Quickly he told the story of their travail in the cabin, the near-brush with freezing and starvation, their capture and eventual rescue by Wolf Voice's Oglalas. "So Belle is back there, in the village," he concluded. "I'm not a religious man, Dancer, but maybe Wakan Tanka was watching over us."

"Wakan Tanka, eh?" Dancer spat out a mouthful of fishbones. With a gesture he offered what was left of the trout to Magpie and the children. "By crikey, it beats all, pilgrim! You don't look nor act nothing like that dude in the clawhammer coat and hard hat come up the river last fall on the *Far West*!"

"I've changed," Martin admitted. He scratched in the dirt with a twig. "But look here—I want to ask you something."

Dancer picked his remaining teeth with a splinter, said nothing.

"I—I don't want anyone to know we—Belle and I—are up here." He struggled for the proper words. "It's just that—well, we've both turned over a new page now, and it's best not to look back."

Dancer nodded, tossed the splinter into the fire. "I get your drift. You don't need to worry none about me. 'Tain't none of my beeswax anyway."

Martin watched smoke curl upward into the trees, listened to the scolding of a jay. After a while he asked, "Where are you bound for?"

"Got me a wife and some younkers by Pompey's

Pillar, up the river. Brulé woman—name's Buffalo
Sister. A mite on the fat side, but a good cook."

Martin grinned. "You told me a long time ago
you had a Cree wife and children at a place called
Whiskey Butte."

Dancer nodded. "Her, too—and them."

"You'll run after anything with skirts!"

Dancer scratched his head. "Don't even need to
have skirts. But that's another story."

"Oh!" Martin said, nonplussed. Then he asked,
"Is Pompey's Pillar near Fitch's Landing?"

"It's on the way."

Martin stirred more dust with the stick. "Could
you take Belle and me with you? To Fitch's Landing, I mean?"

Dancer gnawed off a chunk of Wedding Cake
plug. "What in hell you want to go there for? Since
the mines closed down there ain't anything there
but a few dirt farmers and some falling-down
houses. Fitch's Landing is the absolute asshole of
creation. They ain't even got a decent saloon anymore, or ary whorehouse!"

"Nevertheless," Martin insisted. "Belle and I
want to go there—start a new life, put all the trouble and grief behind us."

The old man stared at him. "Kind of hidin'
out?"

"I guess you could call it that. Fitch's Landing is
far enough up the river so no one from Big Fork is
apt to come on us. We did a great wrong to Giles
Dyson, Belle and I, and that's a fact. But there's no
use crying over spilt milk. Belle and I intend to settle at Fitch's Landing and work out our lives together, try to make a go of it as man and wife."

Dancer scratched his stubbled chin. "Well—"

"I'll pay you!" Martin urged. "I've got money! We'll pay you well!"

The trapper spat. "Hell, I don't need money! How much does it take to buy an old scarecrow like me a plug of 'baccy and a bottle of Green River?"

"Then you'll do it?"

Dancer spat again, wiped his mouth with the back of a hand.

"It's some 'at out of my way, and I'm hurtin' to see Buffalo Sister right quick to get my ashes hauled, but I'll do her. Just don't blat about money any more—it's bad manners amongst friends!"

CHAPTER TEN

The Oglalas knew Dancer as an old friend, allowing him to run trap lines in their ancient lands when the area was forbidden to other Men With Hats. They called him *Wi Na Tsa Ka,* Hair Face, and crowded around to shake hands, clap him on the back, recall old times. Gentle Horse, the woman-man, rubbed his cheek against Dancer's grizzled face and embraced him affectionately. Martin, remembering the old man's Cree wife and children at Whiskey Butte and the Brule woman at Pompey's Pillar, looked puzzled. Dancer grinned cheerfully at him and said, "A feller's got to have a little variety, ain't he?"

Belle, hearing the clamor, pushed her way into the crowd. At the sight of Dancer her eyes widened in surprise. The trapper dismissed Gentle Horse with a pat on the buttocks and shambled toward her, taking off his fur cap. "Miz—miz—" He hesitated. "Ma'am, how by ye?"

Her hand went to her throat in that involuntary gesture.

"I—I'm fine, Mr. Dancer."

"Magpie and I met him in the woods," Martin explained. "He's on his way to—well, to visit someone, and he's promised to see us to Fitch's Landing."

"Is there—is there any news from—"

Martin took her by the arm. "There'll be plenty of time to talk, Belle! Mr. Dancer is probably tired, and would appreicate food and a pot of tea." He gestured to the trapper. "Come along!"

There was no coffee, the Oglalas having run out of this favorite item during the winter. Tea was also in short supply, and neither could be restocked until someone went to Big Fork to trade. With the present tension between the Oglalas and the white men, this was unlikely. Belle served the guest a stew of venison and dock roots, with tea brewed from dried berries. Dancer identified them as "sarvisberries." "Ain't had me a good cup of sarvisberry tea in a coon's age," he proclaimed, wiping his mouth with his sleeve.

Belle's hands trembled. She folded them nervously in her lap. "Is there any news of Big Fork, Mr. Dancer?" she asked. "I mean—have you been there lately?"

The old man sucked the marrow from a piece of leg bone, cast it into the fire. "I come by last month—" His brow wrinkled. "Or was it sooner? I disremember. Anyway, the town don't look no different, though prices has riz higher."

"Did you see Giles? Or Andrew?"

Martin explained how Giles had repented, come to the cabin, found them both gone and concluded they were dead. "Anyway," he said, "that's all behind us now."

But Belle was insistent. "How is Giles? And Andrew, is he getting along all right? Have they started the school yet we were promised? Does Andrew go to school, Mr. Dancer? And about church! I hope Andrew attends Sunday School, at least!"

Her manner was so imploring that Dancer was uneasy. He glanced at Martin, almost as for advice. But when Martin only shrugged, Dancer said, "I can't rightly tell you too much, ma'am. Giles has took this real hard. I know he goes to church right often, and does a lot of praying and good works and things. He's lost some of his heft, and his hair is a mite gray round the edges. Andrew I didn't see. They started the school, and I reckon that's where the boy was when I sashayed into town to buy me traps and bacon and flour and suchlike for the summer."

When Martin and Belle announced their intention to leave the Oglala camp, there was consternation and sadness. He and Belle were friends, and the departure of friends was an occasion for sadness. Belle was a highly-regarded figure about the camp, helping the old, the sick, the unfortunate, always ready to lend a hand, even at the most disagreeable tasks. More important, Martin was great and powerful medicine; they believed that his presence among them gave the Oglalas special favor with the gods. For a time Martin feared they would not suffer him and Belle to depart. His apprehension grew when Wolf Voice summoned him to the great tipi in the middle of the circle of lodges. Martin, feeling the need of an interpreter— his own Oglala talk was fairly fluent but crude— looked in vain for Bull Head to help him. But Bull Head and Little Bear had gone off on some private expedition to the river. Dancer volunteered to assist instead.

The three sat together in Wolf Voice's lodge for a long time, in silence, smoking. After a time Wolf

Voice began a speech. Dancer translated, though Martin was able to get the gist of most of it.

"You are going away from us. I hear this. We are sad you and your woman are going away. You are friends, we like you. When you came, it was as prisoners. But you showed us big medicine. We knew then the gods sent you. We were sorry at the way we treated you and your woman at first."

The chief puffed reflectively on the pipe, sent a wavering blue-gray ring high into the smoke-blackened lodge poles as an offering to Wakan Tanka.

"Then you took that ugly devil-thing out of Star Woman. That was big medicine. Waaagh!" Wolf Voice grunted in amazement. "Great medicine! I never saw a thing like that!"

Dancer took the proffered pipe. He too blew a puff skyward and winked at Martin. "Don't do no harm to butter up Wakan Tanka," he muttered in English. "Anyway, I always like to copper my bets. Maybe Wakan Tanka *is* the big cheese, after all."

"We do not want you to go away," the chief continued, making a sign Martin recognized. Magpie had used it when Star Woman was dying. *Sad,* it meant; *we are sad;* thumb and forefinger of the right hand were joined together to make a small heart, the hand placed over the left breast. Then the hand was swept out and downward. Literally, it signified *our heart is laid on the ground.* "But maybe someone else needs your medicine," Wolf Voice concluded. "So that is all right."

Martin breathed a sigh of relief.

"There is something else," Wolf Voice continued.

He strode about the tipi, hands locked behind

his back in thought. The red blanket was kilted about his waist so that the upper body was left bare. Firelight cast shadows across the Sun Dance scars on his chest, glittered on the shiny armlet of brass wire, lit the blue glass beads of his necklace with a cold flame. For the first time Martin realized Wolf Voice was not as young as he first thought. No longer braided, no longer wrapped in otter fur, the gray-streaked locks fell long about his naked shoulders.

"It is hard to be a chief. A chief is supposed to do good for the people. Sometimes I do not know what is good." Wolf Voice pinched lower lip between thumb and forefinger in a thoughtful gesture. "My young men want to fight. They want to fight right now, before more soldiers come. They want to drive the Men With Hats away, drive them so far they will never again come into our lands." He sat down, crossed lean legs, pulled the bright blanket about his shoulders. Martin offered him the pipe. Wolf Voice smoked somberly, staring into the fire. Finally he jabbed the pipe at Martin, almost like a weapon. "What do you think?"

Martin was caught off guard. For a moment he stammered, trying to collect his thoughts. When he had first come out to the Territory he knew little about Indians except what he read in the Philadelphia *Press* and other Eastern newspapers. Though there were movements favoring the Indian cause, like the National Indian Defense Association, such people were usually reviled as "Indian lovers." The majority of the citizenry believed Indians to be a scourge, wastefully occupying valuable timber lands, railroad rights-of-way, mineral deposits, farmlands. Now Martin was not sure where the equity lay.

"I do not know," he admitted, speaking slowly so Dancer could follow his words and translate in a mixture of Oglala and hand talk. "My medicine does not tell me much about this." Impressed by Wolf Voice's sincerity in speaking of his dilemma, Martin truly wanted to help. "I know this," he went on. "The Oglalas are a mighty people, but the Men With Hats are many more. They have a hundred soldiers for every Oglala brave. They have big guns that will shoot all the way from Fort Schofield to the Sioux villages, kill your women and children. They will come against the Oglalas like a fire that burns the forest, destroying everything."

Wolf Voice's eyes were intent on Martin.

"I am a white man. I have white friends. I have Oglala friends too. I do not want to see my friends fight. I think it is better to sit down and talk to the Men With Hats, try to come to an agreement. There is a lot of land out here. Maybe there can be room for both Oglalas and white men."

Wolf Voice pondered. The ribboned pipe went out. When it made a dry sucking sound the chief laid it aside. After a while he bent his shoulders, pulled the red blanket over his head.

Dancer nudged Martin. "That's all he's gonna say. We better light a shuck."

Outside, it was twilight of late spring. The sun was dying in the west, swallowed in a wrack of cloud. *The Indian nations, too,* Martin thought, *swallowed by a tide of the Men With Hats.*

"I didn't know what else to tell him," he said sadly.

Dancer scratched his chin. "You did good as you could. Ain't no man likely to know the real truth. Anyways, what the hell is truth? My truth ain't likely yours, and Wolf Voice's truth ain't Captain Mapes', down at Fort Schofield. So fergit it, pilgrim! Let's make a flat shirt tail out of here for Fitch's Landing while the chief is of a mind to let you go!"

Wolf Voice gave them horses for the journey, their choice from his own extensive string. Martin was only passably knowledgeable at judging horseflesh, and had never seen horseflesh like the Indian ponies. But Dancer was enthusiastic. "Some of the finest critters I ever seen!"

Oglala boys were gentling unbroken mounts in the stream, riding them back and forth in chest-deep water where the tendency to buck and fight was hampered. The pole corral was filled with Oglala wealth: ponies. Alert, eager, the animals crowded close to the corral fence as they approached. Small sharp ears perked forward, eyes stared curiously at them. To Martin the Oglala horses appeared rather small, legs slender and fine-boned as a deer. But Dancer guffawed at his apprehensions. "Them critters is as tough as rawhide! Look at them big barrels!"

"Barrels?"

"Chests," Dancer explained, fondling the muzzle of a spotted gelding. He pointed. "See, the Injuns allus slit their nostrils when they're babies. Figger it helps their wind when they grow up. Lets 'em drag in more air."

Once Martin had owned a carriage with a pair of

spanking high-steppers driven by a Negro coachman. He peered about the corral, examining the milling animals. "I'm partial to grays, and maybe a sorrel would be nice for Belle."

Dancer guffawed again, slapped his skinny thigh. "Gray? Sorrel! That's the best 'un I've heard for a long time!"

"What's so funny about that?"

"No self-respecting Injun would ride a plain-color critter! An Injun horse has got to be a paint! If 'n they got a good horse that ain't all speckled up like an explosion in a paint factory, they daub spots on it! When you find a gray or a sorrel in this here corral, I'll it eat it raw without no sauce!"

When it came time to leave it was raining, a fine mist veiling the camp, making indistinct the tops of the trees surrounding the meadow. Then the Oglalas came bearing gifts—some people weeping, all very grave. Magpie brought new moccasins for Martin and Belle, stuffed with pemmican for the trail. Star Woman had made Belle a buckskin dress, elaborately beaded, decorated on the hem and sleeves with row after row of porcupine quills, flattened by drawing them between her teeth, then dyed and painstakingly sewed in place. For Martin she had a small hatchet with a carved bone handle that had been her father's. She stood close to him, and with downcast eyes handed him the hatchet.

"I—I thank you," Martin stammered. Suddenly he realized he did not know the word, nor the gesture, for *thanks*. When Star Woman continued to stand there, face cast down, he yielded to a sudden impulse and put his arms around her, planting a kiss on the sleek part in her braids.

Others came with gifts; a leather water-bag painted with brilliant ochre and vermilion and indigo, a shell necklace for Belle, even a coup-stick from High Bear, the Shaman. The old man stared for a long time at the precious stick, bright with ribbons, decorated with hairy tufts. "When I was young," he explained at last, "I struck the enemy many times. The times are all written there, on my coup stick. Now I am old and do not need it any longer." He sighed, handing it to Martin. "I give it to you now. You can use it to count coup on sicknesses, and death."

When their pack-horses were finally loaded with gifts, clothing, Martin's medical satchel and the rest of their impedimenta, the people gathered at the edge of the meadow to watch them depart. As they reached the big rock above the camp, Martin turned to look back. There were no farewells, no wave of hand, nothing; the Oglalas stood silently, individual forms lost in the rain.

"We will never see them again," he said, half to himself.

Belle was weeping softly. He pulled his pinto close to her, put a comforting hand on her arm. Together they followed Dancer's string of mules through the notch and down the rough trail toward the Yellowstone.

"In a way," Belle murmured, "they were family."

As they rode the rain continued, but it was a warm gentle rain and they did not mind. Dancer smoked his pipe, and an aromatic smell of tobacco drifted back to them. The old man ambled on, singing a tune Martin suspected came from Elizabethan England:

"Pore little turtle dove, a'settin' on a pine,
Longing for his true love, as I did once for mine.
I went down in the valley green to win to me my
*   love*
But when I done with that pretty little gal
She turned to a turtle-dove, she did!
Oh, she turned to a turtle-dove!"

"Don't be sad," Martin urged Belle. "It's a new life we're going to, and a better one. After all we've been through, it's *got* to be better!"

Now dry-eyed, she turned to him. "I'm not made out of milk-weed floss! Don't worry about me!"

That night they made camp in a jumble of rocks and junipers. Late in the afternoon the rain had stopped. The sun emerged enough to glint on the swollen yellow waters of the river, far below. Dancer made a small fire and they broiled fresh venison steaks that had been packed for them in a rawhide box lined with moss. There were prairie turnips, too, roasted in the ashes, and a pot of tea made from a dented tin in Dancer's inexhaustible war bag.

"How far have we gone?" Martin asked.

Dancer knocked the dottle from his pipe. "Ten, maybe twelve mile."

"How much farther to Fitch's Landing?"

"In the morning we've got a far piece to go down the mountain yet. Then another ten, twelve mile through the flatlands along the river—if they ain't total under water, that is. With luck, we ought to fetch the Landing late tomorry afternoon." He rose, yawned, stretched. "Better wrap up in your blankets, folks. Sun raises early in this season!"

Martin and Belle obeyed, lying next to each other in the shelter of an overhanging ledge. Dancer picked up his old musket, squatted atop a giant rock, musket across his knees.

"Aren't you going to sleep, Mr. Dancer?" Belle inquired.

"No, ma'am."

"But you must be tired!"

Dancer grinned. "It's the pilgrims that gets tired that ends up with an Injun haircut, ma'am."

Martin sat up. "You mean we're in danger?"

"We're up the river, near Cheyenne country. There's different tribes around, and don't none of 'em cotton to whites. It's allus best to keep an eye peeled." Dipping into his bag, he brought out a plug of tobacco. "Anyway, an old geezer like me don't need much sleep. Someday soon I'll be sleepin' that long sleep anyway."

Finally they slept, and woke to a gray and sunless dawn. It was raining. Though the wood was wet Dancer started a blaze with a pinch of gunpowder. They drank gratefully of hot tea, ate cold meat from the night before. Again they started down the mountain toward the distant river. Martin began to sneeze, and pulled the blanket tight about his shoulders.

In midmorning they reached the Yellowstone, filled from bank to bank with a silt-laden flood the color of mustard. Cottonwoods and willows, looking half-drowned, grew thickly along the river. Following Dancer, they picked their way through rocky shallows, awed by the foaming torrent.

At noon the trail left the river, climbing onto a grassy plateau. At last the fickle sun came out and a breeze sprang up. Patches of blue showed, a battalion of cotton clouds moved majestically overhead. In the lush grass bloomed thousands of wild roses, a kind of phlox, daintily blue in tint, and forget-me-nots. Birds sang, the sweet dry air soon drove the dankness from their sodden clothing. Belle insisted on dismounting to gather a bouquet.

"We're making good time," Dancer remarked. "Ought to be there mebbe by sundown, if this keep up."

Far up the river they saw a curl of smoke. "Cyrus Ong's place," Dancer told them. "Cyrus has got himself a few acres in corn and beans, along with a passel of kids."

It was reassuring to come once more to familiar things: a man with the homely name of Cyrus Ong, a cabin with smoke from a cooking-fire, even a passel of kids. Ambling through the thigh-deep grass, Dancer began to sing again in his high whining tenor. It was all very pleasant.

Seeing the old man rein up in a copse of cottonwoods and dismount, Martin asked, "What's the matter?"

Dancer fished an ancient brassbound telescope from his war bag and put it to his eye, looking toward the Ong place.

"Is something wrong?" Martin kneed his pinto close. "What is it?"

The old man pushed the glass shut and gnawed for a moment at the eyepiece. "Dunno," he said finally, "but something gives me a pricking in my hide."

Martin stared toward the Ong place, half-hidden in the trees. Smoke curled up; through a gap he

could see a patch of plowed field, rich and dark.
Overhead a jay scolded in a tree; the river kept up
its ceaseless rushing.

"I dunno," Dancer murmured. "Sometimes I
just get a funny feeling." Unlimbering his musket,
he laid it across the pommel as he mounted. "You
and Miz—Belle—you and Belle sashay into that
clump of willows yonder whilst I ride a little closer
and see what I can see."

Martin started to protest but Dancer quickly cut
him off. "No sass, now! Do what I say! If it's all
clear I'll whistle." He stuck fingers into his mouth
and made a soft birdlike call. "Like this, only
loud."

"And if it isn't—isn't all right, I mean?"

"If you hear shootin'," Dancer said succinctly,
"get the hell out of here." He cantered toward the
screen of trees, the patch of plowed bottom land.
From the shelter of the cottonwoods Martin and
Belle watched him tie his horse, slip down, and
prowl like an old wolf through the trees.

"Is it—is it Cheyennes?" Belle asked in a hushed
voice.

In spite of the warm sun filtering through the
leaves Martin felt a cold flush in his stomach. They
had no weapons, only the ribboned hatchet Star
Woman had given him.

"I don't know," he muttered. "But surely, so
close to town—"

The leaves of the cottonwoods danced on their
slender stems, showing light and then dark sides as
the wind turned them. His pinto made a whuffling
noise and Martin fumbled for Belle's hand and
gripped it tight. Her hand was cold in his own.

"There!" she whispered, eyes wide. "Did you hear that?"

"I didn't hear anything."

"I thought I heard a whistle."

Creeping to the edge of the cottonwoods, he looked out over the meadow. Nothing; only the tendril of smoke, now grown larger, and a patch of black earth steaming in the sun.

"He said he'd whistle *loud*," Martin said, returning. "Did you hear anything?"

They continued to wait, feeling apprehension grow. The river's rushing seemed louder, and they feared the noise would mask some event they should know about. Straining their ears to hear a reassuring whistle, Belle suddenly jumped, brushing at a beetle crawling on her neck.

"I'm going out there and see what happened," Martin blurted.

"No!" She clung to him. "What could you do?"

He picked up the Oglala hatchet. "Not much," he admitted, "but I'm not going to abandon Dancer. He's done too much for us already. Now he's risking his skin too!"

He tried to shake her loose, but at that moment Dancer emerged from the trees. As though it were very heavy, he lifted his musket and slid it into the saddle scabbard. Then he climbed on the pony and came slowly toward them.

"What is it?" Martin demanded. "We were waiting for you to whistle or something!" Now that the danger was past he felt a twinge of annoyance. "Why didn't you signal us? We were—"

Belle touched his sleeve. He paused, seeing the gray look on the old man's face.

"Cyrus Ong—" Dancer stopped. His tongue emerged from the thicket of whiskers and he licked cracked lips. "Ong and his family has been done in, all of 'em."

"Done in?" Belle whispered.

"Whole passel of 'em! Shot, cut up, cabin set on fire!"

Now they could see the billows of gray-white smoke, even an occasional tongue of flame. Above the rushing of the river they heard snaps and pops from burning timbers. Once there was a louder report, as if an overlooked cartridge had been reached by the hungry flames.

"Good Lord!" Martin muttered.

"Not—not Oglalas," Belle said, hopefully.

"Cheyennes, maybe," Martin suggested. "You said we were near Cheyenne country."

Dancer looked much older. He licked his lips again. "From the way Ong and the young 'uns was cut up, I'd have to say Sioux—probably Oglalas. They got a custom of cuttin' up the enemy—to make sure, mebbe, they're dead, but more likely it's got somethin' to do with keepin' 'em out of the afterworld, or whatever you may call it. No, it was probably Oglalas."

Martin remembered Bull Head and Little Bear had been absent from the camp when he and Belle left. He felt a growing nausea. Belle swayed, looked faint; he pulled her tightly against him.

"What—what can we do?" he faltered.

Dancer looked at him absently.

"What can we do?" Martin repeated.

Dancer took a deep breath. "Do? There ain't nothin' to do but skulk out of here by a back trail

I know and go round the long way to the Landing. Them bucks must have left the Ong place just as I come up. They could still be between us and the Landing, awaitin' to bushwhack us."

"But those people!" Martin protested. "Mr. Ong and his family, all those children! We can't just leave them there, dead in the sun! At least we could bury them!"

Dancer regarded him coldly. "Get on your damned horse, Martin! You too, Belle! This ain't no time for funerals, less'n you want one of your own!" Eyes narrow, he scanned the sunlit meadow. "Up there, in that break in the pines, there's an old hunting trail. The bastard's 'll be layin' for us upstream, so we'll just put a spoke in their wheel. Take us a day longer to reach the Landing, but we'll keep our hair where it belongs."

Quickly they followed him through the meadow, started again to climb the mountain. The path was narrow and rocky and at times the horses stumbled and almost fell. Branches tore at them, catching Belle's hair and tearing Martin's new shirt. At times Dancer disappeared around a leafy bend; frantically they clapped their heels into the ponies' ribs to catch up. *Bull Head,* Martin thought incredulously. *And Little Bear.* Could it be? They had both been impatient with Wolf Voice's slowness in making war on the Men With Hats.

At last they broke out on a rocky ledge far above the river. They were exhausted, and the deep-barrelled Indian ponies were winded. From that vantage point they could look down on the now-silent river, see the burning cabin, contents of the ransacked dwelling scattered about, a slaughtered cow. Too, there were small shapeless bundles of clothing that must be Cyrus Ong, his wife, and the passel of young ones Dancer had mentioned. Belle put her face in her hands.

"That's the beginnin'," Dancer muttered. "Only the beginnin'. Come full summer, there's gonna be blood spattered clear on the moon!"

CHAPTER ELEVEN

Fitch's Landing was a sprawl of shacks and tents that had served the now-abandoned gold mines in the mountains above the Yellowstone. The Landing also served as trading center for a few poor farmers come out from the States to plow the river-bottoms. Now the place was a beleaguered outpost, far up the river, in hostile Indian territory. The townspeople went about heavily armed, looking askance at Belle and Martin in their Oglala garb. One man, a bearlike figure wearing a stained blue forage cap, a shotgun in the crook of his arm, raised a warning hand as they dismounted.

"It's all right, Bert!" Dancer explained. "I can vouch for 'em!"

The man named Bert squinted. "Where in hell they come from, old man?"

To Martin and Belle, Dancer said, "This here dumhead is Bert Scully, the town marshal." Rubbing saddle-galled shanks, he tied his pony to a hitching rail. "Bert, I'd like to make you acquainted with Martin Holly and Miz Holly. They used to live downriver at Big Fork but they was took prisoner in the Chetish by old Wolf Voice. He just turned 'em loose."

"They ain't Indian-lovers, are they?" Scully demanded. "We surely ain't got no use for Indian-lovers around here!"

A small crowd gathered. A sun-bonneted woman fingered the fringe on Belle's Oglala dress, lips pursed appraisingly, while others muttered comments.

"No, they ain't Indian lovers!" Dancer snapped. "They're good folks, and if you'll stop flapping your jaws I'll tell you something else—something more important!"

A tall white-haired man with a face that looked as if it had been hewed from granite joined the group. "What's all this, Mr. Dancer?" he asked. "What's this hoorah all about?"

Dancer took his battered hat. "Mayor," he said, "the Ongs, down the river, has been massacreed. When the Hollys and me come by there, we found the cabin burnt and Cyrus and his missus and the sprats all dead, hacked to pieces." He swallowed, Adam's apple sliding up and down in the lean throat. "Wasn't nothing we could do. The Oglalas was probably layin' for us upriver, so we took the old Hollums trail over the ridge and come down back of town."

There was silence. Someone gasped, a quick intake of breath. A woman covered her face with a gingham apron. The sunny street turned cold. "Not—not the whole Ong family?" the mayor asked.

"The whole lot," Dancer nodded.

"I remember," someone said in a hushed voice, "I remember hearing Cyrus say he run a couple of 'em off his land the other day with a shotgun. Said they were real mean about it."

"He was in here the other day to buy a sack of flower at Burke's store," someone else said, as if this act should have rendered Cyrus Ong invulnerable.

The mayor took a deep breath and bowed his head, clasping big gnarled hands before him. "Lord," he murmured, "take them to your everlasting bosom—Cyrus, Abby, young Bessie, little Alfred—"

His prayer was interrupted by Bert Scully. "Ain't no time for prayin'!" the marshal cried. "It's time for action! Christ, how long we gonna tippytoe around here like rabbits while the damned Indians take over our land?" He raised a clenched fist. "I say it's time to take a stand!"

The mayor looked at him with cold blue eyes. "Bert, you ought to be bored for the simples! We're seventy, maybe eighty people here, including women and children! What can we do except wait for the Army?"

Scully swore viciously. "Wait for the Army? By the time that bunch of coffee-coolers gets here from Fort Schofield, we'll all be dead, topped like a bunch of radishes! No, sir!" He brandished the shotgun. "I say go after 'em now—give the red bastards what for! Fight fire with fire!" He turned to the crowd. "Are you with me?"

There was a chrous of hoarse shouts. Women tugged anxiously at the sleeves of spouses, hoping to dissuade them, but the men were caught up in Scully's oratory. Someone drew a pistol and fired it into the air. Another took out a mouth harp and played Yankee Doodle. Excited, the men crowded around the marshal, slapping him on the back, shaking fists toward the distant bulk of the Chetish and its Oglala inhabitants. No one seemed to hear the mayor's entreaties.

"You're fools!" he shouted. "A bunch of damned fools! There's probably a thousand Oglalas up there in the mountains! It's only God's grace they haven't sacked and burned the town yet!" He raised hands imploringly. "Listen to me! Listen! Don't skyhoot out of here and leave the town helpless! Think of our own women and children, if you can't think of anything else! Think of —think of—"

The crowd's shouts drowned his appeal. Excited and happy, they moved away, milling about Scully. Now there would be action instead of waiting! Scully called out orders. "Billy, round up all the horses you can find! Tom Cross, go over to Burke's store and requisition all the ammunition the old man's got!" He smoothed a wrinkled sheet of paper, scribbled a note on it. "There here is a proper requisition, issued by me as marshal in the face of an emergency. If the old man argues, take the stuff anyway!"

"Idiots!" Mayor Loomis growled, shaking his head.

"Damned idiots!" Dancer agreed. "Well—"

He took them to the house of a widow, a Mrs. Maggie Flood, whose husband had been killed in a rock-fall in the mines. The small white cottage was an anomaly among the rude structures of the Landing. The Floods had come from Massachusetts and brought New England with them. The apple-cheeked old lady bustled about, "redding-up" a room for them and promising a chicken from her flock for supper.

"Laws, ain't it awful?" she asked, voice trembling with fear. "All the men leaving town, with us females defenseless?"

Dancer, assigned to a room next to Martin and Belle, patted the stock of his old gun. "Don't you worry, Maggie," he grinned. "Pretty ladies like you ain't got no call to be feared. I take care of the pretty ones myself, personal!"

Maggie blushed, giving the old man a coy shove. "You ain't changed any, Dancer!" she beamed. "Pa always said you was a skirt-chaser!"

Late in the afternoon the vigilantes rode out of town—a band of thirty, heavily armed; harness jingling, laughing and joking. Bert Scully rode at their head, crossed bandoliers over his chest, Union forage cap on his head. A bugler followed. The rest wore remnants of military attire, some gray, most blue. There were sabers, long-barrelled muskets, modern repeating rifles, a flag that was hasty in concept, with an indeterminate number of strips and crudely-scissored stars.

From an upstairs window Martin and Belle saw the riders. Mayor Loomis stood bareheaded on the sagging porch before Burke's store and watched the parade depart. As they passed, Bert Scully raised his cap.

"Mayor, ain't you gonna wish us good luck?"

Loomis stared at the cavalcade. Then, "Good luck," he called, and turned on his heel.

After the promised chicken supper Martin sat in the parlor with a Rand McNally map of the Territory borrowed from Mrs. Flood. "This is obviously no place for us," he said. "I agree with Mayor Loomis. Those hotheads are just going to cause more trouble. We'll be right in the middle of a full-

scale Indian war before we know it." While Mrs.
Flood dozed over her knitting, he spread the map
flat in the glow of the Argand lamp. "Dancer, look
here!" He traced a line on the map. "This is what
they call the Montana Road. Do you know the lay
of the land out that way?"

Dancer was enjoying the luxury of a Havana
cigar from Burke's store.

"Pretty tolerable," he said. "Not all the way, but
good enough. 'Tain't that much different from
around here. Had me a Flathead woman onct, up
that way."

"I suspect," Martin said dryly, "you've had Indian women of all the tribes known to man or God,
but that isn't the point. What I'm talking about, I
want you to take Belle here and me to—" He
squinted at the map. "To Bozeman, say. Then it
isn't too far to the Columbia River. We've got
plenty of money; I'd pay you well, of course. Then—"
He smiled in anticipation, putting an arm
around Belle. "We could take a steamer to Victoria! That's up in Canada, Belle. From there we
can sail any place we want to in the whole world!
How about the Sandwich Islands?" His eyes shone
with the magnificence of his vision. "Think of it! I
read about it in Stevenson! Palm trees, natives singing and dancing a welcome, our own thatched cottage on a sandy beach! How about that?"

She stared into the lamplight, thoughts far
away. Martin spoke again, almost sharply. "Belle,
are you listening?"

She started. "Yes. Of course!"

"What do you think of it then? The plan?"

She took a deep breath, fumbling with the lace
ruching of the dress Mrs. Flood had loaned her. "I

guess it's all right. I don't know much about geography."

Martin chewed doubtfully on his pencil. "Don't you feel well?"

"I feel all right," she sighed. "I'm just sleepy, I guess." When Maggie Flood dropped the knitting from her lap and woke with a snort, Belle turned to their hostess. "Ma'am," she said, "I'm that worn out, I think I'll bed down."

In spite of Belle's protests Maggie Flood rushed into the small bedroom, lit the lamp, turned down the coverlet, and insisted on brewing Belle a hot cup of tea. "You'll sleep like a baby," she promised. "Poor thing, what you must of been through!"

Martin, in shirt and pants borrowed from the late Mr. Flood, again spread the tattered map before him. Dancer had not noticed his discomfort, or was demonstrating a delicacy not before apparent.

"You was saying?" the old man asked, looking at the ash of his cigar.

For a long time they conferred on the route, supplies, horses, weapons. Finally Dancer's eyelids sagged. Dropping the cigar, he awoke with a yelp as the coal burned his skinny thigh.

"You had better go to bed too," Martin advised. "In the morning we'll go down to Burke's store and pick out what we need for the trip. We can visit the livery stable too, see about pack-horses."

Even after Dancer stumbled off to bed and was snoring an obbligato to Maggie Flood's soprano, Martin sat alone in the parlor, staring at a bouquet of horsehair flowers under a glass dome. The glow of the Argand lamp shone palely on the polished surface. Almost in a hypnotic trance, he was lost in thought. The window was open; a faint night breeze stirred the lace curtains. Somewhere a mockingbird loosed a shower of tender notes. Still he sat, staring at the glass dome. Flowers, only horsehair flowers, but they reminded him of the dogwood blooms, the sprays of forsythia that decorated Philadelphia in the spring. Philadelphia; he would never again see his boyhood home.

Melancholy, he turned down the lamp and went into the small bedroom. Divesting himself of the unaccustomed white man's garb, he sat naked on the edge of the bed, letting the night air bathe his body.

"Martin?"

"I thought you were asleep," he lied.

"I couldn't sleep. I—we should talk."

"About what?" he asked, and knew.

She stroked his naked thigh. "About going to Bozeman, and on to Victoria or whatever it was—on the steamer."

He was silent, staring out the dark window. She went on, voice gentle. "I love you, Martin. I always did, from that first time I saw you on River Street in Big Fork and asked you to help me, with Giles. So, whatever I say now, don't forget that."

Uncomfortable, he said, "Shouldn't you get to the point?"

Belle took a deep breath. Her breasts rose and fell under Maggie Flood's best sheet. "I—I don't want you to run away again. I don't think I—we—ought to go out there."

"But we can't stay here!"

"I know."

"And we certainly can't go back to Big Fork!"

"I think we ought to."

He stared, amazed. "What?"

"We did a great wrong to Giles, you know we did. You admitted as much. Martin, I—we can't go through life living a lie. And there's Andrew to think of, too. He's—"

"I knew it," he said. "You still love Giles. I've known it for a long time. You don't really love me. I don't think you ever really did, Belle."

Long hair streaming in disarray around her shoulders, she rose from the bed on her elbow, clutching the sheet about her bosom. "That's not true!"

Hands clasped behind his head, he lay down beside her, but still distant. "I know what you told me. You can't love both of us, can you? And Andrew into the bargain? No woman's got enough love to spread it that thin."

She pressed her cheek against his. "Martin, don't you see? They're all different!"

Suddenly she was weeping. "Suffering Jesus, can't you see? I love you, Martin, and I love Giles too, and he needs me! Andrew—I worry about him all the time! What's going to happen to the boy?"

Grudgingly he slipped an arm under her head, sighed. "Stop crying, Belle! Tears don't solve anything!"

"I can't help it!" she sobbed. "Suffering Jesus, was ever a woman in such a predicament!"

He tightened his grasp on her shoulders. "Listen, now! Listen to me! This is no time for emotion. We've got to deal in hard cold facts! I'm a doctor, trained in science. In science, facts are all that counts. So what we're dealing with here are our lives, damn it—yours and mine! So we'd better *consider* facts. The fact is, you ran off with me, away from Giles and Andrew, from Big Fork, from everything. Maybe Giles *took* us away, but that begs the question. We wanted to run away with each other. It's too late to do anything about it but press on, find a new life. It would be cruel to go back to Giles, after what we did to him. He's probably adjusted to the loss by now, anyway. Why didn't you think that much about Giles when you were sleeping with me, back there? No, I'm not about to give you up so easily!"

She winced. "You're hurting my shoulder!"

Contrite, he said, "I'm sorry, Belle! It's just that I'm so worked up! Because I love you too, you know that!"

"I—I know," she faltered. "Oh, Lord, what am I to do?"

He pressed her to him. "What you're to do," he murmured, "is trust me, Belle. Love me, trust me! Tomorrow, Dancer and I are going to outfit us for the trip to Bozeman, on the Montana Road. Everything will come out all right, you'll see!"

For a long time they lay in each other's arms. The song of the mockingbird became louder, then dwindled. Somwhere a cat sang to the moon, a far-off dog bayed a complaint; then there was silence. After a while Martin slept. When at times he woke during the night, he was aware Belle was still awake. Once a muffled sob startled him. Bone-weary, he drifted off to sleep again.

Old man Burke smoothed out the greenbacks Martin paid for the provisions and arranged them into a neat pile. "Ain't seen that much real money

in a coon's age!" he chortled. "I been a'carryin'
folks round here so long I plumb forgot there *was*
such a thing as folding cash!"

Martin paid cash also to the livery stable for
three packmules. "I favor mules when I can get
'em," Dancer explained. "They can be stubborn as
a woman, but they got horse sense, which no horse
has got. A mule don't stray off, a mule don't
prance and kick when a snake crosses his path, he
don't fall off a mountain and bust his leg. No, give
me a good stout mule anytime!"

Few noticed their preparations to leave. Most of
the men had left with Bert Scully's avenging troop,
and the women had their men on their minds.
Maggie Flood baked them three loaves of bread
and filled a salt-sack with raisin-studded cookies.
"Sweets always lays easy on the tongue after so
much meat as you'll be eating on the trail," she
said, and gave Martin the rest of her late husband's
wardrobe, along with three dresses and a pair of
kid-and-cloth shoes for Belle. "Too fancy for
Fitch's Landing," she sighed. "I brought them out
from Dorchester when the mister and me come to
the Territory, but I never had a chance to wear
them. Miz Holly, they'll do you real nice when you
get to Bozeman or Victoria or wherever!"

Belle, Martin observed, seemed to have overcome her misgivings about the journey. She joined
him in packing salt and flour and tea into oilskin-
covered packages for the journey. "Summer rains
up there can be real gully-washers," Dancer observed, wrapping precious cigars in a square of
oiled silk. "Best be prepared."

"Wait!" Belle whispered. "What was that?"

They listened. "I didn't hear anything," Martin said.

She went to the window of Maggie Flood's kitchen. "There—again! Didn't you hear it that time? A whistle of some kind, or a horn!"

Martin remembered Bert Scully's bugler. He listened also, and nodded. "That's Marshal Scully and his ragtag army coming back, I'll wager."

They abandoned the packing, joining the rest of those who had been left behind to stream out into the dusty lane. Scully still rode at the head of the troop. He had a bloody bandage around his skull, the forage cap sitting askew. The bugler rested his trumpet on his thigh, but the other arm was in a makeshift sling. The others all bore marks of battle but their spirits were high. As they passed they grinned and held up trophies of the hunt: a painted rattle, a beaded and tasseled rawhide pouch, feathered fishing spears. One man—and then, Martin noticed, several—sported furry objects tied to the barrels of their guns, dangling from saddle-strings. Martin frowned; not fur, but hair, long black hair with ribbons and bone combs and ornaments worked into them. Beside him Mayor Loomis sucked in his breath.

"Scalps!" he muttered.

With a flourish Scully reined up before the mayor. "We're back," he said. "Don't we get no civic welcome or nothing?" He turned to the ragtag troop. "Dismount," he ordered, "and stand easy." Swinging stiffly down from the saddle, he threw the reins over the head of his bay mare and lounged before Mayor Flood.

"I guess I ought to make you an official report," he said, while the women crowded around the returned men and the children stood in open-mouthed awe at the heroic stories being told. "Well, we went downriver and come to Cyrus Ong's place. We buried 'em—all five of the poor creatures. It was a sorrowful sight, I tell you." Reverently he took off the blue cap. "Folks," he went on, addressing the larger audience, "my heart bled for those poor Ongs! And my boys was real moved, too. A sight like that pierces a man's heart!"

Face twisted in a grimace, Mayor Loomis examined a scalp.

"So," Scully went on, "we decided to give the mangy scoundrels a taste of their own medicine. We kept riding downriver, looking for sign. At Murphy's Bar we come on a passel of 'em fishing." Chuckling, he slapped the dusty cap against his thigh. "They never even seen us! We took 'em like old Cump Sherman took Atlanta!"

The mayor looked up from the grisly object. "This—this thing is kind of small, Bert. It looks like it came off a child."

"I wish you could of seen 'em scatter!" Scully exulted. "They run this way and that, like a bunch of spooked sheep! Oh, I tell you they wasn't brave at all when we hoorawed 'em!"

"A boy," Loomis mused. "Or maybe a little girl."

"We run 'em into the river!" Scully crowed. "Didn't waste much ammunition. Sabers and gun butts did for most of 'em!"

Watching the mayor's growing concern, the crowd was mute, restrained. Scully did not appear to notice. He talked on, waving his hands, describing the remarkable exploits of his band. "Exterminate 'em—that's the only way to deal with the dirty skulking Sioux!" He turned to his audience. "Ain't that right?"

There was silence. Martin, disgusted, was nevertheless the professional physician. Not too gently he unwrapped the bugler's damaged arm. "I'm a doctor," he said curtly. "That wound has to be sewed up or you'll lose the arm. It's swollen and red already along that gash where the bone is poking through."

"Lose—lose my arm?" the youth quavered.

"That's right." Martin took the other arm. "Come along with me to the widow Flood's place. I've got my medical kit there." As the silence tightened. Mayor Loomis was examining another scalp. "Small, too," he muttered. "Damned near a baby, I'd say! Were there any men at the river, Bert? Fighting men? Sioux with guns?"

Scully's face colored. "What in hell do you mean by that?"

Loomis stood up straight, white hair blowing in the wind. His features were cold and bleak.

"I mean it looks like you killed a lot of women and children, Bert! They're the ones that usually fish along the river, aren't they—the women and children?"

"Well, of *course* there were men there!" Scully blustered.

"How many?"

"God damn it, Albert, I didn't *count* 'em! We was too busy!"

Loomis threw the small hairy thing into the dust. "You fool!" he murmured. "You damned stupid fool!"

Scully bridled, appealed to the crowd. "They're all alike, ain't they? The women birth the brats, and the brats grows up to be Oglala bucks. What's the difference?"

Loomis shook his big head. "You've killed us all."

Scully stared at him, uncomprehendingly.

"Before," Loomis said, "Fitch's Landing had at least a Chinaman's chance! Maybe we could hold out till that damned Mapes at Fort Schofield sent soldiers. It wasn't much, but it was all the chance we had. No—" He shook his head. "The Oglalas will wipe us out, quick!" He stared at the cliffs above the town. "Soon as they get word of what happened to their people—and a Sioux loves his women and children as much as any white man—they're going to come down us like a swarm of bees!" He spat into the dust. "You mentioned Atlanta. Were you there?"

Scully moved a toe in the dust, uncertain. "I was before Petersburg, with Grant."

"I was at Altanta," the mayor said, "with Logan's Fifteenth Corps."

"What has that got to do with anything?" Scully demanded.

Mayor Loomis glanced at the landing where the *Antelope* was still moored. "Atlanta was a garden spot compared to what Fitch's Landing will look like after Wolf Voice passes this way." He took a deep breath. "We better start to round up our own women and children and try to get them downriver to Big Fork before Wolf Voice and his Oglalas pay us a visit."

That afternoon Martin patched up several of the band. "We didn't want to," an uneasy youth confessed, "but Bert made us do it!"

Martin was brusque. "Were there any Oglala

men with the fishing party?"

The youth shrugged. "A couple. Guards, I guess. They wasn't no older than me. We shot them from that bluff above the Bar. Then we went down to the bank where the rest was kind of—" He swallowed, hard. "Kind of huddled together."

Belle, helping Martin secure the splint on the boy's broken arm, shuddered. Dancer, leaning idly against the door, spat into the yard. Mrs. Flood wiped floury hands on her apron and walked out into her small garden where she looked for a long time at the flowers. Martin smoothed the bulky bandage, rolled down his sleeves.

"Keep it on for two weeks," he advised. "If the bandages seem too tight, loosen them a little. Keep the arm as clean as you can."

When the young man had left Martin slumped in the chair. Belle stood white-faced at the window. "All those women and children," she murmured. "Do you suppose Star Woman, or Magpie, were—"

"I don't know," he said wearily. "But at any rate we'll have to leave for the Montana Road as early in the morning as we can!"

A dawn mist lay over the river as they rode down the street. The little *Antelope* was getting up steam after boiler repairs. "I don't give 'em much chance," Dancer remarked. "Wolf Voice's people know the old hulk is here, tied up. He's probably got outriders along the river already to shoo 'em back to the Landing again." He clapped heels into the paint's ribs, jerked at the lead-rope of a mule. "Well, this mess ain't any of *my* doing! Besides, what good is one gun—" He looked at Martin, his newly-purchased Winchester center-fire in the saddle-scabbard. "One gun, or two, against a couple hundred crazy-mad Oglalas?"

"It's none of my affair either," Martin said curtly. Belle rode behind them, saying nothing.

"There's Scully!" Dancer remarked. "Now what in tophet is that idiot doing up so early? He always liked his sleep!"

In front of Burke's store, still shuttered, Marshal Scully waved them to a stop.

"What you want, Bert?" Dancer demanded.

Scully drew a folded piece of paper from his pocket. "Don't want nothing from you, old man! My business is with Martin Thorne here."

Martin stiffened. "My name is Martin Holly!"

Scully was enjoying himself. Criticized the day before, he was reclaiming status as a figure of authority. "Dunno what name you go by now, and it don't signify!" He shoved the blue forage cap pugnaciously forward. "This morning I read my mail that come up on the *Antelope*. There was this here WANTED circular in it." He held it up. The woodcut was a fair likeness of Martin's face. "Feller I used to know in Big Fork, name of Jack Flanders, posted it upriver to me. Sent back east for it, he said, all the way to Philadelphia. Sent it to me, the marshal hereabouts."

"I don't know anything about it," Martin said in a tight voice.

Scully peered at him. "They got your description down pat, even to that moon-shaped scar on your cheek."

Martin heard Belle's quick intake of breath.

"Martin Thorne, or whatever you call yourself," Scully went on, "I arrest you on authority of the Federal Marshal for the Eastern District of Pennsylvania." He squinted at the poster. "You was a doctor, and done some illegal things. Among others, you botched an operation while under the influence of opium, it says here."

Martin cleared his throat. "That's right,"

"Then run away to escape prosecution." Almost jovially Scully drew the Navy Colt from his belt. "Hand me down that new Winchester, Doctor Thorne! And Dancer—don't you try nothing with that old blunderbuss or I'll give you an ounce of lead right in your bellybutton!"

CHAPTER TWELVE

Fitch's Landing not only had a mayor and a marshal, leftovers from the days when the settlement was a booming town and the gold mines were busy, but a jail also. The jail had real iron bars, brought all the way up the Missouri and the Yellowstone from a St. Louis foundry.

Dancer sat on a stool outside the bars to keep company with Martin, and sipped coffee from a tin cup. "Holly," he mused. "That wasn't your real name, eh?"

Martin shrugged. "Holly was my mother's name. I—I just used it when I had to leave Philadelphia."

"Well it takes a court of law to settle the matter," Dancer sighed. "Besides, a lot of good causes can make a man do bad things. I ain't the one to tell a man how his chip should float!"

Martin grimaced. "I'm grateful for that. Belle wasn't quite so understanding. She says it's a sin to run away from a sin."

Dancer went to the barred window, looked out. "Them hills up there," he remarked "is swarming with Oglalas. They're thick as fleas on a hound dog, all round the town. Ain't no one comin' in or goin' out. Last night the *Antelope* come back stuck so full of arrows she looked like a porkypine. Old

Wolf Voice has plugged up the river."

Martin rubbed his unshaven chin. "What are they waiting for? Why don't they just swoop down and wipe out the Landing?" It did not make much difference to him. After all, what were his prospects? A trial with all his old friends looking on, a long prison sentence, disgrace—physician no longer; instead, a convict. Still and all, he reflected, he would not like them to harm Belle.

Dancer looked into the office where Marshal Scully was writing laboriously in a journal. "Bert," he complained. "I dunno what you put in jail coffee, but it tastes like lye soap!"

Tongue lolling while he wrote, Scully grinned. "If it does," he jeered, "it's the first time soap's been near your hide for a coon's age, old man!"

"So why don't they just swoop down and wipe us out?" Martin insisted.

Dancer threw the rest of the coffee on the floor. "This is probably a big thing with the Oglalas," he theorized. "They got to do it right, not only to put the quietus on the white men for good, but to satisfy the gods—Rock, Thunder, Buffalo, all the rest. They got to dance and pray and get themselves painted up proper. Hell, they know we ain't goin' nowheres! We'll still be here when they're ready!"

Martin lifted the tin plate, stirring the mess with a spoon. The stew, or whatever it was, smelled nauseating. "*You* could get away," he pointed out. "They've got nothing against you. Besides, knowing the land the way you do, you could sneak out, get past them."

Dancer shook his head, lit a cheroot. "When a Sioux gets his dander up he kinda goes crazy. No, I ain't about to cross 'em when they're mad." He puffed a perfect ring. "Anyway, I ain't one to sneak out on my friends. Comes to a fight, I guess I'll stay here, me and my old gun."

Martin was touched. "Well," he sighed, "maybe this jail is the safest place for me after all." Rolling himself in the sleazy blanket, he dozed off. He had been without sleep for a long time.

When he awoke it was afternoon. Slanted shafts of sunlight filtered through the iron bars, laying a pattern on the floor, painting a wandering cockroach with a mellow patina. Hearing a commotion, he went to the window and looked out. Though his view was restricted he saw a scene of frantic activity. Men ran this way and that, carrying heavy logs and building a makeshift barricade across the dusty street. Others dug trenches, fashioning enfilading trenches. Barrels of water were brought, and provisions from Burke's store stockpiled nearby. Men staggered past the window carrying wooden boxes of ammunition. From somewhere an ancient cannon had been propped up on stacked timbers to cover the approach to the town. Bert Scully, loud and profane, directed the acitivity.

Dancer, sauntering about with the old rifle in the crook of his arm, paused by the jail window. "Dummed fools!" he growled. "I told 'em and I told 'em but Scully won't listen! What in tophet make 'em think the Oglalas are going to march down the street like the Army of Northern Virginia on parade? Hell, a Sioux gets to you like a crab in your crotch—he comes in the back way and first thing you know he's bittin' you in the balls!"

"Where's Mayor Loomis?" Martin asked.

"Across the street in his office back of Burke's

store. Him and me been palaverin' till my throat's that dry." Dancer took a bottle of Clubhouse Gin out of a hip pocket and drank a long gargle. "If Bert Scully can requisition anything he wants out of Burke's store, then I guess a duly elected common soldier like me is entitled to a few small items." He offered the bottle to Martin, but Martin shook his head.

"What did you talk about?"

"Loomis wanted me to go up there and talk to Wolf Voice, try to stall him off, buy time if nothing else. He still thinks Mapes and the troops from Fort McPherson are going to ride in, flags waving, and save our hides."

"Is there any chance?"

Dancer snorted. "There's ten Oglalas in them hills and strung out along the river to every yellowleg at Fort Schofield! The army might get through, yes—but it'll be like General Terry arriving at the Little Big Horn. Nothing but corpses to say hello to!"

A gout of dust spurted up from the street. A moment later they heard the distant crack of a rifle. The laboring men stood stockstill for a moment, then ran for cover. Dancer opened the breech of his old rifle to check the load. "Just to keep us on our toes," he remarked.

Suddenly Martin stiffened. His hands clutched the iron bars. "Listen," he said. "Dancer, listen! I'll go!"

The old man stared at him. "Go where?"

"Why, up there!" Martin gestured toward the Chetish, its massive palisades crowned with sunlit snow. "What in hell have I got to lose? I don't want to see all these people slaughtered; Belle and you and Mayor Loomis and Maggie Flood—even that stupid fool Bert Scully! I've lived with those people, and they know me, like me! Let *me* go up there and see what I can do!"

Dancer shook his head. "Martin, I like you. You're my friend, no matter what you did back east. But I tell you it's sure death right now for *any* white man to try to go up there! You lived with 'em for a summer, yes, but I been around Sioux for thirty year or more. And I tell you it won't work! All we can do is scrunch down here and hope we can maybe wing enough of 'em to drive 'em off for a while. After that—" His silence was eloquent.

Martin reached through the bars to tug at the leather fringes of the old man's coat. "What harm can it do? Look, Dancer, go across there and ask the mayor to come and talk to me! You can do that much, can't you?"

Grumbling, Dancer dodged across the street and into Burke's store. Cautiously the workers began to straggle from cover and resume their labors. "They ain't gonna hit anyone from way up there!" Scully encouraged them. "Come on, now, we ain't got all night!"

Mayor Loomis sat on the stool across from Martin and listened.

"After all, there's nothing to lose," Martin argued. "If I lose, if they kill me, then you're certainly no worse off than you were! And if I can hold them off for a while, maybe even convince them they're asking for big trouble from the Army if they attack Fitch's Landing, then it's a good investment!"

Mayor Loomis looked haggard. There were deep pouches under his eyes, and a Bible stuck in his hip pocket. "I've been praying," he said. "It isn't much, maybe, but I'm an old man. I can't do the physical things that Bert Scully and the younger men do." He stared at Martin, ran a hand through his white hair. "But maybe the prayers have brought something."

"That's right!" Martin insisted. "Dancer wouldn't go, and I don't blame him for that! He's an experienced hand in the Territory and knows the Oglalas better than I do. I don't blame him for not wanting to risk it. But sometimes, if you don't know something is impossible—like I don't—then maybe you can do it! Isn't that right?"

The mayor pulled at his lips, eyes narrowed.

"You'd maybe be safer here," he said. "For right now, anyway. Why are you offering to do this?"

Martin crossed his legs, spoke casually. "A while ago I said it would be a good investment for you. But to invest means to put money into a bank, to put money into stocks, to risk capital to make more money. If you want to make this investment, then *you* have to put up something."

Loomis' bushy brows drew together. "I don't follow you."

Martin moved closer to the bars. "I'm in your jail," he said. "I won't try to dissemble. I'm guilty of the charges on that WANTED poster. But I want out of this jail. I want to take my—my wife and go out to the Californias, maybe onto the South Seas, where we can be comfortable, safe from prosecution. So I'll put it this way. Let me out of your jail and I'll go up the mountain to Wolf Voice's camp. I know those people. I lived with them, speak some of the lingo, operated on an

Oglala woman and saved her life. I have friends there. I tell you they'll listen, at least! They may turn me down, may even get angry and roast me over a slow fire! But that's a chance I'm willing to take if—" He paused.

"If what?" Loomis asked.

"If I succeed," Martin said slowly, "I want you to promise that when I come back you'll let me go free, let my wife and me go on west, without let or hindrance."

The mayor's eyes searched Martin's.

"There are serious charges against you. I understand there's a sizeable reward Bert Scully wants to collect. What's to prevent you just sneaking out of the Territory and leaving Bert to hold the bag?"

"My wife," Martin said. "Belle. She's here, staying with Mrs. Flood. I'm not a scoundrel, Mr. Loomis."

The mayor got up, went to the window, stared upward at the chetish. "Seems I haven't got much choice," he muttered. He took the dogeared Bible from his pocket, riffled through it. "Get down on your knees," he ordered.

Wondering, Martin knelt. The old man cleared his throat, read from the Psalms. *"Lord, how are they increased that trouble me! Many are they that rise up against me. But Thou, O Lord, art a shield for me; my glory, and the lifter up of mine head. I will not be afraid of ten thousands of people that have set themselves against me round about. Salvation belongeth unto the Lord; Thy blessing is upon Thy people. Selah."*

The mayor put the tattered Bible back into his pocket.

"I'll go tell Bert to let you out," he said.

* * *

Belle clung to him. "You can't go!" she wept. "It's dangerous! They might kill you! Mr. Dancer says they're really on the warpath!" She turned to the old man. "Isn't that so?"

Dancer shifted uncomfortably, waggled the stogie around his toothless mouth.

"Don't bring him into it, please, Belle," Martin said. "It's my own idea." Gently he pushed her away, holding her by the arms, so he could look into her face. "Don't you understand? It's my—it's our only chance! If I can cool down Wolf Voice and his Oglalas, talk them out of destroying the town, I'll be free! Free, Belle! We can travel to San Francisco or the Sandwich Islands or wherever we want, just like we planned! Remember—I told you about the palm trees, the natives singing, our own thatched cottage on a sandy beach just like in Stevenson?"

She tried to dry her eyes on the hem of the apron she had put on to help Maggie Flood peel potatoes, breath catching like a small child after a bout of weeping.

"I remember. But—"

He placed a finger on her lips. "No buts, now!"

With an almost physical effort she calmed herself, setting her mouth resolutely to still the quivering chin.

"I—I lost one man," she murmured. "Come back, please, Martin. I love you."

"And I you," he said, kissing the tearstained cheeks.

Only when he and Dancer left for a final conference at the mayor's office did her chin quiver and the blue eyes fill again with tears. As they departed Maggie Flood put her arm around Belle's shoulder and offered her a cup of tea.

"There, there, dear!" she comforted. "I know just how you feel. Every time the mister went down in the mines I felt the same way. But your man will be back. I know he will!"

Mayor Loomis presided over the small council of war. "You oughtn't to go alone," he told Martin. "Someone ought to go with you."

"I don't need anyone," Martin said. "They understand a white flag. Mrs. Flood gave me a piece of bedsheet, and I've tied it onto this stick. That'll do to get me into their camp. After that—" He shrugged. "If it comes off all right, fine. If it doesn't, there's no point in risking anyone else's life."

Bert Scully, angry at the mayor's releasing Martin from his jail, growled agreement. "Can't spare anyone else anyway! We need all the men we can get to defend the town."

Dancer, however, cleared his throat. "Guess I'll go with you, Martin. You speak fair Sioux, and I seen you *wibluta* some." *Wibluta* was the hand language common among the tribes. "But this here is apt to be a ticklish kind of situation, and little differences in meaning can be important." He took a deep breath, threw away his stogie. "Hell, I'm near seventy—" He grinned. "Or is it eighty? I disremember. Anyway, I'm independent as a hog on ice. Might as well cash in my checks now as later."

Martin shook his head. "I'm grateful, Dancer, but—"

"My mind's made up," the old man said. "I'm going."

Mayor Loomis was thoughtful. "There ought to

be a representative of the town, seems to me. After all, that's the point, isn't it? We're trying to save Fitch's Landing."

Martin shrugged. Dancer stared at the wall. From high in the hills a bullet hit the iron cannon and screamed into the distance, the wail echoing and reechoing from the canyon walls. There were cries from the workers laboring at the barricades, and a great scurrying about.

"We've got to act fast," Martin warned.

"Indians," Loomis remarked, "put great store on ceremony. Maybe I ought to go too, as mayor."

"I don't think so," Martin said. "The people here need you."

Dancer rubbed his chin, squinted at the ceiling. "Bert ought to come along with us," he suggested. "Ain't he law and order in Fitch's Landing?"

Scully spoke quickly. "I got to finish the barricade and rig up a way to sweep that cannon sideways." He mopped his forehead. "Someone's got to ramrod that job, ain't they? I'd like to go, but—"

"Scared, Bert?" Dancer asked softly.

"Hell, no I ain't scared! I ain't scared of any Sioux that was ever born!"

"Then come along!"

"I told you—"

"Maybe you better, Bert," the mayor suggested. "I'm an old man, and while I'm willing, my legs get cramps."

Scully swallowed, mopped his forehead though it was morning-cool in the room. He looked from one to the other.

"Them fortifications of yours is about done anyway," Dancer grinned, an evil grin. "And you can tell Wolf Voice all about that deadly cannon and how it'll blow his Oglalas to smithereens—if they come in the front door, that is."

"What do you say, Bert?" the mayor insisted. "If these men are risking their lives for us, and they don't even *live* here, it seems to me—"

"All right!" Scully protested. "All right! No brick wall don't have to fall on me!" He got up, pulling the sagging cartridge belt a notch tighter around his belly. "Let's go, then!"

They left quickly, trudging up a winding game trail into the hills. Martin, unarmed, went first, carrying the makeshift flag. Dancer followed, old gun on his shoulder, padding noiselessly in his moccasins. Scully brought up the rear with his shotgun.

The trail was steep, winding in and out of the trees that covered the slope. In spite of the summer season the chill of upper snows reached them in the forest dimness. They were grateful when at times they walked through a patch of sunlight. Jays flitted about, calling raucously. Squirrels paused on branches, tails high and bushy, watching the little procession. The air smelled damp and loamy, laced with the resinous scent of pine and fir.

From time to time Martin waved the flag, calling out, "*Hau, hau!*" in the Oglala tongue, adding: "Friends! We are friends! We want to talk!"

No one answered, except the jays. The squirrels ran farther out on the limbs, peering with bright eyes. Nevertheless, they all knew they were watched. Somewhere in the forest gloom a decision was being made. Would the Oglala scouts shoot, or would they allow Martin and his companions to approach nearer, to speak, to explain their mission?

"*Hau!*" Martin called again, waving the flag. He was sweating, and his heart thudded in his chest. Behind him Bert Scully wheezed for breath. Dancer, too, stopped to lean for a moment against a tree. "Got a little stitch in my side, Martin. Give me a minute!"

From the Landing the mountain had not seemed so high. The sun was almost overhead, however, when they reached the rocky spine of the ridge overlooking the town. Above them loomed the higher reaches of the Chetish, deep in snow. Sun shining on the white expanse made Martin blink. He turned to look down. Far below snaked the Yellowstone. Fitch's Landing was a child's toy town. He could make out buildings, see the little *Antelope* at the wharf, even the black line of Bert Scully's barricade. But from this distance it was impossible to discern individual people. Nevertheless, people *were* there, scattered about, waiting: Mayor Loomis, old Mr. Burke, Maggie Flood—Belle.

"Don't look now," Dancer muttered, "but there's an Oglala over there, behind that scrubby stand of juniper! Just poked his head up!"

Martin didn't see anything but waved the flag again. "*Hau!*" he called. "*Hau cola!*"

"Bert," Dancer grumbled, "stop wavin' that gun around! If your brains was to be put in a jaybird's head he'd fly backwards! Just let it dangle easylike from your hand. You let it go off and we'll all be catmeat!" He shook his head.

Scully spat out an oath. "You got a running off at the mouth, old man! I don't need no advice from a mangy old coon like you!"

"Hush!" Martin ordered.

They were quiet. After a while Dancer asked, "What is it?"

Before Martin could mention the illogical fluttering of the leaves he had seen from the corner of his eye, an Oglala brave rose from the greenery. A single eagle-feather stuck up from a topknot, and the face was painted black for war. Like a statue he stared, unmoving.

"*Hau!*" Martin called. "Friends! We are friends!"

Old Dancer spoke too, voice quick in the choking sibilant Sioux tongue, and made sign talk. Scully raised his shotgun but Dancer pushed it down, hissing a warning.

"*Hau cola!*" Martin repeated. "Here, hold this," he whispered, handing the white flag to Dancer. Slowly he approached the silent figure, holding out both hands to show he was unarmed. "We come to talk," he faltered in rusty Sioux. "Talk! We want to talk!" he gestured. "Talk to my father Wolf Voice."

Among the Sioux the title of father was one of high respect. It did not necessarily imply kinship, but rather a recognition of greatness. With satisfaction Martin found the proper sign coming back to him. *Father*—compressed right hand, back outwards, tips of fingers tapping the right breast. "Talk to my father Wolf Voice."

The iron-hard visage, painted in geometrical swirls and dots, did not change. But—Martin drew in his breath quickly. Was there a glitter of recognition in the hard eyes? Was that—could it be Raccoon, one of Bull Head's good friends, and a persistent suitor of Star Woman?

"Friends," Martin repeated. He squinted in the sunlight. "Raccoon? Is that you?" Hands still held out, he sidled nearer the forbidding scowl. "Do you remember the time we played the button game and I won your best knife, the one with the yellow handle?"

Raccoon rose an inch farther from the cover of the bushes, staring, gun across his chest at the ready. "I know old Hair Face," he admitted. "But who is that other man, the one with the blue hat?"

"Friends," Martin repeated. "We are friends. We come to talk to our father."

Raccoon sighted down the barrel, drawing a bead on Bert Scully. "I do not know that man," he growled. "Tell him to throw down his gun!"

Dancer muttered something to Scully but the marshal only gripped his shotgun more tightly. "If you think I'm goin' amongst those killers without no weapon—"

Like the flick of a cougar's paw Dancer's skinny hand shot out. He knocked the gun from Scully's hand and it fell to the ground beside his own. "We come in peace," Dancer signed.

Still uncertain, Raccoon prowled from his cover, finger on the trigger. He whistled between his teeth and other Oglalas ran from the trees to pick up the white men's guns. "Is it you, White Medicine Man?" he asked.

Martin nodded.

"Why do you and Hair Face come here in this bad time?"

Martin was desperately trying to remember the Sioux words. His fingers fumbled at signs but Dancer spoke for him, skinny fingers weaving an intricate pattern in the sunlight. "There must not be war between the Oglala friends and the white men. We come to talk peace." Martin had not been able to remember the word of the sign for *war;* peace was simply a clasping of the speaker's hands before the body, backs of hands down.

Raccoon, charged with great responsibility to protect the trail into Wolf Voice's camp, was doubtful. "It is late to talk of peace."

Martin found his voice, the words, the signs.

"It is never too late, friend."

Raccoon made a gesture and the Oglalas surrounded the three emissaries. "Then let us go," he said. Stripped of weapons, surrounded by painted faces, they entered Wolf Voice's camp high on the Chetish.

The jumbled rocks swarmed with warriors. Many squatted in the sunlight, smoking or gambling. Some played cards on a blanket with a greasy and well-thumbed deck. Others honed knives on rock ledges, sharpened hatchets, oiled the actions of repeating rifles traded from the white men in more peaceful times. Scrambling up in surprise, Martin's old friends ran forward to greet him and Dancer, shaking hands—Big Leggings, Kills Often, Fool Dog, Stump Horn, Smoke Dancer. "Friends, where did you come from? What are you doing here? White Medicine Man, where is your woman?" A youth, braids bound in otter fur, watched them from a ledge where he sat, new gun across his knees; this was obviously his first war party. "Hair face, do you have any more women?" They laughed, ignoring Bert Scully. "Shoshoni women are good. Do you have a Shoshoni woman to lie in your robes?"

Quickly they were escorted to Wolf Voice's tipi, the only permanent shelter in the rude war camp. "Injun lovers!" Scully jeered. "You, Dancer, and your fancy-dan friend! I suspicioned him from the first, when you brought him and his woman into town!"

Politely Raccoon scratched at the doorflap of Wolf Voice's lodge. "Father," he called, "Hair Face is here, and White Medicine Man! They come to talk to you!"

Dancer spoke in Martin's ear. "Guess you brought it off, pilgrim—so far, at least."

"I didn't—" Martin started to say, but a voice called out from the interior of the tipi. Raccoon gestured for them to enter.

Muted sunlight filtered through thin-scraped and smoke-blackened skins. Wolf Voice squatted on a robe, smoking a pipe, lean body in repose. Beside him stood High Bear, the shaman, in his buffalo-horned hat. Around the two men the older warriors sat, a war-council planning for the extermination of the enemy.

"*Hau*," Martin said, raising a hand in the traditional salute.

"*Hau*," Dancer echoed. Scully stared around, and grunted.

"Father," Martin went on.

"Great chief," Dancer signed; extended palms facing each other before his meager chest, then sweeping his hands outward.

The aristocracy of the Oglalas were surprised to see the party; some were obviously angry at the intrusion into their camp. Martin heard enough muttering to know a Fox Society man was asking his neighbor why they had not already been killed.

Others only glared and fingered their weapons. Martin was surprised to see the youth with the otter-fur braids standing in the dim recesses at the rear of the lodge. Young men were ordinarily not permitted such proximity to the great men of the tribe. Perhaps the youth had done some brave act.

"You come as friends, they say," Wolf Voice remarked. The dim richness of the sunlight washed across the Sun Dance scars on his chest, the raised weals on the tortured flesh.

Martin nodded. "We want to speak with you, father."

Wolf Voice signalled them to sit. Scully muttered in Martin's ear. "I don't understand none of this gibble-babble. But you got me into this mess, you and the old man! You better talk fast and get me out!"

"Shut up," Martin snapped. "Damn it, be quiet or you'll ruin everything!"

In the leisurely Indian way the Oglalas continued to smoke their pipes. Wolf Voice blew wavering rings to the sooty upper reaches of the lodge. High Bear stared heavy-lidded at Martin. The leaders of the warrior societies puffed until the pipes sucked dry, smoke ceased to rise. Wolf Voice cleared his throat, speaking to Martin.

"You were our friend. You saved Star Woman with magic. You lived with us, ate our meat, drank our tea. Your woman helped everybody, and she is sweet in our hearts. But now things are different. The white men come. They keep coming. They take our land, they spit on us, like that bad man that lived on the river and told our people to go away or he would shoot them."

Ong, Martin thought. *Cyrus Ong and his family.*

"Imagine!" Wolf Voice's fist, index finger extended, swept outward from his left breast. "Our own land and that man told us to go away!"

There was a chorus of indignant grunts. Wolf Voice sank back, bare arms crossed across his mutilated chest.

"You were our friend," he repeated. "Now you wear white men's clothes. Are you a white man inside, too? Or do you still love your Indian friends?" He gestured to Martin to speak.

Shakily Martin arose. His mouth was dry and cottony and beads of perspiration lay damp and cold on his brow. He remembered the night he had taken the gun away from Jack Flanders, the gambler, and saved Giles Dyson's life. Laudanum had made him brave that night. Now he must do it on his own.

"Tell 'em," Dancer muttered as he arose. "You got a good case. Don't worry! I'll sign to 'em as you talk!"

Martin cleared his throat, struggling to assemble his thoughts. *There must be no war. The white men are too strong for you. They have men, as many men as the blades of grass, and big cannon that can shoot all the way from Big Fork to your camps, destroy your horses, kill the people.* But in spite of Dancer's reassurance he was worried. The youth with the otter braids still stood in the back of the tipi, silent, motionless. Something in that mute figure sent a chill into Martin Thorne's heart.

CHAPTER THIRTEEN

"Father," Martin began, raising a hand in salute to the members of the powerful warrior societies, to High Bear also. "We come to talk peace."

High Bear's lip curled but Wolf Voice's face was impassive. When some of the Silent Eaters stirred and muttered among themselves at such effrontery, a glance from Wolf Voice silenced them.

"There is bad blood between the white men and my brothers," Martin continued in his halting Sioux. Behind him old Dancer's gnarled fingers danced like butterflies over a meadow. While many of the Oglalas listened to Martin's laborious words, all watched Dancer's hands. That language was eloquent.

I spoke of this before to you, father, when I lived with the people. You asked me then—what do you think about this? I told you then, father, what I thought about the fighting between the Men With Hats and my red brothers. I think about it again and my heart is the same.

Bert Scully grumbled impatiently. In the shadows at the rear of the great lodge the young man in the otter-skin braids stood unmoving, slender arms folded across his chest, a graven statue.

The Men With Hats are as many as the blades of grass in the meadow. They have ten soldiers for every

Sioux, for every Cheyenne, every Ree. Back there—
Martin pointed eastward. *Back there they have
canoes that run on the Big Water and carry hundreds
of people. They have lodges high as the sky.
Thousands of men work in those lodges, live in them.
The Men With Hats have copper strings to knit
spiderwebs to spread over the land, and they talk over
those copper strings to other white men a moon's
horse-riding apart. They have guns so big in the barrel a man could put his head in, guns that shoot for a
day's journey. If they bring a gun like that to Fort
Schofield they will load it up with gunpowder and
iron and shoot high into the Chetish. They can kill all
my Oglala friends—men, women, and children—
without even seeing them! Brothers, you are brave
men! You are right to be angry at what the Men
With Hats have done to the people and their land!
But listen to me. Listen, friends!*

Encouraged at the way the Oglalas seemed to be
receiving his argument he went on, supplementing
Dancer's hand-talk with awkward gestures of his
own. His heart slackened its breakneck pace and he
felt sweat cooling his brow as it evaporated.

*Blood has been shed on both sides! Now it is time
to stop this spilling of blood! There must be a law in
the Chetish. Maybe it is not fair, but that law is
going to be the white man's law. He has many judges,
many policemen, many jails. The white man is going
to hang all those who shed blood, whether it be white
man's blood or Indian blood. That is the way it is
going to be.* Remembering the Reverend Mr.
Willis, the hell-fire Baptist preacher in Big Fork,
Martin added *An eye for an eye and a tooth for a
tooth!*

They understood, but so far he had not convinced them. High Bear spat, making an imprecatory gesture toward Martin. Leaning over, he muttered in Wolf Voice's ear. The chief's face remained carved in stone.

I speak truth, Martin insisted, making the Sioux sign; index finger laid over the heart, then thrust forward; *straight from my heart.* He went on with his stumbling oration, certainly not polished, but heartfelt. *I did not have to come up here to tell you these things. My woman and I were going to go to the Big Water out there*—he gestured toward the west. *But I love my Sioux friends. I wanted to save them from the big guns of the Men With Hats. So I came back here to talk to you, to tell you all these things. Brothers, believe me!*

For the first time he thought he saw uncertainty in Wolf Voice's obsidian stare. High Bull, too, seemed uneasy, and glanced at his chief.

Do not go down there and attack the town. I say fire ends only in fire, and killing ends only in more killing, sadness for everyone—red and white. On both sides blood has been spilled. The gods are satisfied. Let it end that way. He made the sign for *finished*—fists before his chest, knuckles touching, then the two hands slowly withdrawn to right and left. *We have come in peace,* he concluded. *Let us go in peace, friends.* Raising his arms in the ritual gesture toward Wakan Tanka, the Great Spirit, he sat down, his legs weak and trembling under him.

Dancer whispered in his ear. "That was some fine speechifyin'! You gave 'em a hard bone to gnaw on!"

Martin took a shaky breath. "We're not out of the woods yet!"

Again the council lit pipes. High Bear filled the

chief's pipe respectfully from his own pouch and handed it over, lighting it from a sulphur match. Wolf Voice puffed silently. The men of the warrior societies smoked in concert, blowing a long line of regimented smoke rings.

"Wisht I had my old corncob to chew on!" Dancer muttered. "It'd calm my nerves a mite!"

Scully stirred. "How long is this palaver going to go on?" he demanded. "Are we going to sit here all day while these red bastards play dumb?"

Wolf Voice continued to smoke. Outside the lodge a jay scolded, war-ponies neighed. Smoke from a cooking fire drifted in. One warrior called to another, maybe a joke, because laughter followed. Finally Wolf Voice laid down his pipe. When he gestured, the youth with the otter-skin braids left the tipi quickly, as if on an errand.

"We have heard you," Wolf Voice acknowledged. "You speak well." He nodded toward his council. "Our people have thought about these things for a long time." Taking out his carved and painted scratching stick, he poked thoughtfully his graying braids. "The young men always want to fight. The old men know fighting is not always good. So we have to talk about these things." His lean face wrinkled in a grimace. "I told you, that time, it was hard to be a chief. Sometimes a man does not know what is good for the people. So I went into the sweat lodge and stayed a long time. I had dreams, many dreams. When I came out, we talked again, for a long time. We did not want to fight, we decided. We just wanted to be left alone in our Chetish. But then—"

A scratching sounded at the doorflap. Wolf Voice nodded assent, and the slender young man entered, accompanied by two other warriors. Martin's eyes widened. It was his old friend Bull Head, Star Woman's brother, along with Bull Head's bosom companion, Little Bear. Together the two stood near the doorflap, in full war panoply, carrying their weapons.

"But then," Wolf Voice continued, "these two young men rode down to the river. They came on a man plowing his fields and only wanted coffee to drink." Wolf Voice's face hardened. "You know that river belonged to us, and all the land along the river! But—" He shrugged. "We know the Men With Hats have to have some land too. That is fair. So we did not fight when they came to the river, built that camp called Fitch's Landing, dug holes in our mountain looking for gold."

Scully grumbled an oath. "Why don't he get on with it?"

"They only wanted coffee," the chief went on. "But that man drove them off the land, shot at them. So—" Again he shrugged. "Bull Head and Little Bear came back later and killed him."

Killed Cyrus Ong, Martin thought, *and his wife and children.* So it *was* Bull Head and Little Bear who had ridden away from Wolf Voice's camp that day and committed the deed!

"They should not have done that!" Wolf Voice conceded. "Young men are rash, and always want to act big. Maybe it was all right to kill the man, but they should not have killed the women and children too."

There was a murmur of assent from the council.

"An eye for an eye, a tooth for a tooth," Wolf Voice mused. "That is a good law. I like it." He looked appraisingly at Bull Head and Little Bear.

"If there is to be peace in the Chetish and along the river, there must be law. I see that. I hear you say that, and you are right. So these two must obey the law for what they did—obey that white man's law."

Martin was astonished, did not think he had heard aright. Dancer, too was puzzled. "Thin ice, Martin," he muttered. "Look out for cracks!"

For a long time the assembly smoked in silence. Somone brought Martin and Dancer pipes, and they smoked nervously. Everyone seemed to ignore the sweating Bert Scully, and he shifted his bulk, cursing under his breath.

Bull Head and Little Bear must obey the law, the white man's law. But that could only mean the two must hang! A trial in Federal court would be convened at Fort Schofield. Given the mood of the Territory, the verdict could hardly be other than death by hanging. Bull Head, Star Woman's brother—Bull Head, who had shared with Martin and Belle his lodge, his food, his friendship! Suddenly Martin felt sick.

Wolf Voice seemed to read his disturbed thoughts.

"The Men With Hats," he pointed out, "hang with a rope the people who do bad things. But we Sioux kill dogs like that. We strangle dogs with a string when we need meat in winter and there is no meat. That is no way for an Oglala man to die! An Oglala does not die like a dog. He dies like a man, fighting!"

Martin glanced at the two miscreants. Their faces were impassive, without sign of emotion.

"So," Wolf Voice concluded, "I have decided this." With the carved stem of his pipe he pointed to Bull Head and Little Wolf. "Tomorrow, when

the sun is over a man's head, these two die for what
they have done." Only for a moment was there a
convulsive movement in Wolf Voice's cheek, a
shadow that fled almost before it was born. "If the
white men want it that way, an eye for an eye and
a tooth for a tooth, these two will die. They will
ride into town in war paint, on their best ponies.
They will come fighting, like men. Only these two
will come, and—" Wolf Voice paused, clearing his
throat. Again Martin sensed the undercurrent of
emotion. *It is hard to be a chief,* Wolf Voice had
said. It was very hard, with lives at stake, on both
sides.

"They will come shooting," Wolf Voice
mourned. His voice rose in what was almost a
chant, a kind of death-song. "They will die! If it is
the law, it is the law!"

Unbelievable, Martin thought, shocked. *Yet—*

"He could be Solomon, in the Bible," Dancer
whispered in his ear. "That's a fact!"

Wolf Voice concluded. "Then we will go back
into the Chetish. We will not from this day fight
any more unless we have to. If the Men With Hats
leave us alone, we leave them alone."

Martin felt mingled relief and sadness. There
might be peace, but Little Bear and Bull Head
would have to pay for it.

"He wants to know if it's a deal," Dancer whispered.

Martin nodded, made the hand-talk sign.
Agreed; tips of fingers placed to temples, then both
hands swept outward. *One mind, you and me; it is
agreed.*

He started to rise, but Wolf Voice raised a mag-
isterial hand.

"Wait!"

Martin sat down again. Dancer spoke in his ear. "I told you! That coon has got another bullet in his gun!"

"An eye for an eye and a tooth for a tooth," Wolf Voice said. He gestured to the silent youth who was standing near. "This is Long Walker. Do you know him?"

Martin shook his head. Bert Scully craned his neck forward, interested. Dancer signed *no*.

"When our women and children travelled down to the river, Long Walker went with them to help with the nets and carry back fish. Then the white men came, killed our women and children. Long Walker and the other boys tried to fight but the Men With Hats had too many guns. So everybody was killed but—" Wolf Voice pointed to Long Walker. "The white men hit him over the head and thought he was dead. But he crawled back into the hills. When the women and children did not come back, the people found Long Walker and brought him back to our village."

Scully swallowed hard. "I don't like the way things are going," he growled. "What's this all about, anyway? Ain't we finished? Didn't everyone agree?"

Wolf Voice rose, blanket kilted about his waist by the cartridge belt. The Sun Dance scars on his chest stood out in the diffused light that filled the great lodge. Speaking to Long Walker, he asked, "Do you see anyone else who was at the river that day?"

Long Walker pointed.

"This man?" Wolf Voice looked at Bert Scully. Long Walker nodded.

"What's going on?" Scully demanded. He tried

to rise but a scowling warrior pushed him roughly down.

"An eye for an eye, a tooth for a tooth," Wolf Voice mused. "That is a good law, I think. Rock, Thunder, Buffalo—all the gods would like that law!"

Again Scully, suspicious, tried to rise. An angry brave hit him in the mouth with a club decorated in feathers and scarlet ribbons. The marshal's bloody mouth twisted in a grimace. "No!" he cried. "Leave me alone!"

Wolf Voice nudged the groveling figure with the toe of his moccasin. "You die too," he said. "That is the white man's law. An eye for an eye—we all agreed!"

"Dancer!" Scully begged. Scrabbling to his knees, he held out hands imploringly. "Help me!"

Martin started to come to the marshal's defense but Dancer gripped his arm hard. "Stay put!" he muttered. "Our hair ain't on too tight anyway! There ain't anything *we* can do!"

"Dancer! Thorne, or Holly, or whatever your name is—for God's sake help me!" Lurching to his feet, Scully wiped his bleeding mouth, stared around the ring of hostile figures. "God damn it, *do* something! Talk to them! I'm a white man, same as you! Are you going to sit there and let them just *kill* me?" The last words rose in a shriek.

Martin trembled. To Dancer he said "We can't just let them—"

"Sit still!" Dancer's nails dug into his arm. "Don't move! It ain't smart to put *our* spoon in this pot!"

"Take him away!" Wolf Voice ordered.

Screaming, Bert Scully was dragged from the

tipi. They never saw him again.

On a June morning Fitch's Landing awaited two Oglala warriors. Riflemen crouched behind a log barricade. Marksmen were stationed on rooftops, the hillsides, the tailings dumps at the entrances to abandoned mines. Fitch's Landing suspected an Indian trick.

Martin, Dancer, and Mayor Loomis sat on the porch of Burke's store. The women and children of the Landing were safely off the streets.

"I'm not sure I trust them," Loomis said.

Martin differed. "I do. When they make an agreement, they keep it."

"I don't understand them," the mayor sighed. "They're an odd people."

"We never understood them," Martin said. "I guess that was the trouble."

Dancer spat a brown gout into the street. Already the sun had lifted above the surrounding hills. After the dawn chill its ray seemed a beam of hope; the Landing might yet escape an Indian massacre.

"It's no trick!" Dancer confirmed. "I ain't never yet had a Sioux tell me a lie. Anyway, they all figure they got to die some day. They're warriors, and it's a disgrace to die in bed! So what better way to ride up the Starry Road—what we call the Milky Way—than just gallop into town, two against fifty, and go to heaven quick in a good fight? To a Sioux, that's better than pie for breakfast!"

Head bent in thought, the mayor scratched the warm dust with a stick. After a while he said, "Last night I prayed for poor Bert Scully. He was a scoundrel, that's true. Still and all, he was a human being, one of the Lord's children."

"I guess we're all the Lord's children," Martin murmured. "Including Bull Head and Little Wolf."

Loomis walked heavily to the barricade and spoke to the waiting riflemen. "Remember your orders, you men! Don't fire unless you're fired on! Even then, do your best to capture these Indians alive! By rights they're entitled to a fair trial in Federal court!" Silently he walked back, long beard luminous in the sun, to sit beside Martin.

"I don't know whether to thank you or not for those words," Martin said. "Certainly they don't want to be captured alive."

Loomis shrugged. "I don't know whether I *did* a good thing or not. But you said those two were old friends of yours, so I thought—maybe—" His voice broke off and he stared again at the patterns in the dust.

At about eleven a marauding bear broke into a cookshack at the old Lucky Lucy mine, in search of sugar. In his wanderings the bear scrambled onto the tailings pile and loosed a cascade of rubble down the hillside and onto the tin roof of Burke's store. Alarmed, Martin and Dancer and the mayor dived under the porch. Riflemen loosed a hail of fire into the calm blue air. Badly frightened, the bear got away, but the nerves of the town's defenders were shaken.

"This waiting is wearing, very wearing," Loomis muttered. He took out his well-thumbed Bible and read Exodus for a while. Dancer chewed tobacco. Martin took the mayor's stick and scratched his own designs in the dust. Tomorrow he would be free to go west with Belle, along the Montana Road, to a new life. But Bull Head and Little Bear would have to pay for his freedom. He had never intended it to work out that way.

"Nigh on to noon," Dancer commented, squinting at the sun.

The riflemen looked to their loads. Taking a block of matches from his jeans, a man crouched behind an old cannon, loaded with black powder and nails from Burke's store.

"Almost," Martin agreed. "Almost noon."

He was thinking of a hard winter in the snows, of Star Woman's soft body under his knife, of the woman-man Gentle Horse and of old Magpie and her herbs. He remembered Spotted Elk, the camp herald, ambling about the village on a spring morning calling out the news of the day. Martin smiled; the old man yelled so loud he sometimes had to cover his own ears against the yowling.

With a start he realized a peculiar omission in his thoughts. Why had Philadelphia never entered his mind? The old life was there; medical school and the summer girls he loved, St. Anthony's Hospital and the surgery that was his life, the fashionable home in Germantown his skills had paid for. There was a housekeeper for the rising young Dr. Martin Thorne, and a gardener, along with a brace of blacks to draw his *caleche* through the broad avenues and out to Fairmount Park of a Sunday, the handsome lady of his choice reclining beside him on the buttoned velvet cushions. He had not thought of such things for a long time. Was it because home was—*here,* in the Territory? He did not know.

"Noon," Dancer remarked. Apologetically he unlimbered his old rifle. "Don't really intend to do no shootin', unless—" He bit off another chunk of

Wedding Plug, said no more.

Time passed. The wait seemed interminable but actually, Martin realized, it was only a few minutes after twelve. Then a man behind the barricade called out, pointing. "There they are! On the hill behind those big rocks!"

They looked. Among the trees was a splash of color, a thread of movement.

"They're coming!" someone shouted. "Get ready, boys! Look out for tricks!"

Dancer focused his old brassbound glass on the distant ledge. "Like Wolf Voice said," he reported, "there's only the two of them."

Mayor Loomis called to the men behind the barricade. "Remember what I told you! Don't shoot unless you have to!"

A fat man in a checkered waistcoat propped a rifle on the logs before him and squinted through the sights, muttering.

"What was that?" Loomis demanded.

The fat man scowled. "Cyrus Ong was a good customer when I had the notions store! You tellin' me I can't take a shot at those murdering rascals?"

There was general agreement. "They butchered Cyrus, didn't they? And his wife and children?"

"And we killed those Oglala women and children along the river," the mayor said wearily. "The Lord don't look kindly on killing of any sort! It says 'Thou Shall Not Kill', don't it? So do what I tell you—wait till they fire, but try to take them alive."

Now Martin could make out the pair with his naked eye. Bull Head and Little Bear rode slowly down the hill, well out of range but inexorably approaching. Colored pennons waved from upright lances. They carried rifles across the pommels of the high-backed Sioux war saddles. The fine ponies, tails tied up and full of feathers, picked their way daintily among the rocks. A slight breeze scattered puffs of dust as hoofs sought a purchase.

"They're singing," Dancer noted.

In the stillness Martin heard a faraway chant.

"It's a death song," Dancer muttered. "They ain't about to be took alive!" Cautiously he backed into the doorway of Burke's store. "Come back here with me!" he urged Martin. "Leastways you got a doorsill to dodge behind when the lead starts to fly!"

Martin shook his head. Fascinated, he continued to watch the approach of the two Oglala braves.

"There are only the two of them," Mayor Loomis called out. "So it's not a trick! Hold your fire!"

The two figures became larger. Martin could see Bull Head tall and erect in the saddle, beside him his friend Little Bear. As he watched, they dug heels into their ponies' ribs and advanced the pace to a quick trot. Now they were on the grassy river bottoms, only a few hundred yards from the rambling outskirts of Fitch's Landing.

"God damn it, Martin!" Dancer called, "git the hell *in* here!"

The two Oglalas broke into a gallop. Martin heard a war-whoop, a thin and chilling sound. They raised their lances, blades glinting in the sun. Now they were at full gallop, ponies scurrying furiously under the quirt. Little Bear raised his rifle in one hand and shot into the air, yipping like a coyote.

"Damn foools!" Dancer marveled. "But look at 'em come!"

"Don't shoot yet, men!" Mayor Loomis begged.

The racing pair climbed from the green river bottoms to the gravelly road leading into town. Stones rolled under the hoofs of Bull Head's pony. The animal slipped; Bull Head twisted in the saddle and tugged hard on the hackamore. Trying desperately for balance, the animal scrambled upright. Forward the pair galloped, mounted figures looming larger and larger.

Caught up in the drama, Martin vaulted over the barricade and ran heedlessly into the street. "Friends!" he called to the pair. He did not know what he hoped to accomplish, but he could not stand by and watch them die.

"Come back here, you idiot!" Dancer howled.

"Friends!" Martin screamed. He held out his arms. "Wait! Listen!"

As in a nightmare he saw Bull Head's face over the flowing mane of the paint pony. His old companion dropped the ribboned reins and sat swaying in the saddle, drawing a bead with his rifle.

"Wait!" Martin implored. "Wait!"

From the barricade behind him a shot sounded. The cannon roared. The explosion deafened him. Bull Head pulled the trigger and a flower of orange flame bloomed. His old friend's spotted pony swept by him, sweat-flecked shoulder catching him in the chest and knocking him spinning. He fell, stunned, ears rebelling at the furious fusillade that had erupted.

"Don't!" he muttered in protest. "Don't!"

Awkwardly he rolled over, propping himself on

an elbow. Smoke drifted from the barricade. The cannon had reeled backward from the force of the explosion and lay on its side, a dense black cloud rolling upward from its mouth. Men spilled over the high-piled logs, yelling in triumph. A riderless Oglala mount, frightened, jumped the barricade and ran neighing shrilly about the street. When a man attempted to seize the bridle the animal kicked wildly out, breaking a window in an abandoned feed store.

Someone helped Martin to his feet. "You hurt?" the man asked, peering into Martin's face.

"I don't think so."

The man dropped his arm in disgust. "You was a fool! Might of been killed, running out there like that!"

Slowly Martin walked to the two crumpled figures, sprawled in the dust like rag dolls thrown away by an uncaring child. The man in the checkered waistcoat looked up as Martin approached. "I got this one," he said proudly, nudging Little Bear's body with a booted toe.

Dancer shoved the man away. "Git out of here!" he snarled, "before I brain you with the butt of my gun!"

Mayor Loomis stood beside Martin, looking down at the bodies. "They came shooting," he said. "I tried to hold the men off, but—"

"Your men did what they had to do," Martin said wearily. "Bull Head and Little Bear did what they had to do, too."

Loomis thumbed his tattered Bible. "They weren't Christians, but it seems to me they ought to have a Christian burial." He looked keenly at Martin. "You sure you're all right?"

"I'm all right."

"Well," Loomis said, "I guess you're free to go."

Martin felt very tired. His ears still rang. "What?" he asked, almost absently.

"We made a bargain." The mayor pointed up toward the great bulk of the Chetish, crowned with snow in the noonday sun. On the rocky escarpment above the town a file of mounted Oglala warriors inched along the trail. Wolf Voice and his people were leaving.

"They're going," Loomis said. "You're free to go too, with the thanks of the town. I'll tear up that WANTED poster and swear I never saw it."

Martin didn't answer. Squatting on his heels beside the two dead men, he murmured, "Goodbye, friends." He was, he knew, saying farewell to many things.

CHAPTER FOURTEEN

Belle did not understand. Sitting in Maggie Flood's parlor she stared at him, eyes brimming with tears at his account of the deaths of Bull Head and Little Bear.

"But I don't know what you're saying!" she protested. "You—we—were going to the Sandwich Islands, you said! Now—"

"What I'm saying, Belle—" He took her hand in his; it was cold and nerveless. "What I'm saying is this: I've decided not to run away any more. I'm going back to Philadelphia to face charges, stand trial for whatever I've done."

Agitated, she rose to pace the faded roses of the carpet. "I can't stand the thought of you in jail!"

He took a deep breath. "That's the penalty! Of course, I have some money, and can hire a good lawyer. But there's no doubt I'll spend time in jail, Belle."

She swung to face him, hands desperately locked together. "I know *I've* sinned, Martin, and I want to pay the piper too! But why did you change *your* mind?"

Standing beside her at the lace-curtained window, looking down at the town, peaceful under the summer sun, he felt fulfilled. It was a strange feeling, one long denied him. The log barricade had disappeared, the cannon had been removed to a shed to rust away its martial life. People went about their business, women called pleasantly to each other, men smoked pipes on the porch of Burke's store. The Indian threat was over, perhaps for good.

"Why?" he asked. "I don't know! A lot of things, I suppose. A man gets tired of running. Then, too, there's a crumb of conscience in the hearts of all of us. Sometimes it takes time to bring it out. What happened to me, up there—" He gestured toward the Chetish. "Maybe up there, talking to Wolf Voice and his people, a change came. I told them, you see, that there had to be law, the white man's law. People, red or white, couldn't just go around any more and do whatever they had a mind to. No, I said, there had to be law." He held her in his arms, looking into the sunflower-blue eyes. "Maybe I convinced myself too, Belle. Isn't that funny?"

Weeping, she clung to him. "Martin, I don't want you to leave me!"

He touched the shining hair, lit with flame where the sun leaked through the curtains. "But I *have* to, Belle! You *made* me!"

"Me?" Puzzled, she drew back.

"You! Belle LaTour! You've finally made a man of me."

"But—"

Gently he put a finger to her lips. "When I first came to Big Fork I was chased by demons. I drank laudanum, thought of suicide, almost lost my mind. Then I met you. My life changed. I fell in love. You cured me of being a doper. In that winter in the Chetish you nursed me, cared for me, saved my life, taught me what it means to prevail, *how* to prevail." He lifted the heavy sheaf of notes on Indian medicine. "With your help I began to pick up the raveled threads of my life and see there was still something worth saving. And now—" He smiled. "Your teachings are showing themselves in the pupil. It's not so mysterious after all, is it?"

Eyes wet, she said in an almost inaudible voice, "You give me too much credit!"

"Well," he said, "I know what was in me then, and what is in me now!"

Together they sat on the flowered sofa brought all the way from Massachusetts by the Floods. "What will happen to me?" she asked.

"I have a plan," he told her.

Her eyes searched his.

"We loved each other," he said, "and I am forever grateful for that. But it was passion, Belle, not the real and abiding thing. Deep down in your heart you still love Giles. I know that. And Andrew is always on your mind."

"But—" Her voice trembled. "I lost them!"

"Tomorrow," he said, "you and I will go downriver on the *Antelope*. We will stop over at Big Fork while the boat takes on wood. We, you and I together, will go to Giles and throw ourselves on his mercy. I will tell him you never loved me."

Under the ruching her breasts rose and fell, quickly.

"Do you suppose he would take me back?"

"Giles Dyson," Martin said, "is a better man that I ever was, and *I* would take you back and count myself lucky!" Rising, he took her hand. "Now let's go and say goodbye to Dancer. He says there are too many people along the river these

days. He's going out the Montana Road himself to
have a look-see."

From the deck of the *Antelope,* downriver bound
to Bismarck and Omaha and Kansas City, Big
Fork looked much the same as Martin remembered it from almost a year before. There was
River Street, the Empire Hotel where he had spent
his first days of exile, the Ace of Diamonds Bar
that was old Dancer's favorite resting-place. He
could see Giles Dyson's smithy, dilapidated and
sagging, and on the hill the small house where
Giles and Belle and Andrew had lived in happier
days.

Hand in hand they walked up River Street. Otis
Spinney saw them first and goggled in surprise.
"Mr. Holly!" he blurted. "And Miz—Miz—"

"Hello, Otis," Martin said.

"You were dead!"

"Not exactly," Martin said. "It was all a—well,
a misunderstanding, Otis."

"But—but—"

They passed on, leaving Otis pale-faced and
scratching his head in perplexity.

As Martin had observed from the *Antelope,* the
blacksmith shop was closed. A heavy brass
padlock secured the door, and the windows were
cobwebbed and dirty. Together they walked up the
long grassy slope toward the house, sun hot on their
backs. At their passage grasshoppers rose from the
long grass and carromed into flight. A meadow-
lark sang, and they strolled through patches of
harebells, forget-me-nots, and astragulus.

The old house was dark and shuttered. Paint
peeled from clapboards. One corner of the porch

roof sagged where a post had rotted away. From the chimney a crow flapped, cawing at them. Martin knocked.

"Giles?"

There was no answer. He knocked again. "Giles? Are you in there? It's me, Giles—Martin! And—and Belle."

There was no sound. He was about to rap again when he heard footsteps inside. They were light and hesitant, surely not those of Giles Dyson. Martin was about to knock again when the door opened and a small face peered out.

"Andrew!" Belle cried.

The boy looked at her uncertainly.

"Andrew!" she repeated. "It's me, mama! Don't you know me?"

Incredulously Andrew eyed her. Then he threw wide the sagging door and dashed into her arms. "Mama!" he cried in a choked voice. "Mama! It's you! You've come back!"

Weeping, she hugged the tow-headed boy to her bosom.

"I knew you would!" Andrew insisted. "I *knew* you would! Pa said you were dead, you and—" Over her shoulder he stared at Martin with tear-bright eyes. "They said you were dead, but I knew you'd come back!"

Giles Dyson stood in the open doorway, a thin and gaunt caricature of the man they had known. His mouth twisted, he turned pale. "Belle—" For a moment he swayed on his feet, and reached for support. "Belle! No, it can't be! I—I—"

"It's me!" Belle said. She rushed to support him, to lead him, fumbling and awkward, inside. Martin followed.

The formerly neat and tidy house was a

shambles. Dust lay everywhere. The curtains hung yellowed and lifeless. A tin plate of half-eaten food on the table was covered with flies that buzzed angrily as they approached. Over all was a general miasma of neglect and decay.

"I—I don't understand," Giles muttered, a hand to his brow as if to wipe away a cobweb.

Martin helped him sit on a three-legged chair propped up by a chunk of firewood.

"We didn't die, Giles," he explained. "Thanks to Belle here, we lived. And we went on from that old cabin in the Chetish to a lot of other things. But there's no need to go into that now."

Deep fire burned in the sunken eyes. Giles started to rise from the spindly chair, hands propped on the littered table before him. "You stole my woman!" he cried. "Damn you, Martin Holly, for what you did to a man that never did aught but befriend you!"

"My name is Thorne now," Martin said quietly. "Martin Thorne."

Weak, Giles sagged back on the chair and put his head in his hands. "I thought you was dead," he muttered, "the both of you. When I come on the old cabin and saw those few rags and Belle's old shoe, tore by animals, I—I—" Putting his unkempt head on his arms, he wept.

"Giles." Tenderly Belle touched his shoulder. "Please, Giles, listen to me." Sitting beside him, a new reticule from Burke's store on her lap, she talked while Andrew, now inches taller, stood near, eyes shining. From time to time he touched his stepmother's hair as if finding her presence unreal, likely to vanish.

"Let me start from the first," Belle said.

In her gentle voice she described their adventures, ending with the story of Martin's saving the town of Fitch's Landing. "And so—" She hesitated. "So Martin and I—we decided to come back."

"And to face," Martin added, "whatever is in store for us."

Head pillowed on his arms, Giles was silent. Belle's face was suddenly strained and weary. She made a little gesture of resignation.

"Anyway," she added, "I love you, Giles! I always did! What happened with Martin and me was one of those things that just—just happens. But you don't have to take me back. Just forgive me."

Giles raised a haggard face. He looked at Belle, looked at Andrew, love shining from the boy's eyes. He looked at Martin Holly, now Martin Thorne.

"Like Belle told you," Martin said steadily, looking straight-faced at Giles, "I'm going back to take my punishment. But I swear to you that Belle never loved me, never *really* loved me! She loved you, she always did, even when we were in that cabin together, on the Chetish in the deep of winter!" He swallowed hard. "When I go back to prison or whatever fate, it would be easier if I knew that you—she and you—" His voice failed him and he looked away, filled with emotion.

Giles stared at him for a long moment. "I—I believe you," he said. "Damned if I know why, but—" He reached out and took Belle's hand. "I guess we all make mistakes," he confessed. "It must of been hard on you, Belle, me not taking care of you the way I should, spending so much time in the shop and then gambling away all my—" He swallowed, hard. "Gambling away all *our* money in the Empire back room. I was at fault too!"

Belle's eyes shone. "Then you'll—"

He clasped her in his arms.

"Welcome home, Belle," he muttered.

The *Antelope* was getting up steam. Martin, Giles, Belle and Andrew waited on the dock for the whistle to blow for departure downriver.

"You'll come back?" Giles asked Martin. He had shaved, the first time in a long time, and put on the clean shirt which Belle washed. Andrew clung to his mother's hand, dressed in a blue cotton coat and pants he had worn, long before, when Belle made him dress up for Sunday School.

"It may be a long time," Martin said soberly. He looked down at his physician's satchel. "I don't know how they'll treat me, but the fact that I came back and turned myself in ought to have weight in the trial. Besides, I still have friends in Philadelphia. They'll help me get a good lawyer, I think, to defend me—if there's any real defense for what I did."

From a corner of his eye Martin saw a figure lurking in the cargo shed along River Street. It was Jack Flanders, the gambler; the man he had taken the gun away from that night at the Empire to save Giles Dyson's life. Flanders had not been satisfied Martin was dead, and so circulated the WANTED poster in the belief the man who humiliated him was too clever to die, must still be in the Territory.

"Jack!" Martin called. "Jack Flanders!"

In the blackness of the shed Flanders stood stockstill.

"Come here!" Martin called.

Uncertainly the gambler stepped into the sunlight, one hand inside his coat. His face was pale.

Holding out his hand, Martin walked forward. "I just want to tell you I hold no hard feelings."

Flanders licked his lips; fingers played with the ruffles of his shirt. The gambler was always, Martin remembered, a fancy dresser. "I—I heard you were back," Flanders stammered. "Otis Spinney said he saw you and—" He glanced toward Belle Dyson, neat and composed in a pink dress she had rescued from a pile in the old house, washed and ironed.

"Shake," Martin invited.

Suspicious of a trick, Flanders blinked. Then, slowly, the groping hand emerged from the shirt front—near the derringer, Martin supposed—and took Martin's own. It was cold and wet.

"No hard feelings," Martin smiled. "Goodbye, Jack."

Finally the whistle blew. After tearful farewells, he went aboard. Indian pharmacopoeia under one arm and the satchel in his other hand, he stood on the after deck, high above the wash of the paddles in the muddy spring-swollen Yellowstone, watching Big Fork grow smaller and smaller. Just before the *Antelope* rounded the bend that would take him out of sight of Big Fork—forever?—he took a last look at the town, at the small group still waving farewell from the dock. Barely, just barely, he could make out Belle LaTour's—Belle Dyson's—pink dress in the fading light.

Sighing, he went below decks. He felt sad, yet somehow comforted.